Melody of the Heart

A Contemporary MM Romance Novel

Blake Allwood

Blake Allwood Publishing

Printed in the United States of America

Box Elder, SD

First Printing: May 2022

E-book ISBN: 978-1-956727-25-8

Print ISBN: 978-1-956727-26-5

Library of Congress Control Number: 2022907903

Acknowledgments

Special thanks to the following amazing people who helped me get this book finished and into your hands.

Jo Bird: Editor
Renee Mizar: Editor
Alma Alexander: Editor
Ann Attwood: Proofreader

And of course, a big thank you to my husband who puts up with my endless stories and handles the formatting and final publishing of all my books.

Jonas Ludwig

"Son, you are being a snob." My father chuckled.

"No, Papa, this isn't music... It's banging."

My father shook his head and sat down with me. "Lizzy tells me you are too young to understand, but I don't think that's so."

He stood up, leaving me sitting on the sofa, and sat at the grand piano. "Listen..." he said as he played a piece I hadn't heard before.

"What do you hear?" he asked. This was a common question; one I'd become accustomed to answering.

"The music is flowing down the scale," I said, and was proud when he smiled at me.

"Indeed. Now, what do you hear?" he asked as he switched to playing a requiem that he'd forced me to practice.

"It's the same thing, the music is going down the scale."

"And how does this make you feel?" he asked.

I thought for a moment. "It's sad, Papa."

"Yes, it is. For six hundred years, since the fourteen hundreds, people have listened to music that goes down the scale, and associated it with sadness." He began playing the blues... the type of music I had told him I didn't like, which had started this conversation. "What do you hear?" he asked.

I listened, even though I wanted to argue again. "Um, it's the same chord going... going down," I said, and was rewarded by my father's bright smile.

"And now?" he asked as he switched to a jazzier piece.

"It's the same."

I laughed when he switched to a pop song I recognized from television. "It's the same too."

He stopped then, and turned toward me. "You think music can only be music if it's the classics." He sighed deeply. "I suppose that's my fault. You are too young to think music is only valuable if it's written from the masters." My father's suddenly serious tone had me sitting up a little straighter. "Listen to me, son. Melody of the heart... some people will feel the melody in the classics, and for others, the blues. Even more will feel it in the more modern pieces. Don't be a snob. Let yourself find that balance."

I nodded. At ten years old, I wanted to earn my father's approval more than anything else in the world. "Yes, Papa," I said, and the world was set right once again as he drew me into his arms.

2

Orlando Hancock

"**H**OLD ON, I'M COMING!" I yelled out of the bathroom as I finished drying off, and quickly pulled sweats on.

Before I could get to the front door, whoever it was knocked again.

"Geez, really?" I asked as I pulled the door open.

I froze as Tommy, my boyfriend, stood facing me, with two rather unsavory-looking Pittsburgh policemen behind him.

"Um, what's up? Tommy, you okay?"

"Sir, can we come in?" the tallest cop asked.

"Sure," I said, moving away from the door. Unfortunately, the small motel room didn't give us much space.

"What's going on?" I asked dumbly as the three men entered my room, and faced me.

"You know what's going on, you piece of shit," Tommy yelled at me, pointing his finger in my face.

"Um, no, if I knew why you and two armed policemen were at my door, I wouldn't have asked." Why, after driving all this way to meet him, was Tommy now pulling this kind of shit? He sure knew how to get my dander up.

He swore then, and acted like he was going to come at me. Of course, I stood a good six inches taller than him, and worked with my hands. He didn't, so I knew it was more for show than an actual threat.

Despite that, the cops held him back. The gesture was almost funny, considering it wouldn't take two strong men to hold him.

"Mr. Hancock, where were you tonight?"

"Well, I've been here… since I got to town, at least."

"Can anyone corroborate that for you?" the shorter cop asked.

I thought for a moment, then looked at my phone. "Um, I haven't been here long, I just got out of the shower, but don't y'all track phones these days? I mean, you can check that."

I noticed a small grin slip past the taller cop's lips before he managed to gather himself again.

"We can look into that," he said, looking at his partner. "Someone wrecked Mr. Jones's car this evening. Do you know who it could've been?"

"No." I looked at the cops, then at my boyfriend. "Tommy, where were you?" I asked.

Tommy hmphed, then turned slightly to the right. He only did that when he was guilty of something.

"Officer, where did this occur?" I asked the cops.

All three men shifted uncomfortably at my question. Considering I'd met Tommy at a bar just across the street from a bathhouse, I knew exactly where his car wreck happened. I waited for one of them to confirm my suspicions.

"The Pittsburgh Club," the taller officer said.

I nodded. "So, you were at the bathhouse downtown when someone wrecked your vehicle, and you just assumed it was me?"

Tommy looked at the floor. I took a deep breath and let it out slowly.

"Officers, I assure you I haven't left the room since I checked in, and more importantly, until just now, I didn't realize my worthless, dick of a boyfriend was cheating on me, so I didn't have a reason to go out."

Tommy's chin jutted forward, like he was going to argue with me, but before he could, I said, "Unless you have evidence, besides this lying, cheating asshole, I'd like for you to remove him from my room."

The cops nodded, and said they'd come back if they had any other questions. "That's fine, officer, and don't worry, this man has nothing I'm willing to break the law for."

I waited until all three were outside, and then called out, "Oh, and Tommy, regarding your proposal of marriage, I have your answer now. Hell no!" I slammed the door behind them.

3

Jonas

M Y MOUTH FLEW OPEN when I heard the offer. "*How much?*"

The gray-haired man lifted his arrogant nose, so he could stare down it at me, and repeated the ridiculously low price.

"Sir, this is a Steinway D-274," I said, lifting myself up to my full height, which, if I was being honest, wasn't all that tall.

"With a cracked soundboard," he interrupted.

"Which is fixable. To offer such a low price is an insult. Please, leave."

The man nodded slightly, probably a remnant of good manners taught to him long ago, but the sneer never left his face. He knew he had me over a barrel. Very few people, at least in the industry, weren't fully aware of my financial difficulties.

I didn't bother to see the old man out. Instead, I closed the piano, and used a polishing cloth to rub it down, as my father had dictated time and time again. "You must never forget to care for her. She is your lifeblood, she is your child, she is worth more than you." His words reverberated in my mind. Then, he'd chuckle and pull me into his arms, tickling me and kissing me at the same time.

Damn, I missed my dad. The welcome memories always came with the same emotions—deep sadness and loss, and an intense love for him.

My dad was seventy when I was born. I was the result of an affair he'd had with a young German woman from an extremely conservative family. She was forced to hide the pregnancy, and gave me to him to raise as a single parent. I'd never met her, and her family was very clear I wasn't welcome. It never bothered me.

My dad died a year ago, then my very grumpy housekeeper, Letti, who wasn't much younger than him, had died last month. She loved me fiercely, and between the two of them, we'd been a close family.

My father had taught me how to do one thing, and to do it very well, but managing money wasn't it.

I thought of the Ponzi scheme I'd stumbled into that had robbed me of so much. What little inheritance I had left was running low. I just didn't know what to do about it. I felt vulnerable and stupid, and, well, now I was basically broke.

The rent on our New York apartment was significantly more than I could afford, even after the building superintendent halved the rent for my father, then me.

We should've moved long ago.

Was I feeling sorry for myself? Yes, I suppose I was, a little, but I wasn't going to let my misfortunes dictate my life. Somehow, I was going to find a way out of this mess.

I went to the living room and began packing the last of my father's things. The concert-grand piano was the only thing of real value I owned. Now, I'd been low-balled, and not just by one, but by several piano dealers in town. In nineteen ninety-seven, the sister to my Steinway had sold for one point two million. It was the most a piano had ever sold for. Now, I'd be lucky to get six figures, but not because of the cracked soundboard. It was one hundred percent, because it belonged to me, the late, great Stephan Ludwig's loser son.

I could go to Europe, and maybe find a small orchestra that might overlook my last performance, but no, that wouldn't work. Even in Europe, the pay for a low-level performer wouldn't cover my bills, and besides, I didn't have the money to move.

I could take on more students, though I hated teaching entitled children just to pay the bills, and all of my current students fell into that category. I charged well over three hundred dollars per lesson, which was great, but it also meant I was expected to create a virtuoso after just ten lessons. I had a couple of students who were okay, but none of them would make it that far.

The knock at the door announced my next student, and I opened it and led the kid over to the piano. As he played, I thought about how I needed to think outside the box, but I wasn't distracted enough to not notice numerous mistakes in his attempt at Tchaikovsky, a composer his Russian father had demanded he learn. "Chad, you're still messing up in the same place as last week," I chastised. "It doesn't matter how often you come for lessons, unless you practice, you'll never hit the correct notes."

I listened as the teenager argued he didn't have time to practice. It was the same argument he'd made since he'd become a teenager. I wanted to yell that he was wasting my time, and I needed to stop working with students who couldn't care less about what they were doing. Instead, I grimaced internally, while maintaining the professional façade I'd perfected. "I'm sorry, then you may need to reconsider your lessons with me."

As he turned away, and without instruction from me, started playing the piece again, I sighed. I really hated teaching disinterested kids from wealthy families. Oh, well, I doubted I'd be able to attract these students much longer anyway since word of my concert debacle was spreading. Besides, people wanted prestige, and benefitting from my father's reputation could only go so far.

After Chad had been picked up by his mom's assistant, I plopped down on my sofa, and stared out the window as I weighed my dwindling options. I could auction the piano. I mean, that was the most logical solution, and the representative I spoke to from the elite auction house assured me it could be anonymous. Still, everyone who could buy the Steinway would know it was my father's. They'd know it was me selling it, and I'd be in the same situation of being lowballed, except I wouldn't be able to tell the jerks to leave.

Of course, there was always the insurance money. If anything happened to the Steinway, it was... heavily insured. I hadn't even allowed my mind to consider it, but damn, the options were gone. I shook my head, trying to shake out the desperation that was taking over.

I looked at my father's pride and joy, and paled. I could almost hear him screaming in my mind at the very thought of intentionally damaging his precious Steinway. "Stop, Dad, stop!" I yelled to the empty room. "I can't do anything anyway. The insurance company would figure me out, and I'd be ruined."

To distract myself, I picked up a magazine that was at least a decade old, left over from when my father had taught lessons. As I absently flipped through the pages, my eyes landed on an ad for the contest my father had been involved in. I thought a local university had sponsored it as some sort of fundraiser. A piano was loaned to the winner, and they received lessons from a variety of prestigious pianists.

Hmm... why couldn't I do the same? I stood up and began pacing. Why not? Why couldn't I conduct a contest? The winner could have my loaned piano delivered to their home. It meant only those who had room for the instrument could win, but that could be made an entry condition. Even with the cracked soundboard, the piano sounded fine... not perfect, but fine.

I could use the money from the contest to fix the soundboard, and have enough left over to survive for more than a year. If the worst happened and the piano was damaged in transport, the insurance would pay. It was a win-win.

My father's voice became quieter in my head, but I could still feel his disapproval. Despite that, it was the solution to all my problems.

4

Orlando

I IGNORED RAY'S PITYING looks as I checked in the last customers scheduled for the day.

He and Angela had both talked me down after I'd called Ray on my way home to tell him what'd happened with the idiot I was dating. "Can you believe he was cheating on me, and had the audacity to accuse me of stealing and wrecking his car?"

Ray had been my best friend since high school, and Angela, who I'd also gone to school with, was his wife. I considered both of them my family.

"Honey, he wasn't right for you anyway," Angela argued. "Any man who'd force you to drive all the way to Pittsburgh just to see him doesn't understand you, or the life you live here."

They'd managed to make me feel better, at least somewhat, before I hit the mountains and lost cell phone coverage. I ended up spending the rest of the drive back to Monongahela, thinking about what Angela had said.

She was right, of course, but frankly, there was no one I wanted to date in my tiny hometown. Sure, there were a few guys who'd shown interest, but one was married, and the other was older than my dad. The rest were just creeps looking for a fast hookup. None of that appealed to me. I wanted a relationship like Ray and Angela's.

The next day, I was back at work with my head under the hood of a car. I leaned up after Ray had been rambling on about something. Only catching part of what he'd said, I asked, "Contest?" Then, I felt guilty for ignoring him, still caught up in my head about what'd happened with my now ex-boyfriend. "What kind of contest?"

"Not sure, some New York fancy pants is doing it, and the winner gets to keep his equally fancy pants piano for a year, while they receive lessons from him."

"Ray, you live in Monongahela, West Virginia. No New York piano teacher is going to bring his piano out here to teach your kid how to play."

"Dude, Hela isn't so bad. Why you dissing it?"

"The very fact that you can't even pronounce the name of our town is a good indication of what I'm saying. We're a backwater, a beautiful backwater with people I'd all but lay my life down for, but we are not New York City."

Ray sighed. "I know, this is all Angela. She's convinced Ella is going to be the next great concert pianoist."

I ignored the mispronunciation and went for what he was really getting at. "Ray, I've told you, she has the ability, but she doesn't have the drive. Ella's a tomboy. She'd rather be in here working on that motor with you than playing piano in some concert hall."

Ray chuckled. "You need to convince Angela, not me."

"You both need to talk to Ella," I said again, for the umpteenth time.

Ella was an eight-year-old fireball with wild, frizzy hair, which fit her personality to a T, a face full of freckles, and one-hundred-percent energy. She did play piano well, and I think she enjoyed it to some degree, but her real passion was anything she could get her hands into. I doubted she'd ever stay inside and practice long enough to raise her skill level much higher.

"Well," Ray said, lifting himself completely out of the ancient Ford Explorer to look at me. "The contest requires the piano teacher to send a letter of recommendation. Angela will be impossible to live with if I don't at least ask you. So, will you write the letter?"

I chuckled. The New Year before last, Angela and Ray had been at my house when dad talked me into playing to impress his then fiancée, Lydia. After that, Angela wouldn't leave me alone about giving Ella lessons. It was cool, although I knew the girl would rather be here in the garage messing with motors than playing piano. Still, there was little I wouldn't do for that kid, or her parents. "Sure, just tell Angela to email me the information. I'll do it tonight."

Ray's smile beamed bright enough to light up the dark garage. "I'll text her now."

I shook my head as Ray bounded outside, the only place you could get decent cell coverage. I couldn't help but feel sorry for the poor girl. Angela really wanted Ella to be less like Ray and more like her. The truth was, though, I'd known Angela all her life, and if I remembered correctly, she was just as rough and tumble when she was eight as Ella was now.

Between Ray's genes and hers, there was no way Ella would've been anyone other than herself.

5

Jonas

I CONTACTED SEVERAL REPORTERS who covered the arts, and they all took to my idea immediately, so much so, I'd been approached by the *Morning Show* to announce the contest publicly on television.

I quickly pulled my Pradas on, buffed them to ensure I looked my best, and dashed out the door to my waiting taxi.

"It's not every day a pianist as renowned as yourself creates such an offer," the TV station manager said.

"It's to honor my father," I said, and forced myself to ignore the guilt that swept through me. I'd always been determined to make it on my own.

My father had taught me that lesson. "Stand on your own two feet, son," he'd told me. "That way, you'll never be stuck in my shadow."

As if the Ponzi scheme debacle wasn't embarrassing enough, the rest of my financial woes could be traced to my stupid ex, Rodrigo. He was the conductor for the orchestra I'd been contracted with and thanks to his underhanded scheming at our last concert together, I was essentially not hirable.

Thinking of Rodrigo depressed and angered me. Those emotions were not great, particularly when combined. Dredging them up when about to go live on-air was even less so. Luckily, the taxi pulled up to the station, before I could go much further down that road.

"Mr. Ludwig, thanks for coming," the woman who met me at the front desk said. "If you come this way, I'll get you to makeup."

I had done this multiple times over the years, so I knew the routine. Each time I won a prestigious award, both national and international, I'd been paraded out as a feel-good piece on the *Morning Show*. I frowned as I thought about the last time I'd been here. It'd been with Rodrigo. He was announcing my contract with the orchestra. *Asshole.*

Just as I thought of the man, I caught a glimpse of someone who looked remarkably like him. My heart skipped a beat, and I stopped in my tracks, ignoring the woman who was speed walking in front of me. She didn't notice. "Rodrigo?" I asked as I looked inside the small makeup room.

I saw him smile his sly asshole smile in the mirror before he turned to me. "Jonas, it's such a pleasure to see you again."

"Why are you here?" I asked, avoiding the fake pleasantries.

"Oh, didn't they tell you? We're doing this interview together."

My blood turned to ice in my veins, and I quickly stepped back. I was about to turn around and leave the studio, when Rodrigo said, "I wouldn't leave if I were you. I'm here to offer you... well, you could call it a way out."

I stood stock-still and closed my eyes a moment, anger boiling inside me. This was exactly what happened before. Rodrigo had instigated it to get a reaction.

The horrible memory resurfaced before I could respond. The last time I'd seen Rodrigo, he'd paraded and kissed his boy toy in front of me right before telling me he wanted to break up. It had happened literally moments before we were called on stage.

Rodrigo had been everything to me up until then. I had even been naïve enough to believe we were going to be married. Instead, I fucked the concert up so badly, I ended up walking out after the first piece.

It wasn't until a few days later, after I'd been suspended without pay, that Jamie, the first-chair violinist, called, and told me Rodrigo's boy toy had taken my place. I'd been set up.

"Rodrigo, you can't make right what you've done. You can only make it worse." My voice was tense and mirrored my body language.

I turned to go again, but he approached before I could exit the room. "The board isn't happy and wants to make things right. I told them it was ridiculous, but well, what can we do? You don't want it made public that you were sleeping with the conductor of the orchestra you worked for, and the organization doesn't want to be sued. So, since you are technically still under contract, they have a proposal."

I was so angry I could feel the pulse in my neck. "I don't want anything to do with you or them. Go to hell, Rodrigo."

"Ten grand a month, starting now, and ending in one year. We fix your piano, and sponsor the winner of your contest if they perform in Salzburg next year."

"What?" I asked, stunned.

"I think you heard me. The board sees this as a way to satisfy you, prevent you from filing any... uncomfortable lawsuits, and it gives them some much-needed media attention. If you let us sponsor it, you can also forgo the exceptionally high admissions requirement." Rodrigo looked arrogantly toward me and smiled. "That's why I'm here, to announce the orchestra's involvement as you announce the contest."

I thought for a moment. Ten grand was a considerable sum when I had little money left and no prospects. Plus, if the piano was repaired, I could sell it. Even if the contest was a bust, as long as the press coverage was good, I could still sell it, and avoid the buzzards circling overhead.

It might also help me avoid the desperate insurance scheme I had been considering as a worst-case scenario. "Do it," I heard my father's voice say in my head.

"What's the catch?" I asked, trying to sound as disinterested as possible.

"No catch, you simply sign a nondisclosure agreement not to sue the board or publicly disclose our *involvement*, and abide by the terms of the contest. Easy, no?"

"Easy? No, I seriously doubt it'll be easy. I won't work with you, Rodrigo. Not even a little. If you show up, the deal's off."

Rodrigo smiled before walking back to rifle through his messenger bag, and returning a moment later with a folder. "Look this over while you're in makeup. If the terms are agreeable, sign it, and we'll make the announcement together."

I took the folder, hoping Rodrigo couldn't see my shaking hands, and turned just as the woman who I'd met at reception appeared before me, looking worried. I nodded toward her, and left without looking at the son of a bitch again.

The board's terms were as Rodrigo had explained. I still didn't trust him, though, so I carefully read through the agreement again while the makeup artist got me ready.

It really was cut and dried, and without any big fanfare. Entrants must be amateur pianists and electronically submit paperwork that their piano teacher also had to sign, and send a live recording of a performance.

The top performances would be uploaded to the orchestra's website, and I'd select the winner. The process was a bit more than I'd planned, but it worked, and no one could accuse me of being biased.

Once the winner was selected, I'd spend a year working with them personally to prepare them for a prestigious competition in Salzburg, Austria, on February tenth of next year. The orchestral organization would repair my piano, and have it delivered to the place I was staying, while training the winner. Oh, and of course, the winner would have to be approved by the board of directors. That didn't concern me too much. I knew what they'd be looking for, and now that the contest was a serious one, I'd be looking for the very same thing. Hopefully, someone young, with moderate talent who actually wanted to improve, and who wouldn't be able to afford the opportunity otherwise.

I could agree to those terms, but only under one non-negotiable condition. I quickly wrote, *Rodrigo Everett will not be involved in the process, nor will I work with him in* any *capacity during the term of this contract.*

I signed it, and handed Rodrigo the folder as I walked out of my makeup room. "It's done, but you'll have to initial the handwritten section to agree. I will not deal with you, Rodrigo, not in any capacity."

He looked angry for a moment, then his scheming mind must've figured out a way around the clause, because he smiled and signed the document. "Then it's settled," he said, and handed the document to the lady who'd escorted us in, asking for copies.

I forced myself to smile during the interview, but emotions swarmed inside me. Relief, concern, and anxiety over what Rodrigo had planned all swamped me. Regardless, for the next year at least, I wouldn't starve, and more importantly, my father's Steinway would be repaired. If I didn't let Rodrigo screw this up, maybe, just maybe, I'd find myself free of the crap I'd let him get me into, and finally be free of him altogether.

6

Orlando

"**O**RLANDO, ARE YOU IN here?" Ray called from my front door.

"Yeah, I'm in the kitchen. Come on in."

"Hey, Ella isn't gonna make it tonight. She's got, well, she's not feeling up to it."

I chuckled. "I warned you. That girl wants to play in the woods, not sit here playing piano on one of the first sunny days we've had in weeks."

Ray shook his head. "I know, but seriously, I don't like her canceling last minute."

"Have you and Angela asked her what she wants yet?" I asked, and Ray blushed.

"No, but she pretty much told us how she feels last night."

"Good, then you need to leave the poor girl alone, and let her get on with the things that inspire her, and stop forcing her to come over here and bang on that old piano with me."

I looked over at my great-grandmother's honky-tonk piano and grinned. The woman had died at ninety-eight and had been a live wire all the time I'd known her. She'd been even more so back in the day, scandalizing the community and her parents by playing in every bar this side of the Mississippi.

Even now, the old piano had grooves in the keys where she and many others had played it all those years.

Ray plopped down on my sofa. Chuckling, I pulled a beer out of the fridge and brought it over. "You and Angela are great parents. I don't want to make it sound like I don't believe you are, but for real, you need to see her for who she is, what she's already got going on, and stop trying to force her to be who she isn't. You see that, right?"

Ray nodded. "Yeah, dude, I see it, and I think after Ella gave us both what for, Angela finally sees it too."

"Good, and it's about time," I said, and clanked bottles with my best friend. "Now, let's talk about getting your baby girl into some coveralls and to the garage, to learn how to wrestle a motor."

Ray cringed. "That's more than her mom can handle right now, but let her get a few more years on her, and I'll see if I can't push that a bit more."

I laughed out loud at Ray's anxious expression, but he and I both knew sooner or later, the girl would be working at the garage with us. I almost felt sorry for Angela, but again, it's not like Ella wasn't a chip off the old block on both sides of the family.

"Oh," Ray said. "We heard back from that fancy New York piano teacher. Ella's in the final selection process. I guess we'll have to tell them she's out, huh?"

"Yep. Shouldn't have entered in the first place, but my stubborn friend never listens to me."

"Hey, shut up. You don't have to raise a kid, and Ella's not exactly the easiest kid to raise."

"Ella is awesome, and we both know it, but you should probably send an email letting them know you're withdrawing her. That way, they can put another kid in the final process. It's only fair."

Ray nodded, and that was that, or at least that was what I thought.

7

Jonas

*N*O *SURPRISE*, I THOUGHT, when I read the caller ID on my ringing phone. Tatiana must've finally gotten wind of the contest.

"Hello?" I tried to sound as sleepy as possible.

"Why didn't you tell me about the contest?" she fussed.

I hadn't told her, because I'd been actively avoiding this conversation. I knew my friend well enough to know she'd be able to pull information out of me that I didn't want her to know, like my unspeakable hope that I'd end up with insurance money for the piano.

"Tatiana, you're busy, I'm busy. It's two o'clock in the morning!"

"You are such a prat. Tell me."

And I did. Well, I skipped most of the details, and cut to how the orchestra was already putting demands on me that went beyond our agreement.

"Why are you letting them push you around?" she asked.

"Because, I'm broke, and I need the chance to redeem myself, Tatiana. It seems the entire musical world has turned against me. I can't get a job as a janitor cleaning the stage, much less performing on one."

"Pssh, it wasn't so bad. You missed a couple of notes, it's not like you forgot the whole thing."

"I don't miss notes. I've won every competition I've entered since I was sixteen, Tatiana. I have fallen from the horse, and now I'm a pariah."

"A horse of your own making. You could join me in Germany, return to your family's roots. We would embrace you." When I didn't respond, she sighed dramatically. "Tell me what they added to the requirements."

I laughed. "Well, they're making the top selections instead of me, and letting me pick the winner out of those. Also, I have to prepare the student to play one of the most technically difficult compositions ever written for piano."

"Ugh, you signed a contract to do that?" she asked, and I could hear her annoyance aimed at me.

"No, they're adding things as they wish. I was supposed to be involved in the entire selection process, but the finalists have already been chosen. I agreed to Salzburg, but not to the choice of music."

"Then you should ignore that. What else?"

"Just that. They aren't really doing much more, yet."

"Come to Germany, Jonas. I miss you, and you would blossom here."

I sighed deeply and lay back on my bed. "I thought about it, but that doesn't feel right. Besides, you're wrong. They're less forgiving there than they are here. I can't even begin to think what they'd put me through."

"Jonas," Tatiana said. "You'd be given a teaching position, no questions asked. In fact, I could talk to my dean."

"No, I don't want to teach. I'm a performer. Just... this is going to work. I have a good feeling."

I appreciated that my friend didn't bring up the fact that I'd said almost the exact same thing when I went to work for Rodrigo.

"Well, so the board has taken over the selection process, tell me who they selected," she said.

I picked up the list of the three finalists the board sent me. "So, one lives in public housing in San Francisco. Rent for a small apartment there is twenty-five, twenty-six hundred. The student suggested a private room in the apartment complex, and the manager agreed to allow us to store the piano, but that doesn't really work, and to rent an apartment large enough for my piano could be twice my budget, so that one is out. I just can't afford to live there to give her lessons."

"Okay, who's next?" she asked.

"Mumford, Texas."

"Dear God," Tatiana said, "that sounds horrible."

"Worse. The moment they find out I'm gay and from New York, the community will likely spit roast me."

"So, I'm hoping the third option is better?" she asked.

"It's definitely the most promising. Small town, a tad smaller than Mumford. Ever heard of Monongahela, West Virginia?"

Tatiana laughed. "No, I can't say I've had the pleasure."

"It's just outside a national forest, beautiful scenery, and the best thing is it's less than a day's train ride back to New York."

"Then, your decision is made."

"I think so. I've not been to Monongahela, but my dad and I traveled to Martinsburg once. They have beautiful waterfalls not far from the town. Dad performed a charity concert at the base of one of the falls shortly before he died."

"So, maybe this is providence," she said.

I chuckled. "That's rich, coming from my most-ardent, atheist friend."

"Baby, I'm your only friend," she said.

"Providence or not, I can afford it. It's close to New York, and I don't think I'll be strung up by homophobic cowboys. So, Monongahela, here I come."

After hanging up, and because I was now wide awake, I went through Ella's entry paperwork, and watched her performance video again. The girl had talent, and if she worked hard, she'd be able to perform well enough that I wouldn't be embarrassed by her performance in Salzburg.

As I'd gone through the application the first time, I'd been surprised to learn that her piano teacher was, in fact, an amateur himself. I'd ended up Googling him, and was even more intrigued to learn he owned an auto repair shop. Our selectee was the student of a grease monkey, of all things.

The press was going to love that if they ever got wind of it.

The next morning, I got my coffee, flipped open my laptop, and typed out an email to the board of directors announcing my final decision.

Ella Frankford of Monongahela, West Virginia, is the winner of the contest.

Please make arrangements to have the Steinway moved to my accommodations in Monongahela when repairs are complete. I will notify you of the address once I've secured an apartment.

Sincerely,

Jonas Ludwig

Once I hit send, I called the Frankfords. "Hello?" a woman answered.

"Hello, is this the guardian of Ella Frankford?" I asked.

"Yes," the woman answered warily.

"Good. I'm Jonas Ludwig. I'm calling to congratulate Ella. She has won the contest you entered for a year of piano instruction."

"No, it's too late," the board president repeated. "We've already made the announcements. Either you will be in Monongahela, West Virginia, or you will have to reimburse us for the repairs."

I knew I was on a conference call, and could imagine the entire board sitting around the conference table, all nodding in agreement.

"What do you want me to do? You already know I don't have the resources to pay for the repairs on the piano, and the girl's family has said no. They thought they'd withdrawn from the contest."

"Jonas, darling." The sound of Rodrigo's voice sent a cold chill down my spine. "You will have to think of something. Surely you don't want another blight on your reputation disrupting another contract with the orchestra?"

I sat in silence, choosing my words carefully. "I guess I could hire an attorney, and we could fight this out in court."

I could hear murmuring, before the board president spoke again, "We'd rather avoid that, as I'm sure would you. Why don't you go to Monongahela and meet the child and her parents? Maybe something could be worked out."

"As you wish, but I can't force the girl to participate if she doesn't want to, and if you push me any further, I won't have a choice but to fight you in court. I've already been pushed to my limit."

"*You* have?" I heard the anger and derision in the woman's voice, and immediately knew it was Mrs. Rita Covington, a longtime patron and board member. The woman was practically made of money, and had her finger on the pulse of numerous arts projects in New York.

I heard shushing, then Rodrigo spoke again. "What about the piano teacher? I looked him up. He's quite a colorful character." He was addressing the board members, describing the man as a self-taught mechanic. "He'd be such good publicity. He's young, handsome, and lacked the opportunities that would've been given to him had he grown up in a more affluent family."

"Wait, I've not heard the man perform," I countered. "He might not be able to play anything other than chopsticks." I didn't really believe that, since he'd taught Ella, who clearly possessed skills to build upon. But, I wasn't going to allow myself to be railroaded into something by my asshole ex.

"Well, sir," I heard Mrs. Covington say. "For your sake, either the girl or her teacher had better agree to the program, or it'll be my own personal attorneys you'll be facing in court."

At that, the line went dead. The damn woman had ended the call before I could reply, but I also knew no one on the board would challenge her. She paid most of the bills, so her word was law. Rodrigo was her pet. I was a threat to her pet, so I had already lost the argument before it even began.

The knot in my stomach grew. I felt as if I could puke, but since I'd barely eaten in days, it'd probably only make me feel worse.

Why had I been such a stupid fool? I knew that low-down pond scum would end up screwing me again.

I'd closed my dad's apartment just the day before, and had to finish packing my belongings. I'd donated several of his things to various museums around the city after he'd died. I'd also sold most of the valuables I'd kept.

My remaining possessions were worthless, except to me. They were my treasures, the only things I had left in the world. The old tweed jacket my father had worn since I'd been born. Several handwritten music scores he'd composed, but never published. Small things that reminded me of the man I'd adored, then lost.

The moving van was arriving later to take my things to storage. I had already packed what little I'd be taking with me to Monongahela.

After the moving men came and went, I inspected the only home I'd ever known one last time, before closing the door on a chapter of my life. As I went from room to room, I let the emotions wash over me—anger, frustration, guilt... mostly guilt. I'd failed to hold onto nearly all my father had worked for and left to me, all because I'd trusted the wrong people. First, my father's account manager who'd proposed the Ponzi scheme, then Rodrigo, who appeared hellbent on destroying me.

Now, I was leaving all I'd ever known. I could only hope and pray I wouldn't completely stain my dad's legacy, as my own future seemed to be swirling down the proverbial toilet.

I tossed the bags into the back of my waiting taxi, and left for the train station. I had seven hours to get to Monongahela, West Virginia. Seven hours to come up with a plan to talk little Ella Frankford into becoming my student, fulfilling the stupid contractual agreement I'd foolishly made with the orchestra, and saving my pitiful hide before all my deepest fears were realized.

8

Orlando

"I'M SORRY, SIR, BUT she's already decided. The conversation is over."

I walked into the shop to see my six-foot-three broad-shouldered best friend, who was usually a teddy bear, directing a frustrated gaze at a much shorter, much-less built, blond man with wire-rimmed glasses. The guy was attractive, despite the agitated look on his increasingly red face that was angled up at my friend.

"Um, what's going on?" I asked Ray.

"This man is from the contest we entered. He's saying it's too late to back out now that Ella's been selected."

"The ball is already in motion. We can't change direction now," the man said, and from the way he was wringing his hands together, he appeared to be on the verge of some sort of breakdown. I could sympathize, but this was ultimately Ella's decision, and we had to support it.

"Sir, I'm sorry, but the girl isn't interested. I'm her teacher, and I know she's not going to pursue piano any further. You're wasting your time."

The man visibly deflated in front of me, and I fought an inexplicable urge to wrap a supportive arm around his shoulders. "You're her teacher?" he asked.

I nodded and he hesitated a moment, like he was making mental calculations, then asked, "How well do you play?"

I was taken aback by his question, and the suddenly hopeful glint I saw in his beautiful eyes. "*Me*? How well do *I* play?" He nodded and waited for me to continue. "I'm fair, but not great. Why does that matter?"

"Because, the board has given me the option of enrolling you into the program if Miss Frankford doesn't agree to the offer." His expression was serious.

"You're kidding. I'm a mechanic." I laughed so hard I thought my sides would split. It had to be a joke, right?

Ray's eyes lit up, and he came over to where I stood as my laughter gave way to shock. "This is totally your guy. He's been a protoget since he was a kid."

"Prodigy," I corrected. "I'm not a prodigy. I'm barely literate in music. I know almost every blues song ever played, and do okay with "Stairway to Heaven" on the piano, but I'm certainly not an ideal student for your fancy lessons. I'm sorry."

I turned to leave when I felt the man's surprisingly strong grip clamp down on my elbow. "You don't understand. I've invested everything into this. If it doesn't work, I'm ruined." He sounded slightly panicked.

I looked down at the man's perfectly manicured hands as I pried his fingers from my elbow, but didn't let go. "Look," I said, holding my own hand next to his, palm up. "Take a nice long look. Your fingers are long, delicate, and soft. I'm sure you've never done a hard day's work in your life. Mine... they're scarred, and stained with oil that'll likely never come off, even if I stopped working on cars today. I have calluses thicker than leather hide. Trust me, mister, I'm not your guy."

I released his hand and walked away without looking back. I was sure as I closed the door to my office that this was all a farce Ray had drummed up to give me shit about later. Things were beginning to make a lot more sense, now I thought about it that way.

Ella, winning some elite contest when she barely played. I mean, she played well enough for an eight-year-old, but there were certainly a lot of kids her age who played better, and were more committed.

The clincher was me taking her place. *What the holy hell?* I wondered if maybe there'd been a hidden camera somewhere, especially considering how angry Ray had been. That had to be an act, right?

I opened my office door, ready for the camera reveal, but Ray was back under the hood of Mr. Johnson's Chrysler, and the stranger was nowhere to be seen.

"So, what's the gig? I mean, no cameras?"

Ray chuckled. "Hey, it's all legit. Crazy, but legit."

"I don't buy it, Ray. There's got to be some sort of angle here."

"Nope, I checked the dude out before we entered the contest. He's an award-winning pianoist from New York and everything."

"It's pianist, there's no o in it. So, why would he make up shit about me being his student for a year?"

"Don't know, but he was pretty adamant. Even after you left, he tried to get me to talk you into it. Said he was going to lose his pants if you didn't."

"He said he was gonna lose his pants?" I asked, quashing a highly inappropriate mental image of the attractive man not wearing pants.

Ray laughed. "Not in so many words, but that was the gist of it."

"You don't think this is some sort of scam?"

"Maybe, but his bags were with him, so if it is, the man is full-out committed."

"Damn you, Ray, this is all your and Angela's doing. Let me go find him, and see if I can't get to the fucking bottom of it. God, I hate you sometimes." Part of me wanted to just let it go, but I remembered the look on the man's face, and the panic in his voice. I was drawn to him enough to want to put things right.

"You do not. You've a right to be pissed, but you adore me, and you know it. Besides, you owe me after..."

"Don't go there. I know I do, but after this shit, we're even, got it?"

Ray winked at me and gave me a thumbs-up as he disappeared back under the hood. Not that I'd ever really be even with Ray and Angela for all they'd done to literally keep my ass off the streets.

One main street ran through our town, and there weren't many places he could go on foot, so it only took a few minutes for me to find him sitting in Libby's Park, next to the river. He was looking out over the rapids. His glazed expression told me he was staring, but not really seeing them.

"So—" I said, startling him. "—what's the real story, and don't try to bullshit me? I know how to recognize bullshit a mile away."

He shook his head and sighed deeply, the look on his face all but resigned to defeat. "It's just what I said. The contest requires me to teach someone for a year. We selected Miss Frankford, and she's declined, so it's my neck on the line to get chopped."

"And, tell me again, what that has to do with me?" I asked.

The man sighed again, this time almost making me laugh at how dramatic he was. "That's more a dig at me. My former boss, well, he was my ex as well as my boss. He threw you into the mix as a way to embarrass me. I shouldn't have brought it up, but I got a little desperate in there."

"So, your former boss was also your lover?" I asked, intrigued, not only by the story, but by the admission, intended or not, that he was gay.

"Yeah. Oh wait, you aren't a homophobe, are you? Because, that would be excellent. Getting my ass kicked would just be the cherry on top of this shit pie." He sounded more resigned than apprehensive at the possibility I'd take issue with his sexuality. My smiling at him likely helped ease any uncertainty.

"No, I'm gay. But, isn't that like sexual harassment, or something?"

His chuckle was bitter. "Yeah, and I've already talked to my attorney. I'll probably win in court, but it's going to destroy my fucking career. No one will ever hire me to perform again."

"Yeah, that sucks, but you'll win, that's something."

He shrugged. "Well, I might as well go face the music. I'm sorry for the insane morning, Mr..."

"You can call me Orli. Everyone around here does."

"Well, Orli, I wish I could say it's been a pleasure."

He stood to go, and before I knew what I was doing, I asked, "So, what is it they want me to play?"

The man slowly turned around. "Have you ever heard of Beethoven's *Piano Sonata No. 29 in B-flat Major?*

I shook my head.

"What about *La Campanella* by Liszt?"

I shook my head again.

"The Oriental fantasy *Islamey* by Mily Balakirev?"

"No, sorry, I don't know much classical."

He chuckled mirthlessly. "They're some of the most difficult pieces ever written. They gave me one year to teach Ella—and in her absence, you—how to play these technically impossible pieces well enough to qualify to play in Salzburg, Austria."

"So, it really is a vengeance quest against you then?"

He appeared shocked by my being so forthright, but slowly nodded. "There's a lot to it, but yes, I suppose it is exactly that."

"Can you really teach me?" I asked, fully regretting the decision I'd already made internally.

"Can you play?" he asked.

I laughed. "I was taught by my great-grandmother who played in honky-tonks, but I'm not horrible."

The man looked torn between hope and resignation. "Do you have a piano, so I can hear you play?"

I nodded and remembered the three cars I'd agreed to have done by the weekend. *Oh well*, I thought, *Ray might get to work some overtime, since this was his damned fault anyway.*

"Where's your car?" I asked.

He shrugged. "I'm from New York. I don't have a car. I rode the train to Martinsburg, and had an Uber drop me off here."

"Well, you're going to need a car if you're here for long, 'cause we only have one Uber, and Sally only works when she needs money to buy yarn to pay for her knitting obsession."

"Let's hear you play before we commit to anything," he said, and followed me back to the shop. We set off for my place in the wrecker I drove most of the time, since we only had one tow truck operator in this town too, and *I* was it.

9

Jonas

T HIS DAY WAS AS horrible as I'd predicted. I hadn't slept on the train, my Uber was over an hour late, and the drive to the town where Ella's father listed his employment took another hour. By the time I got there, I was fit to be tied.

The father ended up being some linebacker who was nice enough, but my anxiety had taken over when he'd closed the door on Ella participating, and I handled everything really badly. If he'd hit me in the face, I'd have deserved it.

Then, the freaking teacher walked in, and I blurted out that he could take Ella's place. I quietly chuckled to myself as I rode with him toward wherever he was taking me to hear him play. It was a wonder he hadn't batted my hand away when I'd grabbed him by the elbow earlier. I never lost control of myself in public like that, meltdowns involving my asshole ex notwithstanding.

If I had any sense of self-preservation, I wouldn't have gotten in this stranger's vehicle to begin with, let alone agreed to go to some unknown location. But, he hadn't called the police on me for being a hysterical mess earlier, which made me feel strangely comfortable being with him in his run-down tow truck headed out of town. Besides, now that I'd calmed down and learned he was gay, I noticed just how attractive he was. In a grease monkey sort of way, of course.

When he pulled up to a cute cottage on a hill overlooking the majestic river that ran through town, I admit I was a bit surprised. If this was his home, I was expecting vehicles on blocks with their rusty hoods standing open.

However, this was anything but that. Instead, the cottage was painted light green with white trim. I mean, I didn't really like green, but it made this little home look all the more adorable.

There were flowers planted along a walkway leading up to a front porch, with a rocking chair and a swing. It was almost like looking at a picture. "Do you live here?" I asked.

He smiled without looking at me. "Yep. Not what you expected?"

"Um, not exactly."

"Don't judge a book by its cover. Isn't that the saying?" he asked, and appropriately chastised, I followed him inside.

If it'd been cute on the outside, it was an utter disaster on the inside. Walls were missing, and sheetrock dust was everywhere. "Um, definitely have to agree about that book cover," I said, and realized that sounded arrogant. "Sorry, you're doing some rehab?"

The man blushed. "Never-ending, I'm afraid. I've redone this three times since my grandpa died ,and I can't get it right. Well, anyway, you didn't come here to hear me complain about my shortcomings as a designer. Follow me upstairs. That's where I actually live while I'm working on this."

I nodded and did as he instructed, following him up a wooden staircase covered in plastic that looked like it'd been there for half a century. I knew it made me a bit of a perv, but I couldn't help but notice how nice his ass filled out his dark-grey pants.

The moment we got to the top, however, things were quite different. He'd converted a front bedroom into a living room, and when I followed him in, I saw the tiny spinet piano sitting in the corner.

There was a picture going around social media a few years back of a piano beaten to within an inch of its life. You could tell it'd spent more than a few nights outside in the weather. Old, wrinkled hands were playing it, and despite the piano's condition, I'd always thought the image was cool, real in a way the world of classical music often wasn't.

The spinet resembled that photo. I cringed inwardly as I thought of what it would sound like.

However, after the guy, Orli, he'd said to call him, took my coat and placed it over the back of a midcentury-looking sofa, he sat down at the little piano, and before I knew it sound came pouring out.

My first thought was, how could such a little piano put out so much noise? My second was this guy really knew how to tear up the keys. I sat and listened to him go through one song after another. Some fast, some slow.

When he began singing, my heart leaped into my throat. "When the sun broke this morning, I was lying down across my bed." His voice had that rich Southern-blues sound I'd heard when I'd spent a month in New Orleans with my dad.

I'd been so intrigued by how different the music was from what I'd been forced to play all my life. My dad had laughed at me, and said that to be a good musician, I needed to learn more than just the classics. After that, he had me taking lessons from several of the old-timers we'd heard perform.

Of course, I sucked. Too many years of playing classical prevented me from being able to learn the funk. One old man had told my father, "He's just too white."

I'd been so offended back then, but my dad had laughed, and replied, "You may be right."

After that, we'd returned home, but I'd spent another two years trying to figure out how to get the rhythm I never seemed to have.

That was until my dad died. After his death, I gave up on that, and went back to perfecting my classical performances.

I sighed as Orli finished playing. "You're good, really good, but you're far from a classical pianist. So, you really don't know any classical?" I asked.

"When he shook his head, I hummed Beethoven's Für Elise, a composition forced on nearly everyone who's ever taught a child classical piano. He smiled before clunking it out on the spinet.

"Yes, that's the one, but it's not something to be played like one of your blues hits. If you're going to play classical, you have to be able to play legato, as well as staccato."

The blank look on his face told me all I needed to know. He was a good player, but knew little about music.

"Okay, have you ever had silk slide through your hands?"

"Yeah," he said tentatively.

"And you've run your hands over denim, like the jeans you've got on, right?"

He nodded.

"*Für Elise* needs to be played like silk flowing gently over your palms, not a coarse material like denim. Try again, and this time, let the music flow."

He surprised me when the music was gentle, almost touching, although that could've been wishful thinking on my part.

"Decent, but here," I said, reaching over to push him up into a proper posture. "Don't slump, sit up straight like you have a rod going from your ass to your neck. Good, now scoot up, so you're only sitting on half the piano bench. That'll give you more leverage and keep your body supple. Great, great. Now, let me see you play it again."

This time when he played, I could hear the difference, and see his body move with the piece. Maybe, just maybe, there was hope.

When he stopped, I nodded. "Now, look at your hands. You're playing like your hands are a rigid board. Fingers, like your body, must be able to move with the music. Rigidity in the fingers stifles the music." I showed him how to make a relaxed bow with his hands. "Imagine you've got a baseball sitting in the palm, and you're playing around it," I said and pushed the back of my hand into his rough palm.

I'd done this literally a thousand times with student after student, but the feel of his coarse hands on the back of mine caused a jolt of sexual desire to course through my body.

My muscles tensed, but I forced myself to ignore the reaction, and after clearing my throat, I continued the lesson. "The hands should maintain that shape, unless you are reaching with the pinky to hit a note far away, but the hand should always come back to that position." He tried, and I couldn't help but laugh when he struggled. "No worries, this is the kind of thing that takes practice."

I sat down on the sofa, and looked at him for a long moment. Honestly, I needed time to get my libido back under control. "You know, working with a younger student would be easier. They are more malleable. They often haven't had time to learn the wrong techniques that they then have to unlearn. In my experience, bad techniques are harder to unlearn than to learn correctly in the first place. If you take this on, do you have time to practice? Do you have the motivation to learn?"

Orli shook his head. "No, I've not thought about it, to be honest. My great-granny was my teacher, and I loved her, so I was always eager to learn. I never practiced 'cause I wanted to be a master musician, I practiced 'cause I loved it, and knew my great-granny would be sitting somewhere, grinning as she heard me learn to play the old songs she loved so much."

"I can't say learning these pieces will be fun or nostalgic. The truth is, they're ruthless, forcing you to move your fingers in almost impossible ways. If Ella were willing to try, I'd have had a long conversation with her parents about the endless hours of practice it would require. She'd have to practice every night after school, several hours a day on weekends, and there would be very few days off. I'm afraid since you're literally going to have to battle old habits you've been using for years, it will be even more time-consuming."

"Are you trying to talk me out of it?" he asked furrowing his brow.

I smiled and shook my head. "No, I really do need you to agree to this. If you don't, I could lose my father's Steinway piano. That's something I can't... *won't* let happen." I pushed down the flaring feeling of guilt. I'd created this contest as a way to collect the insurance money, not that I would ever admit it out loud. I faced Orli again. "But, you should know the commitment you'd be making if you decide to do this."

"Do you think I can learn to play the hard songs?" he asked.

I sighed and leaned back against the sofa, looking out the window toward the road. "To be honest, no. I mean, I think I can help you learn enough to get you into the Salzburg competition, the one I'm required to prepare you for. Luckily, the actual pieces aren't listed in the contract, so technically the board can't force me to use them, but even I struggle with them, and I've been playing since I was old enough to sit on a piano bench."

"Then, why don't you just teach me how to play well enough to fulfill the requirements of the contract? We won't worry about the hard songs."

I laughed, but it felt hollow. If only this situation were that simple, not that I had much choice either way. If he was actually willing to learn, perhaps I should give this a real chance. He already appeared more eager than most of my students, and he hadn't even fully agreed yet.

"Trust me, it'll all be hard to learn, but..." I felt myself begin to fidget as an electric feeling of hope began to take hold of me. "So, is that a yes then?"

I internally chanted *Do it! Do it! Do it!* as I waited for his response, until he smiled, and said, "I have a full-time job, and often I have to work weekends too, but I love to play. I play every night anyway, so I don't figure it'll be much different than what I'm already doing."

I nodded, knowing it wasn't going to be anything like what he was already doing, but decided to keep that uncomfortable truth to myself. "Then, we have a deal?"

"Maybe." He stood up and went over to an old book-case built into the wall. He pulled out a notebook and opened it, handing it to me. "Those are fifteen children I currently give lessons to. Every evening, Monday through Thursday. If I'm gonna need to practice as much as you say, then someone's gonna have to take over teaching duties for me."

I cringed, unable to hide the involuntary response. "I usually get paid three hundred and fifty dollars per lesson. Can those kids afford that?"

He laughed and his rich, deep voice sent a surprising current of desire through me before I could suppress it and get myself under control.

"Those lessons are free, but that's my one condition. If you want me to commit to this, you'll have to commit to them, and no, you can't charge them. None of them have the money for that."

I stared at the list, negotiating the mix of feelings. The contest was for one student, not sixteen. I *hated* teaching, but then I thought of my father's piano, of the ten grand a month, and the potential to get my tattered reputation back on track.

I closed my eyes for a moment and took a deep breath. "Okay, it's a deal then, and please, call me Jonas," I said. "I'll teach them, and I'll teach you. How bad can it be?"

His approving grin was dazzling, though not quite enough to ease my dread about just how bad I knew it would be.

10

Orlando

"Ray, you are an SOB, and you're working over-time to help me get my work done."

"But..."

"No, dammit, there's no but. You and Angela got me into this mess, now the least you can do is take up the slack at the shop."

"Okay," he said, sounding just like he used to when his mama would get onto us as kids.

"Okay. I'm going to take Jonas, my new piano teacher, over to the school, and introduce him to Ms. Phillips, and let her know he's taking over my students."

"You know that's gonna go over like a lead balloon."

I laughed inwardly. "Yep, but that's the deal I struck with him. I can't be teaching if I'm gonna learn to become a maestro."

"Ugh, okay, you're already becoming snobby. Can't you just tell him to go away?"

"Snotty, jeez, Ray." Then, I thought for a moment about what he'd asked. "I could, but do you want to be the reason the man loses his job, his dad's piano, and his livelihood?"

I could see my friend shaking his head. Ray was nothing if not empathetic. "Then, I'll be taking this on, you'll be taking on more responsibilities at the shop, and the kids Ms. Phillips assigns me will have a new piano teacher."

"If you say so, boss," Ray replied, and I laughed.

"Yeah, and don't you forget it."

I'd driven Jonas over to our town's lone motel, and chuckled to myself when I noticed him cringe as we pulled up. The place was certainly dated, but Mr. and Mrs. Khatri were diligent with cleanliness. Deferred maintenance had become more apparent as the couple had aged, but for the most part, the place was fine for a few nights.

I was waiting for him to come back out, and had called Ms. Phillips first, then Ray. Just as I hung up with Ray, I saw blond hair duck out of the room, lock the door, and rush back over to my tow truck.

"Everything okay?" I asked, when he climbed in.

"Okay enough, but I need different accommodations. Sooner rather than later," he said with a huff. I smiled as I realized he was even cuter when flustered.

"I'll ask around and see," I said, before driving us over to Monongahela Elementary School. Ms. Phillips had been my music teacher growing up, and since she was as old as dirt, I wasn't at all sure she hadn't been my father's teacher as well.

Age hadn't withered her commitment to her students, and when she got her clutches into you, well, you did as you were told, otherwise, it could get painful. Ms. Phillips ensured all her kids had equal opportunities, regardless of their financial or familial status.

"Jonas, this is Ms. Phillips," I said as we walked into the school's main office. "Ms. Phillips, let me present Jonas Ludwig."

"Who is Jonas Ludwig?" she asked as she turned to open her mail.

"He's going to be the new piano teacher for a while," I said.

That made her stop and look up. "And why do we need a new piano teacher?" she asked, boring a hole through me with her piercing gaze.

"Well, because I've agreed to become a student myself, and I'm not going to have time to teach."

"Hmph," she said, and I had to work hard to hide my smile. "What are your credentials, Mr. Ludwig?"

He looked at me, then back at Ms. Phillips with what appeared to be some annoyance. "I've won over sixty awards for my performances, I've earned a degree from Juilliard, and I'm classically trained by my own father, Stephan Ludwig. What else do you need to know?"

"Can you handle pre-teens, Mr. Ludwig?"

"Um, handle?" Jonas asked, and shrugged. "Most of my students are older, but I assume it's similar."

I cringed and quietly apologized for the conversation to come.

"Are elderly old men and teenage boys the same? What about a young girl of sixteen and her mother at forty? A child before his or her teenage years is quite unique, Mr. Ludwig, and if you aren't aware of their differences, then you are most certainly not qualified to teach them."

Seeing as Jonas looked like a deer caught in the headlights, I guessed he'd never been dressed down like that in public, or at least not by the likes of a no-nonsense elementary-school teacher. Ms. Phillips slipped around us and was about to walk into the hall, when I said, "So, the piano program is delayed until next year then?"

"Most certainly it is not. You'll just have to find time for your own training *and* teaching."

"That is ridiculous, and you know it." Mrs. Stewart came into the office, and went straight to her mailbox slot. "You are not Orli's boss, and you should show more respect for someone who is volunteering to do a job you got tired of doing yourself."

Mrs. Stewart was five foot two and tough as nails. As the physical-education teacher, she was in every way Ms. Phillips's nemesis.

"I beg your pardon?"

"Then so be it begged, but most certainly not pardoned," she said, dismissing Ms. Phillips's objection. "Mr. Ludwig, it's a pleasure to meet you. I was in Angela Frankford's salon a few weeks back, and she was saying how Ella was entering a contest. If I remember correctly, the contest was sponsored by a Mr. Jonas Ludwig, is that you by chance?"

"Yes, ma'am," he said, sounding relieved to have found an ally of sorts, and took her hand.

"Then it's an honor to meet you. I did some research, and you've had quite the illustrious career. I, of course, can't speak for my colleague—" Mrs. Stewart said, pointing at the now fuming Ms. Phillips, "—but I'm sure the parents of our piano students will be honored to work with such a skilled musician."

"He's not qualified," Ms. Phillips said through clenched teeth.

"That won't be a problem. I'm happy to supervise Mr. Ludwig as he tutors our students. I am, after all, head of the arts and physical-education departments."

I'd been a party to their feud before. For the most part, the arguments tended to run fast and hot, but never lasted long. However, I'd never seen Ms. Phillips so angry. "I'm the school music teacher," she said, spit flying from her mouth. "Or, have you taken that position over as well?"

At Ms. Phillips's raised voice, the principal came out of her office with a concerned expression on her face.

"Then—" Mrs. Stewart said, "—by all means, why don't you train Mr. Ludwig if you have concerns about his ability to work with our students. Since both he and Mr. Hancock are volunteer teachers, we should do what we can to ensure they are... welcome."

I honestly thought Ms. Phillips's head was going to spin as the principal rushed over to intervene. "Mr. Ludwig? Why don't you come into my office and fill out the necessary paperwork? Orli, um, Mr. Hancock, why don't you go help Ms. Phillips with her incoming class?"

I nodded as the poor woman gave me a pleading look, and glanced over at Jonas just in time to see a baffled expression. I almost laughed, but knew it would be my funeral... or more likely, his.

"Ms. Phillips, may I escort you back to your classroom?" I offered. "It's the kindergarten class at the moment, correct?"

The woman wilted. She hated teaching five-year-olds, and I couldn't blame her. Music for kindergarten involved twenty children banging various instruments, and would be taxing on anyone.

"Yes, Orlando, that would be quite lovely," she said.

The moment we walked into her classroom, Ms. Phillips turned to me. "Why did you spring that young man on me like that?"

"Because, if I'd done it in private, you'd have forced me to do more than I'm able."

She smiled. "Okay, you may have me there, but you are so good with the children. I don't want some snotty musician coming in here and ripping the joy those children have at playing the piano away from them."

I sighed. "I know, and I'm sorry, but he's in dire straits, or at least he says he is. I tell you what, if you agree to work with him next week, I'll get him started now. Between both of us, I think we can whip him into shape. Deal?"

She nodded. "What made you want to take lessons from him?"

I explained my weird morning to her, and she sighed, "So, this isn't your idea?" I shook my head. "And he didn't want to work with your students, but that's the agreement you made?" I nodded. "Damn," she whispered. "Okay, but my feet swell if I'm here after five, so if my feet swell, Orlando, I'm calling you to massage them."

"Eww, Ms. Phillips, you know feet terrify me."

"Which—" she said smiling, "—is why you're going to ensure these lessons don't last later than four thirty, so I can leave early enough to get home and get these piggies up!"

"I swear to do my best."

Just then, the room began filling with five-year-olds, and I looked over to see Ms. Phillips take a deep breath, let it out, and begin helping the rambunctious little ones get settled in for their class.

Jonas

"U M, I'M NOT REALLY sure about all this," I said as I was escorted into the principal's office, and noticed the *Principal Jenkins* name plate on her desk.

"Oh, don't worry about those two. Ms. Phillips just got voted out of a position she's held for probably thirty years, and to her rival, no less. Now, Mr. Ludwig, did I say that correctly?" I nodded. "You wish to volunteer in our music program, so I'll need you to fill out this paperwork. We'll have to run your name through the database, to ensure you are safe to work with the children. If the grapevine is operating correctly, it's my understanding you have a degree from Juilliard. I'd like to have that on file as well."

Over the next thirty minutes, I filled out paperwork and answered the principal's questions. By the time she escorted me to the music room, I was emotionally stretched to my limit. I'd been riding a roller coaster since I'd first learned about this cursed town.

Not only had my world been turned upside down, but I'd lost the only home I'd ever known, and I was being harassed by my ex, and the board of directors he controlled. I was barely holding on financially, and my fate was strangely wrapped up with a mechanic who could play a wicked blues piano, but didn't know Beethoven from Mozart.

I couldn't help but feel completely overwhelmed, dismayed, and yet, somehow hopeful.

As Principal Jenkins and I approached the music room, I heard the most horrendous racket coming from that direction. "What is that?" I asked.

"Oh, the kindergarteners have music right now. I should've given you some earplugs, but—" she said, looking at her watch, "—they should be finishing up by now."

Sure enough, I heard Ms. Phillips's voice, a voice I was sure would haunt my dreams from this point forward, calming the children down. "Place your instruments into the designated boxes," she said, and I heard chaos on the other side of the door.

"There," Principal Jenkins said, "you've been spared." She smiled as she led me into the chaos, and pointed toward the only adult chair in the room. Orli was helping organize the instruments, while Ms. Phillips was helping get the little ones in line.

Within seconds, a flustered young man showed up, and the children began following him down the hall. When they were gone, Ms. Phillips and Orli picked up the remaining instruments, then came toward me.

I cringed as they approached, and waited for another dressing down by the nasty teacher.

"Mr. Ludwig, I owe you an apology. You must think I'm quite the monster."

I looked at Orli and he just shrugged, but gave me a kind smile. "Um, I didn't mean to..." I began.

"Oh, don't apologize. Mrs. Stewart was correct. I was out of line. It's just that Orlando is one of the best teachers I've ever encountered. I swear he can get these kids to give one hundred percent, and that's no easy feat. I was taken aback and was rude to you as a result. I'm sorry for that."

She sat at her desk, and turned her chair toward me. "If you're willing to try, so are we. Orlando and me, that is. You will most certainly not be getting your training from Mrs. Stewart. I swear the woman thinks discipline is letting children throw balls at one another until they're black and blue."

She shook her head, and I could tell she was working out her frustration. "Orlando will sit with you this week, help you grasp the nuances of his teaching style, and I will work with you next week. You won't be allowed to be alone with the children, until you're cleared with the state anyway, so this is a good time for you to learn."

Just then, a group of students arrived at the classroom door. "That would be my third graders," she said as she stood up, and began to give directions for the children to take a seat.

She turned back to me then, and said, "I look forward to getting to know you, Mr. Ludwig, and I hope you won't judge me too harshly from your first impression."

I nodded and smiled, but deep down, I knew I'd totally judged the woman from my first impression. I swore, as soon as humanly possible, I'd get out of this distasteful teaching gig, and turn it over to someone less likely to get skinned and roasted in her old witch-in-the-forest's oven.

12

Orlando

"**W**HAT DO YOU MEAN a grand piano?" I asked, completely unsure of what to do with this new information.

"It was agreed when the Frankfords applied," Jonas said.

"Well, Ray and Angela live in a five thousand-square-foot home built in the mid-eighteen hundreds. Their house would fit a grand piano. Mine? Well, you've seen mine."

"Regardless, when the repairs on my piano are completed, it must have a place where it can be kept safe."

I thought for a moment, wracking my brain for any place that could work. The problem was, besides Ray and Angela's house, I couldn't think of anywhere.

"Can't you store it until the contest is over?" I asked.

Jonas drew in a deep breath, letting it out slowly while scratching his head. "I suspect I can, but the idea was the student would have the benefit of using a Steinway D-274. It's one of the most valuable Steinways ever made, and has been featured in some of the most prestigious venues in Europe. When it made its way here to the States, it continued that tradition. It should be utilized, not stored."

"The only place I can even think would work would be the apartment above the shop."

I forced myself to look at the disgust that crossed Jonas's face. "You must be kidding. It cost close to a hundred grand to repair. You can't possibly consider having it placed in a drafty space above an auto repair shop..."

"Come look at the space, then when you say no, you'll understand why you have to store it."

He shrugged, but followed me upstairs to the apartment my father and I lived in, until I inherited my mom's parents' cottage.

"Well," Jonas said as he walked around. "It's a lot bigger than I would've thought, but I can smell the fumes from below. I can't take a chance on that getting into the wood."

He was about to leave when he turned to me, and asked, "Who is living here now?"

"No one, it's been vacant since my father moved out."

He wandered around the place again, and sighed. "I need a place that isn't a motel room. How much would you charge me to live here?"

I shrugged. "Well, since you're giving me lessons for free, why don't you just stay here. Maybe you can put some sweat equity into the place, and get it ready for me to rent out sometime in the future."

I had no intention of ever renting the space out. It had direct access to the garage below, and I'd never trust anyone with clients' cars. Well, except maybe a fancy-pants New Yorker that I imagined would do everything in his power to avoid the actual auto repair shop if he could.

"Good, that's a deal. And my first sweat equity, as you call it, will be to have the place deep cleaned. Is there a cleaning agency in town I can hire?"

I couldn't help but laugh. "Agency, no, but Mrs. Perkins sometimes does cleaning for the local real estate company to make an extra buck or two. I can give you her number. I repaired her Pontiac last month, so I should still have it somewhere."

"That'd be excellent," he said, looking around the place again. "But, really, what do you plan to do with all this stuff? Shouldn't you move it into storage or something?"

I shook my head. "No, I'm afraid if you take it, you'll have to accept it as is. Anything you don't want in plain view, like family photos and such, can be stored in my old bedroom."

"Your bedroom? You lived here?"

I nodded. "Grew up here. My mom's father passed away a few years ago, and I inherited his house. Dad got remarried in March and moved to Cleveland to live with his wife. So, yeah, this was my home."

"You don't mind if I move things around then?"

"Nope, make yourself at home."

He nodded, but I could tell he wasn't convinced. The only decent thing about the place was the new floor. Dad had dated some woman who'd convinced him to have the carpet replaced with hardwood, but the walls were still the dingy color they'd been my entire life. My mother painted the walls when she'd moved in thirty years ago.

Oh, well, free rent was free rent. If the guy needed to save money like he said, he could either live here as is, or he could get some paint and go to town.

"I'll take it, but I'm not moving the Steinway here. I'll try to make arrangements for it in New York, and now that I won't have to pay rent, I can probably afford to have it stored. It might be prudent to have a piano installed here, though. I'll need to practice, and it might be easier for you to have your lessons here, instead of at home or the school."

I nodded. "I'll see if I can find you one, but don't expect a Steinway," I said chuckling. He'd be lucky if we found a piano that stayed in tune. Regardless, I'd ask Ms. Phillips if there was a decent piano for sale somewhere in town.

13

Jonas

AFTER ORLI HANDED ME the keys to his old apartment, I stayed and surveyed my new territory. A few months ago, I'd never have considered staying in a place like this. That was the truth of it. As it was, I'd have preferred to hire workers to make it livable, but couldn't justify the expense. Not knowing what might happen if things fell apart with the fragile deal I'd managed to create, I didn't dare spend any more money than absolutely necessary.

I had phoned the orchestra office that morning, and alerted the secretary that Orli had agreed to be my pupil, and asked that the board be informed the program was moving forward, and to hold off shipping my piano here.

I shook off the thoughts of my evil ex laughing hysterically at the news. As if attempting to prepare a child to compete against top-notch amateurs in Salzburg wouldn't jeopardize my reputation enough, I'd be swapping the kid for a backwoods mechanic raised on saloon music. No doubt Rodrigo would delight in this turn of events. *Asshole*.

Now, I just had to figure out how to live in a tattered old apartment over an auto repair shop.

I sat on an old recliner, careful not to sit too far back, considering how dirty it looked, and flipped open YouTube for ideas about painting the room. As I watched the video, I decided it didn't look too difficult, and since I didn't have to start teaching until Monday, I had today, Friday and the weekend to paint.

I put my phone in my pocket and looked around the apartment again, deciding to remove nearly everything in sight, including the disgusting furniture. I'd buy paint for the walls and an air filter in hopes of filtering out the oily gasoline smell that seemed to permeate the place.

"You can do this," I said, mostly to convince myself, then got to work stuffing empty cardboard boxes I thankfully found scattered around, and shoving as much as humanly possible into Orli's old bedroom.

14

Orlando

T HINGS WERE BEING MOVED around upstairs, and Ray raised an eyebrow several times when we heard something heavy being dragged across the floor. I just shrugged. "I told him it's his place to do with as he pleases. My guess is he is trying to make it his home."

"Okay," was all Ray said, and when we heard something crash above us, he just shook his head.

The truth was, I didn't really care what happened to most of the stuff up there. Besides the family photos, nothing held any sentimental value. I'd bought the shop and the building from my dad when he got married, and most of its contents came with it. My father was an okay guy, but there wasn't a lot of love lost between us. He seemed to care more about himself than me, the kid he got stuck with raising as a single parent, since my mom died when I was born.

Fortunately, I'd had my grandparents, who I lived with on and off most of my life. Dad had taught me mechanics, though it felt more like I'd been forced to learn it. He'd never approved of the piano, saying it was for girls.

The apartment was a sore spot, and I had no idea what to do with it. Dad had basically abandoned everything in it, when his new wife told him she didn't want a bunch of trash in her home, like our family photos were trash?

Well, they probably were to him anyway. I should've taken them with me when I'd moved out, but maybe I could relate to my new stepmother, in that I didn't want the old to mess up the new. Redoing my grandparents' cottage had opened up a new life for me.

My grandpa had even said as much when he'd told me his house would be mine. "You'll have a little money in your pocket when I go. Most of that was left to me by your great-granny, and she'd have wanted you to have it anyway. You make this home your own. Don't try to hold onto the past."

I'd done just that, although I was still struggling with what making it my own really looked like.

Ray and I were still running behind after all the chaos from yesterday, but we made up for it by working through lunch, and everyone had picked up their cars by closing time.

"Wanna come over to join Angela and me for dinner? She just texted and said we're having chili dogs."

I laughed. "Well, as hard as that is to say no to, I think I'm gonna go and check on Mr. Piano Man upstairs, then go home and take a long, hot shower, and order a pizza."

"That sounds good. Well, the shower and pizza sound good." He looked up toward the ceiling of the shop. "I'm not sure what you can expect from up there."

I smiled. "I'm guessing from the sound of things, a lot of changes, but that's good. He's cleaning up what I should've done a long time ago."

"I still say you should've turned that into a man cave, and rented it out for bachelor parties."

"Yeah, beer-stained floors and furniture are just what we need up there."

"Your loss, dude, you could've made a fortune!"

I shoved my best buddy out the door, making him laugh. "Tell Angela I'll try to have y'all out this weekend for a barbeque at the house. Maybe we can invite New York up there to join us, let him get to know some folks, so it's not just all work and no play."

Ray's smile dropped. "Yeah, that's good. Okay, well, see ya tomorrow," he said, and climbed into his old pickup truck.

Just as I was getting ready to lock up for the night, my phone buzzed. I took it out and saw Tommy's name. "Ugh, I needed to block the fucker..." I said to the empty office.

I pushed the button to ignore, locked the door, and counted out the till. When everything was locked in the safe, I went up and knocked on the apartment door.

"Hello?" I called.

A moment later, a very disheveled Jonas answered the door. He was smiling from ear to ear, and it looked good on him.

"Hey, I'm glad you came up. I have some questions about some of the stuff you have here."

I nodded and followed him in. All the furniture had been shoved against the back wall, and what he could lift had been stacked, making the space look much larger than before.

"I filled all of the empty boxes and put them in your old bedroom. I had to take the bed down and lean it up against the back of the closet to make everything fit, but I packed everything well, thanks to whoever left all the packing material. You don't have to worry about any-thing being broken, I hope. I watched several packing technique videos on YouTube, so I think it's okay."

He rambled on, speaking fast as he showed me a solid wall of boxes in what was my old bedroom. Strangely, I was touched that he'd gone to so much trouble, packing everything, so it wouldn't be damaged. For some reason, I assumed he'd have just thrown what he didn't want in there. I never imagined he'd have carefully packed it all, much less watched how-to videos, so he could do it well.

"Is that okay?" he asked, biting his bottom lip.

The unguarded gesture sent electric pulses through me, and it was all I could do not to stare at his mouth. Even when the man told me he could lose everything, he hadn't looked as vulnerable as he did now. It was as if he needed my approval, and I couldn't deny him.

"This is... well, it's incredibly thoughtful. I appreciate you took care with... with my father's stuff."

Jonas blushed a bit, before leading me into the kitchen.

"So, I'm hoping you won't mind if I paint your cabinets. I did a lot of YouTubing today," he said, chuckling to himself. "I guess if you prime everything, you can paint, and it'll get rid of a lot of the smell from the shop, and painted cabinets will make these look much more up-to-date. In fact, if they look like some of the ones I saw today, the kitchen will be nice."

I smiled, impressed by his vision for improving the admittedly shabby place. "If you're willing to do the work, I don't mind."

He almost looked bashful as he nodded. "So, do you think you could drive me over to the hardware store? It's too far to carry the paint back, and from what I can tell, I'm going to need three five-gallon buckets. I'm going to paint everything off-white, so it retains a neutral feel, and it'll go well with your floors. The cabinets I'm going to paint white on the top and gray below. Once I'm done, maybe you'd like to replace the pulls, but if not, I did find where people have painted them, and they looked okay."

"Sure, do you want to go now?" I asked.

"If you're willing. I only have the weekend to finish all this, and if I'm going to live here, I'd like it to be nice before I move in."

I nodded hesitantly. "Okay, yes, but let's eat first. I'm starving. Do you like pizza?"

Jonas shrugged. "A little."

"Then, let me treat."

We started to head out the door, when Jonas stopped by the pile of furniture. "Um, I wondered if you were attached to the furniture. I'm going to be here a year, and none of this is really my taste."

"Dude, it's nobody's taste. I think most of this came from second-hand shops, or stuff my dad found on the side of the road. You can toss all of it."

I swear, the man lit up like a Christmas tree. He looked both excited and relieved. "Really, you don't mind?"

"Why would I mind? In fact, maybe Ray and I can help you haul it down to the street tomorrow morning. Most of this is still decent, so if it's placed on the side of the parking lot, with a free sign, it'll probably get picked up, but what are you going to do for furniture?"

He gifted me with another smile. "Well, I did some searches and found the perfect replacements in Morgantown. You letting me live here for free makes it affordable to add some of that sweat equity, you mentioned, and I'm getting a really good deal on the stuff. It's second-hand, but is coming out of a show home."

"How will you get it here?"

He smiled. "They're delivering it on Sunday."

"You were confident that I'd let you get rid of the furniture then?"

"Hopeful," he said, his eyes twinkling adorably.

As we walked down to my truck, I couldn't help but notice the difference in Jonas since just yesterday. His arrogance had been what you'd expect from an award-winning concert pianist, but now he seemed so much more friendly. It was almost as if redoing the apartment was opening up a different, if not better, side of his personality.

It was good to see. I was dreading having to work with him for a year, but if this person, the one whose eyes twinkled as he discussed furniture deliveries and painting old cabinets, could be who I was stuck working with, I might actually enjoy learning classical piano.

I drove him to the hardware store first, knowing Jimmy would've closed the place by the time we got done eating at Mo's Pizza. Mo's was good, but notoriously slow.

I offered to pay for the paint, but he waved me off, saying our agreement was he lived there for free, but he did the work.

I helped him put the paint in the back of the truck, then drove us over to Mo's.

After ordering and sitting down, it only took a moment for the day's work to overtake him. "You look tired," I said.

"Yeah, I'm used to hours of practice, but not so much hours of physical labor."

I smiled. "Well, if you want, I can have them split the pizza and I can take you home. The paint will be fine in the truck until tomorrow."

Jonas yawned at that very moment, and with watery eyes, nodded. "Yeah, I might have to do that. I don't think I knew how tired I was."

He looked adorable as a smile flitted across his face. We chatted about his plans for the apartment, until the pizza was ready, and I had the kid working the counter split it into two separate to-go boxes.

By the time I dropped Jonas off at the motel, he was asleep on his feet. Had we known each other better, I'd have walked him in, and my mind even conjured up images of me tucking his tight little body into bed, before kissing him goodnight.

Damn, I thought. *I can't be fantasizing about my piano teacher.* Yeah, he was cute, especially when he smiled. I'd noticed that, of course, but this? My weakness for men who weren't afraid to get their hands dirty must be clouding my judgment.

Thinking of his hands, led me to wonder what else he could do with those delicate, talented fingers. As I drove toward home, I shook the thought off. I wouldn't get involved with another Tommy. You'd think after the shit I'd gone through just a week before, I wouldn't be so quick to jump in the sack with another twink.

Yeah, the piano man was very much my type, but I was very much burned to the core when it came to men, especially men who looked like him.

15

Jonas

E XHAUSTION. M Y BODY WAS experiencing a total, bone-deep weariness like I'd never felt before. My dad, although he'd truly let me do what I wanted, never allowed me to do anything physical that might risk injuring my hands. "These are your tools, son. You must protect and care for them," he'd said.

Despite my body's protests, I enjoyed prepping the apartment much more than I thought I would. The best thing was once I got rid of the crap, and there was a *lot* of crap, the space was actually quite cute. I guessed the building had been built in the late twenties or early thirties, judging by all the subtle art-deco elements still present.

Had this apartment been in New York, even with the unpleasant fumes, it would've cost thousands upon thousands of dollars to rent. With that in mind, I convinced myself to let go of my miserly ways, and invest at least minimally in the apartment.

Then, I started having fun. By the time I'd dumped what had to be the hundredth can of trash into the dumpster behind the building, I began packing what might be something of value to Orli, and moving it to his bedroom. I suspected his framed family photos must be especially important to him, since he'd mentioned them when showing me the apartment, so I took special care in boxing those.

I surprised myself by humming as I worked. My muscles ached, but the ache felt good, as did the feeling that for the first time in a long time, I was making progress at something, and that somehow, my efforts would lead to my life being slightly better than it had been just yesterday.

Unfortunately, by the time I sat down with Orli to eat at the pizza place, I was wiped out. I ended up crashing on the motel bed the minute I finished my shower, and hadn't even thought of eating my dinner.

That was a bad idea, because I woke up at four a.m. starving and aching all over. I downed a couple Tylenol I found in my carry-on bag, left over from who knows when, and devoured the now-cold pizza.

I'd never liked pizza that much. I mean, it was okay, but I hadn't tried it until I was at Juilliard. My father didn't like it at all, and I rarely ate without him, but this morning, nothing tasted better than that cheesy, meat-laden, veggie-topped combination of flavors.

When I'd finished, I dressed and headed out across town toward the shop. I doubted anyone would be there at this hour, but I'd seen a diner between here and there, and hoped they'd be open, so I could get a cup of coffee. I then planned to let myself into the apartment, and finish packing up the kitchen, so I could get started painting as soon as Orli arrived.

Finishing the kitchen was my top priority, because having a clean and decent place to prepare my own meals was a must. I knew if I allowed myself to eat pizza and God only knows what else, I'd end up as big around as I was tall. Pictures of my dad's parents and siblings, all of whom had died before I was born, showed me that genetically, we grew wide. Since I didn't love working out, despite forcing myself to run at least a mile a day, fixing healthy food was essential to my staying in shape. Luckily, I found the diner open, so I went in and sat on a barstool at the counter. A sassy young woman sashayed up, winked at me, and filled my coffee cup. "Nothing to eat?" she asked, and smacked gum just like the waitress on an old TV show my father used to watch.

"Um, well, I ate half a pizza this morning, so probably not, but why don't you give me one of those giant cinnamon rolls to go."

The woman winked at me again, turned around, and put the monster roll into a to-go container. "Oh, wait, the other one will probably eat that, so you'd better give me another roll."

She laughed. "Well, Ray Frankford is going to whip your butt, but he's late coming in, so he snoozes, he loses."

"You're joking, right?" I asked.

"No, Ray comes in every Saturday to get one of these. Angela, his wife, won't let him have them except once a week. This is our last one."

I grinned and could feel the Grinch-like quality of it. "Well, poor Ray. Tell him the piano teacher from New York bought it."

"Oh, you're trying to start trouble." She grinned back at me. "I always did like trouble."

"Barking up the wrong tree, I'm afraid," I said as I paid her. "I'm, as they say, queer as a two-dollar bill, but I appreciate the rolls and coffee."

"Damn," she said. "Why are all the cute guys around here gay?"

I smiled and shrugged, before dashing out the front door. I had to go through the office side of the shop to get up to the apartment, at least until a key could be made for the backdoor up the stairs. Snagging a pen, I wrote Ray's and Orli's names on the to-go boxes, and hoping it would endear me to him a little more, on Ray's I added, *You owe me!*

I knew he disliked me, or was at least leery of me. He and his wife were the reason I was in this predicament, since they could've alerted us that Ella was no longer interested after she'd been chosen for the final three. Oh, well, it looked like things might work out now, and I didn't want to live in close proximity to a guy who hated me. I'd had to deal with that kind of thing my whole life, someone wanting to destroy me, and waiting for the right moment to pounce.

If I could avoid that situation here, that would be best. So, if that meant leaving a cinnamon roll peace offering for Ray to find on the office desk, so be it.

I was finishing up the last of the kitchen packing, when I heard movement downstairs. The garage doors were loud, very loud, as they came up in the mornings. Thankfully, the shop would be closed on Sundays, which was the one day I let myself sleep later than five or six a.m.

Usually, mornings were my time to practice. If I could get five hours in before my day began, then the rest of it was mine to spend how I wanted. Now that I wasn't performing, I'd already decided to knock my practice time down to two hours. Since the shop opened at seven, it meant I could be up by five, and done before anyone arrived. It was another concession I hoped would make my downstairs neighbors not hate me, assuming Orli came through with finding me a piano for the apartment.

I stopped packing and stared out the window. I really needed this to work. I still hadn't had an official lesson with Orli yet, but I was fairly confident that if he kept his word, we could get him ready for the competition. He didn't have to win, he didn't even have to place, he just had to compete, which meant he had to qualify.

That was a stickler, because even the competition to qualify would be tough, but doable. At least, if luck was in my corner.

The knock at the door startled me. "Come in," I called, knowing it would be Orli.

"Hey," a voice said. I looked up to see Ray.

"Hey, thanks," I said, when he put paint buckets next to the door.

Orli followed a moment later, and placed the rest of my supplies next to them. "Well, got my day cut out for me," I remarked.

I smiled at them, but when I saw Ray's expression, it fell. "Everything okay?" I asked.

Ray nodded. "Yeah, um, well, I wanted you to know how sorry my wife and I are about dragging you and Orli into this. We both feel bad. And, thanks for the cinnamon roll too." His face broke into a slight grin as he admitted how much he loved them.

"Mr. Frankford, it appears it's all going to work out. I mean, thanks to Orli, at least."

"Yeah, he saved my butt, and yours too."

"He did." I smiled at Orli, then went to look through the stuff. "Oh, do you have any sandpaper? I forgot to pick it up, and I'll need it for the kitchen cabinets."

"Yeah, I think so, but it's for cars, not wood. I'll see what we have, and if it'll work, one of us will bring it up later," Orli said.

I turned to head into the kitchen, when a throat cleared. I turned around to look at Ray again. He was standing there alone, shifting his feet nervously. "So, um," he began, and for a moment the huge man looked like a little boy who'd gotten into trouble. "Angela, she wanted me to invite you over for supper. Orli too, so we could apologize and welcome you here. She's a really good cook."

I smiled and put my hand up to stop him. "There's no need to apologize, everything is working out, but I'd love to come to dinner, just let me know when."

"Angela said if you're free tonight..."

I looked around the apartment at all the work I had to do, and sighed inwardly. I'd have rather worked throughout the evening to get it done. Still, relationships were important, and something told me in this small town that was even more the case.

"Sure, what time?" I asked.

When he told me six, I almost sighed out loud, but instead, I forced a smile, and nodded. "I'll be ready. Shall I meet you downstairs?"

"No, you can ride with me," Orli said as he came back into the room, carrying what looked like sandpaper. "I'm guessing you'll want to go back to the motel to shower and change, so I'll pick you up there."

"That's perfect, thanks," I said, and the two men nodded and left.

Oh well, I thought to myself. I had until six to transform this kitchen. According to the YouTube channel I watched, sanding was to be done with heavy paper first, then switch to light. Luckily, Orli must've known that, because he'd brought me two types of sandpaper.

I smiled as I mentally thanked him, and tried not to read too much into his thoughtfulness. After I had removed everything from the kitchen, I started taking down the cabinet doors and sanding them in preparation for the primer.

16

Orlando

W E WERE STILL SLAMMED with work. It wasn't like we weren't always slammed, since most of the folks around here drove older model vehicles, but our customer load tended to come in waves. This week was exceptionally busy.

By the time we hit the lunch hour, both Ray and I were famished. We locked the front door, which was the only way we could get any peace, and after cleaning up, we dug into the sandwiches Angela had sent.

I appreciated that whatever she fixed for Ray, she tended to fix for me too. That had started shortly after Ray had come to work at the garage full-time. He'd been a bulldozer operator who worked repairing highways before that. When the dozer rolled over on him, breaking his arm, Angela had been so concerned, that Ray had started looking for other work around here.

Ray and my dad were like oil and water, or more like gasoline and fire. Neither man liked the other, but even Dad couldn't deny Ray's skill as a mechanic. Work became a much calmer place after I purchased the garage, and Dad had moved away, and it only tightened my friendship with Ray. The truth was, lately I'd been seriously thinking about asking him to become my business partner.

We already had more work than the two of us could handle, and a service station that was bigger, newer, and had more modern equipment, was coming on the market within the next year or so. Its owner had approached me last month, saying he was getting ready to retire, and since our businesses more or less overlapped, he'd like to sell to me.

I was seriously considering it, but there were several factors to consider, Ray's possible partnership being a significant one. I would also have to sell this building to afford it, and I'd still need a loan to cover the rest. Before the whole concert-pianist debacle, I'd intended to approach Ray and Angela this weekend to float the idea. Of course, that was on the back burner now, at least until our guy upstairs was settled, and I knew more about what my life was going to look like over the coming year.

Just as we were finishing our sandwiches, I heard a crash from upstairs. "I'll go," I said. "You open the shop back up."

Ray nodded, and I dashed up the stairs to see what'd happened.

The moment I opened the door, I saw Jonas in the kitchen, staring at the empty wall where a row of cabinets had been. "You okay?" I asked.

"Um, yeah, I-I'm sorry, I'm not sure what happened. I was taking off the last door and put a little weight on the bottom of the cabinet when the entire thing came crashing down onto the counter."

I chuckled. "Well, my father installed these, so we can guess he fucked it up. Unfortunately, that's pretty much destroyed them, hasn't it?" I asked, seeing the cheap cabinets had shattered on impact.

Jonas just stared pale-faced toward the mess. "Hey, come over here." He did as I asked without question, and I checked him over for any injuries, careful not to touch him, despite the overwhelming urge. "You aren't hurt, right?"

"No, it didn't fall on me. Um, what am I going to do about cabinets?" he asked.

I didn't need to think about it. "Lucky for you, I still have the old kitchen cabinets from my grandparents' place, and they're in good condition."

"Really?" When his flush of embarrassment morphed into a hopeful look, I knew I couldn't blame the sudden feeling of butterflies in my stomach on indigestion from Angela's sandwich.

"Yeah, and they're significantly newer, since they were installed in the nineties, instead of the seventies like these were," I said, gesturing to the wood heap. "They're modern and clean, and I think you'll like them a lot more."

"Um, you aren't going to use them?" he asked while biting his bottom lip, which I was quickly discovering was a major turn-on, at least, when he did it.

I shook my head. "No, I gutted the kitchen and removed all the walls to give the cottage an open floor plan, so those cabinets won't be reused. I was thinking about donating them to Habitat for Humanity in Morgantown, but I can just as easily donate them to you."

Jonas shook his head in dismay. "I-I appreciate it, but painting was a big deal for me. I can't even begin to imagine putting up cabinets, it's not something I can do."

I had to grin at that. "Well, luckily, after building and ripping out the first floor of my home three times, I'm now quite an expert, so I'll do the work in the kitchen. You can focus on the rest of the apartment until I get time to tackle this."

Jonas nodded and gave me a faint smile. "Okay, if you think it'll work."

"I know it will. The cabinets are already painted white, and they look really good. My grandmother had them installed before she passed, and my grandfather never cooked, so they're like new."

He nodded again. "Thanks, and I'm really sorry about all that," he said, and waved toward the broken cabinetry.

"No problem. Do you need help getting things out of here, so you can paint?" I asked.

"I will, but I'll have to do it tomorrow. I'll focus on the main bedroom, bathroom and hallway. Maybe you could help me tomorrow morning? I'll start taking the smaller stuff down later today, but I'll need help with the larger pieces."

"That sounds like a plan. We can discuss it tonight over dinner."

He cringed, then apologized when he saw I noticed. "Sorry, I forgot about dinner. I should've taken a rain check until I got this apartment done. I wanted to have it finished before the furniture is delivered tomorrow. At this rate, there's no way..."

I clapped him on the back. "Don't worry, these things have a way of working themselves out. You need to get to know the natives, so to speak, especially since you're gonna be here a whole year. Besides, Angela is the unofficial, town welcome party. You're not gonna be able to avoid her for much longer anyway, might as well get it out of the way now."

Jonas's smile was more of a grimace, which amused me, but I was telling the truth. He would do good to have Angela on his side, especially as he navigated small-town life. She was one of the major cornerstones, and if she liked Jonas, I had no doubt the community would come to embrace him too.

17

Jonas

DEPRESSION BEGAN TO SET in after the kitchen cabinets literally exploded on me. I was finally hitting my stride, accomplishing something basic, and making progress I could physically see, when it all went to hell. So much for that fleeting sense of healing, in a world I felt I'd lost all control over.

Of course, Orli had rushed in like a knight on horseback, but that didn't make me feel much better. I was beginning to see a pattern of the guy having to dig me out of the shit I shoveled into his path. I had never been a burden on anyone. I didn't like the feeling, and wanted it to stop now, before things got even worse.

So, I pressed on with my plan. I managed, albeit badly, to paint the bedroom, before crumpling to the floor in a full-out crying fit. Unfortunately, YouTube hadn't prepared me for what I didn't know about painting a room. So, not only had I destroyed the kitchen, but my paint job was going to look like shit too.

I was in the middle of a full-on pity fest, when someone cleared their throat behind me. I was still sniffling as I peeled myself off the floor, then stood up quickly to see a beautiful woman standing in the doorway. "I'm sorry, the front door was open. Orli asked me to come up to see if I could help you take some measurements for the kitchen."

"No, it's okay. I'm just having a breakdown. I'm almost over it now."

"Honey," the woman said in a soothing tone as she approached me, and began rubbing my arm. "What's going on? Is it the competition?"

I shook my head. "No, not just that. I thought I could fix the kitchen, then it fell apart, then I thought I could paint, but it's a lot harder than it looks."

She chuckled. "Oh, it's a lot harder than it looks. I'm Angela, by the way."

My face blushed as I realized who had caught me in my mortifying breakdown. "I'm so sorry, Mrs. Frankford, you must think I'm an idiot."

She smiled. "No, love, I think my husband and I put you in a bad situation that you're doing what you can to work through. Orli also told me you're worried about getting this done. So, as of now, dinner plans are off, and since Ella is spending all day at a friend's house, I'm all yours."

"No, there's no need—"

"There is," she insisted. "And I'm an excellent painter. In fact, I was going to take the rest of the day off to prepare dinner, so I can put that off and help you instead."

I sighed. I couldn't argue with needing help to get the place done before the furniture arrived. "If you're serious, I could clearly use the help."

"I am. Now, let me run home and change into clothes I don't mind getting paint on, and of course, I have to cover this hair. For what I pay to have it look this good, baby, there's absolutely no way I'm going to risk it."

I chuckled. Her long flowing hair was flawless. I'd had a friend at Juilliard who worked as a hairdresser while in school, and specialized in Black women's hair. I knew based on that friend's experience Angela wasn't lying about having a small fortune invested in it.

I thanked her, and she disappeared out the door. I collapsed to the floor again, and snuggled back into the only corner of the room I hadn't painted yet, pulling my feet up to my chest. Despite Orli and Angela both offering to help, I couldn't shake feeling this entire venture—the apartment, the competition, showing up my asshole ex—was a lost cause. I laid my head down, and just let myself give in to the despondent feelings.

By the time Angela returned, I had all but decided to quit now and cut my losses. Yes, I'd lose my dad's piano, but I couldn't learn to live with yet another disappointment. Life was no longer throwing rotten tomatoes at me, it was throwing daggers, and I was tired of being stabbed.

"Hello," she called out, and I got up and made my way to the living room, ready to tell her I was giving up. When I walked in, however, I saw three other women and two teenage boys with her. "These are my friends," she said, and introduced me to each of them.

I was so overwhelmed that I didn't hear the names, so I just nodded. "We're going to get this whipped out for you right now. Boys, start taking the rest of those cabinets down and haul them to the dumpster out back. Mr. Ludwig, if you can help them, the girls and I will get started on the painting."

I stood in amazement as the apartment became a hive of activity. Dumbly, I followed the boys into the kitchen and began helping them take the rest of the cabinets apart, which was surprisingly quick and easy. The two very large teens didn't even seem to break a sweat as they hauled the cabinets down the back stairwell.

In less than an hour, all the cabinets, with the exception of the one attached to the sink, were removed. "Good," Angela said as walked into the kitchen. "Orli can disconnect the plumbing when he and Ray finish for the day, then it can be hauled out too."

"Now, let's get all this out of here as well," she said, gesturing to the furniture stacked up against the wall in the living room.

"Orli wanted all this to be placed at the side of the parking lot with a free sign, so people would pick it up," I said.

"That's a good idea. Boys, take everything down to there, and make sure nothing is in the way of incoming traffic. Dump the mattress and box springs in the dumpster, though, since no one will want those."

The boys nodded, not saying a word. "Thank you, Angela, I can't..."

"It's the least I can do. Now, I think the girls and I will have the bedroom finished in a few moments. Do you want us to do the bathroom or the hallway next?"

I was so overwhelmed I wasn't sure what to tell her, so I just shrugged. Fortunately, she had no issue taking the lead. "Well, bathrooms are essential, and because it's small, it'll also be a beast to paint. Why don't we do that first? Then, when it's dry, you can concentrate on making it tidy, and, well, better than it is now."

I smiled at her reference. The bathroom looked as if it'd been updated fairly recently, but it wasn't exactly clean. So, once it was painted, I would most certainly be doing a deep clean, or at least hiring someone to do so.

"Thank you, Angela," I said.

"No problem. Now, why don't you help the boys, and we'll get the painting done."

I smiled, grabbed an old end table, and took it down the stairs. I was more than happy to see people were already pulling up to look at the stuff the boys had brought down.

"Hey," an older man said as he got out of a battered white van. "Do you got any living-room furniture you're getting rid of?"

"Yes, actually a lot."

"Well, I might be willing to take it off your hands."

I nodded and escorted him upstairs to see the pile.

"Elmer Franks, are you pilfering again?" one of the ladies who was painting asked as we walked into the apartment together.

"Alli, now don't you go causing trouble."

The two razzed each other, until it became clear the man was the woman's uncle. "I should've thought of him. I'm sorry, Mr. Ludwig. He's always looking for stuff he can sell down at the flea market, or in his antique store. I'm guessing you'll take all this, huh?" she asked him, and he smiled.

That was how the rest of the day went. I liked the women, and even the teenagers who'd come to help out with my disaster of a life. When Ray and Orli came up after closing time, they made short work of the sink.

I ended up calling the diner and ordering food for everyone, which Angela sent the boys to pick up. We all sat together on the living room floor to eat.

I smiled as they all cut up with one another, and answered a few questions that came my way. When nightfall came and we all broke apart, I felt overcome with emotions, and barely able to keep them in check. "I-I was ready to give up and go back to New York when you all showed up. I don't know how to thank you for all you've done."

"Well—" Angela said, "—you are going to repay them." I tensed as I waited for another shoe to drop.

Angela laughed at my expression. "These three ladies all have kids you've agreed to teach."

I glanced at the women and was met with three smiling faces. "You can just consider this our thank you in advance," Alli, the one related to the old junkman, said.

"Well, thank you. There's no way I could've done all this, no matter how much YouTube I watched."

As everyone left, I slipped a fifty into the hands of both teenagers. "Thanks, guys," I said, and they both smiled, before disappearing down the stairs.

Angela came over and patted my back. "That's going to help them more than you know. Their dad just lost his job and the family's trying to live on their mother's income alone. Every penny helps them right now."

"I'll reimburse you for what—"

"No, you won't. You're going to let us help out, so we feel like we aren't quite as horrible for getting you into this mess," she said, and I nodded.

"Thank you."

"Well, that's enough of that. Tomorrow, I hear we've got a couple more people coming to help, and if the kitchen cabinets fit like Orli thinks they will, then our buddy Jimbo Pipkin has already agreed to install them for you. If everything works out smoothly, by tomorrow night, you might have a good place to call home."

"It already is," I said, and Angela smiled, hugging me on the way out. Ray came up to me then and shook my hand.

"Looks like you've been welcomed in," he said.

"Yeah, that was... unexpected."

"Don't get too excited." Orli said as he came in behind us, "It's nice for a minute, then they'll start being all in your business, and trying to fix you up with the ugliest people they can find. But, hey, on the positive side, at least they're focusing on someone besides me for a change."

My face must've registered panic, because he slapped me on the back and laughed. "Only joking, well, a little anyway. Welcome home. See you tomorrow."

18

Orlando

AFTER THE KITCHEN PROJECT had fallen apart, I worried about Jonas. As happy as he'd been the night before, that's how miserable he seemed today, so I immediately called Angela, and asked her to check up on him.

Part of me felt guilty. I should've done more to make him feel better, but the truth was, I was just as bad as Ray at helping someone navigate their emotions. In the end, I'd made a good call by calling Angela. She took the bull by the horns, which she really was an expert at doing, and the next thing I knew, people were filing up the stairs to help put the apartment back in working order.

I waved at the Johnson boys when I saw them hauling the old kitchen cabinets out to the dumpster, then laughed when old man Franks showed up right on cue to haul all my dad's junk off.

By the time Ray and I made it upstairs, the place was coming together. "Hey—" I asked Ray, "—why don't you have that friend of yours Jimbo come by my place tomorrow and get the kitchen cabinets out of my shed. I'm guessing he could use the work, and I think our Mr. Piano Man could use a new kitchen sooner rather than later."

"You know he'll charge you out the nose for anything last minute."

"Yeah, wait, isn't his niece one of my piano students? Emily, right?"

Ray nodded. "Let's have Angela call him. If anyone can whip that money-grubbing narcist into shape, it'll be her."

Narcissist, I thought. I smiled at the mispronounced word, but didn't correct him this time. I'd swear it was a losing battle. "You know he's not the same bully he was in high school, right?" Ray said.

"Well, who charged widow Scott twice what it should've cost to take out her old kitchen?"

Ray cringed. "Well, the insurance covered most of that."

"And the soup kitchen? Who was going to charge them eight thousand dollars to install cabinets they already had?"

"Okay, okay, I get it, but I'm still saying you should give him another chance. Not all of us are the same people we were in high school."

"I am. You are," I said.

"No, dude, we aren't. You were a miserable SOB, and I've just become more charming, but you know we've both changed."

"I guess, but you know I had a reason to be miserable, losing my granny, and everything that went down with my dad..." I paused as a lump formed in my throat, thinking about the time things had gotten so bad at home.

"Hey, it's okay," Ray cut in and put a hand on my shoulder. "You know that's what friends are for, right?"

"No, I don't think most friends are like y'all. You two were at war with your own parents, and still took my sorry ass in."

He chuckled. "Well, my parents love Angela more than me, and hers? You know they just expected her to leave Monongahela, and become a high-powered something. They weren't ready for her to settle down with the likes of me."

"They love you well enough now."

"God, can't get rid of them."

I laughed and got back to working on the car. Ray and Angela had gotten married the day after Ray turned eighteen, against their parents' wishes. Angela was already working at her mom's salon, and Ray had started college, intending to get a business degree, but dropped out to attend trade school instead.

Problems with our parents was something we had in common. I'd told my father I was gay when I turned fourteen, and he'd thrown a fit. Our lives only fell back into a normal rhythm, because there weren't any guys around I was interested in, until I met Billy Buckley. He was an idiot of epic proportions, but he had abs like a washboard, and lips like a succulent piece of fruit, and the combination was irresistible.

My dad caught us kissing behind the shop, and ended up punching Billy in the face. He would've hit me too if Ray, who was considerably bigger than my father, hadn't shown up and shoved him away long enough for Billy to run, and for us to get the hell out of there.

Dad got arrested, and spent a night in jail for assaulting Billy, and I moved in with Ray and Angela. Their place was a tiny one-bedroom apartment in what used to be a boarding house by the railroad depot. It was a craphole, and you had to fight off the rats to dump your trash, but they'd saved me.

Grandpa's dementia had progressed enough that he'd gone into the nursing home, and his cottage had been boarded up. I still could've stayed there, but to be honest, I needed the sense of physical and emotional safety that living with Ray and Angela provided. I hadn't realized it then, but it was at that point that they'd gone from being my friends to my family.

So, I stayed six months with my newlywed friends. That was a debt I doubted I'd ever repay, no matter what I'd said about taking piano lessons from Jonas.

"Hey, Angela wants to know if you're sure the cabinets will fit?" Ray asked from outside the garage door.

"Pretty sure, but I'll double check tonight when I get home."

A few minutes later, Angela came into the garage, and said Jimbo was willing to install them for free as long as they fit.

"Miracle worker," I said, and Ray snickered.

"What?" she asked.

"Nothing, sweetheart, just admiring your ability to get things done," Ray told her, and she smiled.

"Jimbo was easy, if that's what you're talking about. You know he's mad about that niece of his. All I had to do was tell him this would keep the famous piano teacher here in town, and he was all for it."

"I stand by what I said, you're a miracle worker," I said, then I winked at Angela before I dove back into the car repairs.

"Well, you're both needed when you finish here. We've got most of the work done and prepped for to-morrow, so it shouldn't take much time."

"We're happy to help," Ray said, and kissed his wife, careful not to put his greasy hands on her.

I had to admit, seeing Ray and Angela together always gave me hope. The two had been madly in love long before we graduated high school, but even now, they moved together like a perfectly choreographed dance.

As always, when I saw them together, I wondered if I would ever have a relationship like theirs. My track record suggested it wasn't likely, not when I was attracted to idiots like my ex, Tommy, who talked me into traveling all the way to Pittsburgh to see him, only to discover he'd been out fucking someone else while I waited in the motel room.

I was, and always had been, a bad judge of character when it came to men. Even the cutie upstairs was a bad bet. I liked him, was attracted to him, and was almost sure if I pursued him, he'd be at least willing to consider it... consider me, but it'd only be playtime, and nothing serious would come of it. Not that I wouldn't welcome that kind of release, but it would only complicate an already complicated situation. In the end, it would come to nothing but trouble.

Some people like Ray and Angela got the fairy tale, and others, like me, we got shit. Then, again, if my version of a happily ever after entailed ending up with somebody like Tommy, I'd rather be lonely.

19

Jonas

ONCE EVERYONE HAD GONE, I lay on the floor and stared up at the ceiling, just letting all the day's pent-up feelings flow through me.

"You okay?" Orli asked from the doorway.

When I looked over, I saw concern on his face.

"Better than I've been in a very long time," I admitted.

Orli came over and sat down next to me. "This place has never been this nice," he said quietly.

The sad tone of his voice had me sitting up. "*You* okay?"

He laughed. "Yeah, just wondering why my dad never went to the effort to make the place look like this. Oh, well, no use getting worked up about it. Want a lift back to the motel? If you're still hungry or need a drink, we can stop along the way."

"I could go for a drink. I can't do pizza or hamburgers again anyway. My stomach wouldn't be able to handle that tonight."

He chuckled, before saying, "Believe it or not, the café has a nice salad bar, with more than iceberg lettuce, if you can believe it. I like to eat there after a busy day, but they have a decent beverage menu too. Wanna join me?"

I shrugged. "Sure, I guess. At some point, I'll go shopping to fill that refrigerator up, but yeah, there really isn't much more to do here."

He stood and reached out to pull me up after him. He pulled slightly too hard, and I ended up chest to chest with him.

I was startled by the sudden contact, and could feel the heat coming off him. When I looked up, I saw longing in his eyes that I knew matched my own. Without thinking it through, I lifted up onto my toes and kissed him.

The kiss started out tentative, but quickly grew more intense as I all but clung to him. *God, who knew the smell of oil and gasoline on a man was so delicious?*

When he pulled back, I almost fell back onto the floor. I was that absorbed in his kiss.

"Sorry, no, I mean, I like you, but I can't..."

Blushing, I nodded. "Yeah, sorry, I shouldn't have."

I tried for a reassuring smile, but inside I was mortified. I turned to go wash my face, and hopefully scrub away the feeling of rejection as well.

"Wait, Jonas, it's not you. Really, this is all on me. I just got out of a horrible relationship."

"Hey, no problem. I get it. I shouldn't have kissed you. I think I'll skip that drink, though, if you don't mind," I said as I rushed to the bathroom.

I ended up sitting on the closed toilet seat and having a good cry, not over Orli though. The kiss had been impulsive, and I knew better than to try mixing business with pleasure. I'd pushed when I shouldn't have, and I'd need to clean that up later. No, the tears were over Rodrigo.

I hadn't really let myself feel the loss of our relationship since he'd pulled that shit the night of my botched performance. Not that the asshole deserved my tears, but having Orli pull away, even if he had every right to do so, made me feel that sting and humiliation all over again.

"You suck at relationships," I whispered to myself. God, if Orli was still in the living room, hopefully he hadn't heard me sobbing. As if I needed a single thing more to be embarrassed about.

After I'd washed my face and cleaned myself up, I came out to find Orli had gone. Well, that was good, since I wasn't ready to have that conversation yet. I sure as hell didn't want him to see me looking like a fucking crybaby either, since I knew he'd think my tears were about him.

I locked up and slipped out the back door, glad Orli had gotten the lock replaced during the day, so I could now come and go without going through the office downstairs.

I avoided the café, eager not to run into Orli, or be seen by anyone if I could help it. Luckily, I made it back to the motel without being spotted.

I got a bottle of water out of the refrigerator, chugged it, then took a Tylenol before crashing on the bed.

As I lay there, I thought about all I'd lost in the past year. Rodrigo was a shit, but the truth was my losses started long before I got into a relationship with him. Losing my dad, then my housekeeper and pseudo-mom, Letti, my home, and life as I'd known it back in New York. Other than Tatiana, I'd never developed long-lasting friendships, which only added to my feeling of being alone. I felt that even more acutely today, as people I didn't know worked their asses off for me, a complete stranger.

I wasn't an idiot. I knew they'd done that because of Orli and Angela—probably Ray too. Their friendship transcended them, and landed on me. I'd been pulled in their orbit, because my fucking life was so fucked up, and they felt guilty about it, maybe even responsible for it, but it was up to me to enjoy the ride.

I flipped onto my back, and stared at the dated and stained ceiling above me. "Well," I said out loud, "I can sure as hell change this whole victim thing right now. As of Monday, I'm going to become the best piano teacher this town has ever seen, and that goes for Orli too. He might've gotten tricked into this, but I'll be damned if he doesn't get the payoff before I'm done."

The newfound resolve bolstered my confidence, and by the time I fell asleep, I knew what my life mission was, at least for the next year. That, in and of itself, was a blessing, and I intended to take full advantage.

By some miracle, the entire apartment was painted, and the kitchen cabinets installed by midafternoon the next day. I even had a working dishwasher now, after the guy Angela called Jimbo worked his magic on the broken appliance that morning.

I looked around the space and felt like I could cry again. What a complete transformation in just a few days. Even the old bathroom looked better. One of the women who'd helped yesterday brought a friend, who ended up scouring the bathroom without me even knowing, then she went to work doing the same to the kitchen.

Mostly, I spent the day learning to paint, staying out of everyone's way, and trying not to weep, because my brain struggled to comprehend all these strangers being so willing to help out. Angela, her friends, and Jimbo had come and gone by the time the furniture was delivered.

It wasn't until the large moving truck pulled into the parking lot that afternoon that I realized I had no idea how much I'd purchased. Was it really enough to require such a huge truck?

I was relieved when the men opened the back, and it wasn't full. "We've got to hurry," the man told me then. "Got to be in DC by late afternoon."

"No problem, can I help?"

That's probably not something I would've offered before the weekend, but somehow the small-town mentality had already begun to infiltrate my city mindset. The man smiled and said I could bring up the cushions while he and the younger guy, who I assumed was probably his son, carried the sofa.

In less than an hour, the furniture was unloaded and put where I wanted it, and it was freaking beautiful. I still needed to hang the art I'd purchased with the set, but the furniture looked like it'd been made for the apartment. Modern with nice lines that complemented the art deco feel of the place.

I began placing the artwork where I'd eventually hang it when I heard someone come in downstairs. I knew the shop was closed on Sunday, but I figured Orli probably came in to do some paperwork. I knew I was a coward, but I decided not to go down just yet. I was in too good a mood with how great all the furniture looked.

So, I went to the bedroom and began making the bed with the sheets I'd also managed to get in the deal. The owner had assured me everything was clean, and she'd packed it in a bag, so I knew they'd made it to the apartment in the same condition. Not having a washer or dryer, I decided they were as clean as anything at the motel, and made the bed, then I crashed on it, happier than I should be with my little apartment. It was half the size of my old one in Manhattan, but with freshly painted walls, pretty faux-hardwood floors, and a nice, if slightly used, kitchen, it would make a comfortable home.

When I heard the door open and shut, then raised voices, I decided to check out what was going on downstairs. Could there be a thief on the property?

I dashed down to the office, just in time to see Orli pulled down into a lip-lock with a guy about my height and build.

Orli must've heard me, because he pulled back, and looked right at me.

"Sorry," I said, and dashed back upstairs, mortified at what I'd unwittingly witnessed.

"Jonas, wait!" I heard Orli say, and then the stranger said something about me being a side piece. I had no desire to stick around to hear any of that. I'd assumed, wrongly, that Orli was not in a relationship. He'd even told me as much, but who knew what to believe. *Damn,* I'd fucked up worse than I thought.

I closed the door to the apartment and locked it, mostly as a way to make myself feel better, then I dashed out the back door, locking it too, and headed toward my motel room. Now that the apartment was refurnished, I could officially move in, but as I rushed back to the motel, I decided it would be in my best interests to pay for another day, and stay the hell away from the shop and apartment, until Orli and his boyfriend could work things out.

They sure as hell didn't need my ass in the middle of whatever was going on between them.

20

Orlando

*S*HIT AND *FUCK* AND all the other cuss words I could think of. I'd overslept, fully intending to be at the shop in time to help Jonas with his furniture delivery. Unfortunately, when I got there, Tommy, of all fucking people, was standing inside my office.

God, I'd forgotten I'd given the idiot a key to the place. Why did I do stupid shit like that? Seriously, he'd only been to Monongahela once, and I'd acted like the fool I was, giving him a key to the shop, and telling him how much it meant to me the idiot had been willing to visit.

"Tommy, why are you here, and more importantly, why are you in my shop?"

"I wanted to surprise you," he said, trying to make his voice sound sultry. It made my skin crawl.

"You need to leave, Tommy. We're over, I told you that."

"Oh, honey, we're men, gay men, you know how it is."

"I know you're a cheating, lying, snake in the grass."

"Oh, honey, come on, you know you've missed me."

I'd put distance between us, but he came over while I checked the register and shop to ensure he hadn't taken or gotten into anything. When I turned around, he lunged and kissed me before I could pull away.

I pushed him off just in time to look into the face of Jonas. *Fucking fuckity fuck.*

"Sorry," Jonas said, and darted up the stairs.

I called after him, just as my idiot ex said, "Oh, so I'm not the only one with a side piece."

"Shut the fuck up, Tommy. Leave now and give me the fucking key. You're not welcome here."

"Now, now, don't be so hasty."

"No, we're through. Leave now before I call the sheriff."

"Well, if I'd known you were going to be a princess about it all, I never would've driven all this way."

"You had to know... no, forget it, think what you like, just give me the key and leave. Tommy, if I ever see you again, it'll be too soon."

Tommy pulled the key out of his pocket and threw it at me Then, as dramatically as his queenly little ass could carry him, he marched out the door, slamming it, or trying to, on his way.

Luckily, the old shop door had been replaced with a commercial door, so it didn't slam as he'd hoped. Seeing him storm away even more pissed off, because of the door, was immensely satisfying.

I watched him leave, then called my buddy who'd come out yesterday to replace the lock on Jonas's apartment. *Jonas's apartment.* Wow, when had I begun thinking of it as his?

I arranged for my buddy to come back and replace the lock on my office door, knowing Tommy had probably made a copy. I had no doubt he could come back and create all kinds of havoc, now that he felt spurned.

Besides, I felt better knowing the locks were replaced. Everyone in town, it seemed, had a copy, and while that had never been a problem before, it seemed like an invasion of Jonas's privacy, since he was living here now.

Lucky for me, my locksmith friend was recently divorced, and usually his Sundays were spent drinking and watching TV, so he didn't hesitate to say he'd come over.

Once all that was arranged, I climbed the stairs and knocked on Jonas's door. When he didn't answer, I tried opening it and found it locked. I mean, that shouldn't have surprised me. Hell, I shouldn't have tried walking in without an invitation anyway.

I guessed now was as good a time as any to learn that little piece of good manners.

I slumped back down the stairs, fell into my office chair, and wondered if I had it in me to try to get some paperwork done. I still had to get receipts together for the accountant, but dang, I would rather do anything besides crunch numbers.

That was when it hit me that Jonas wasn't ignoring me. He'd probably gone back to the motel to get his things. That was something I could and would help with. I locked the deadbolt and grabbed the opener for the garage door, thinking that would give me a way in, and keep Tommy out.

My friend wouldn't be by to change the locks for a couple of hours, so I had time to spare.

I jumped into the truck, and drove over to the Monongahela Motel without thinking.

When Jonas opened the door, his expression told me just how much I didn't consider before rushing over here.

"Hey, you okay?" I asked.

"Yeah, I'm great, but you probably shouldn't be here, especially with your boyfriend in town."

"Oh, he's an ex, and I mean *very* ex. I'm sorry you had to witness his misguided, and unsuccessful attempt at getting back together with me."

Jonas backed up then and let me into the room. "I'm the one who's sorry, Orli. I shouldn't have come downstairs, and I sure as hell shouldn't have kissed you, not without knowing if you're taken or not."

The way he said it with such earnestness was sweet. He was sweet. "I liked kissing you," I admitted.

"Orli, you backed away like I was a snake or something. I mean, I don't blame you, but you can't say you enjoyed it when you clearly didn't. Besides," he said, stopping me from interrupting to protest, "I shouldn't be kissing you anyway. You're my student, my life literally teeters on your willingness to do the contest, and I'm in no way ready to be in a relationship anyway. Not when my freaking ex is dictating my life at the moment."

I thought about what to say, and chose my words carefully. "You met Tommy this morning. He's my ex as of last week. The police literally showed up at my motel room when he accused me of stealing his car while I was waiting for him to show up. I'd driven all the way to Pittsburgh to be with him, and instead of coming to the motel when he got off work like he'd said he would, he'd gone to the local fuckplace and got his rocks off. When someone stole and wrecked his car, he assumed it was me lashing out at him for cheating."

Jonas's lips turned down in frown that mirrored mine at recounting Tommy's betrayal. "Damn, that's almost as bad as my ex. He broke up with me, and locked lips with my soon-to-be replacement just as I was about to perform. Oh, and did I mention he's the conductor of the orchestra I was contracted with? The same orchestra that's sponsoring this contest."

"Oh, yeah, that's truly bad too."

He chuckled. "So, we both suck at picking men. That's a solid reason for us not making out, especially when one of us has his entire life on the line."

I nodded and acknowledged, inwardly at least, how I'd hoped, maybe in time, I could let go of my horrible past and give love another chance.

"You're making sense. So, for now, let's be friends, okay?"

He looked at my outstretched hand, then up at my face. "I've not got many of those either, but okay, why the hell not?" he said, and grasped my hand. "Friends."

I totally wanted to kiss him again. I wasn't proud of that, but I couldn't deny the truth of it. Instead, I asked what he wanted me to carry out to the truck.

"Huh?" he asked.

I waved my pointer finger around the room. "After all that work, you aren't moving in?"

"Oh, I was going to give you and who I thought was your boyfriend some alone time."

"God, I've had all the time with him I want. Let's get you moved in. You'll be a lot more comfortable there than here."

"No doubt," he agreed, and didn't waste time throwing his luggage together. In way too little time, he had everything packed and in the back of the truck. We made a quick stop at the grocery store on the way back to the apartment, to ensure he'd have a few days' worth of food, until I could take him to a larger store with more selection in Martinsville.

We finished unpacking the groceries just as I heard knocking on the door downstairs, meaning the locksmith was here.

I rushed down and he wasted no time installing a new lock on the office door. After paying and thanking my buddy multiple times, I ran back upstairs to see if Jonas wanted to join me at Angela and Ray's for a cookout.

When I reached the top of the stairs, the door to his apartment was open. I looked inside to see him passed out on the sofa. Damn, he was even cuter while he slept. I quietly closed the door, backed down the stairs, and headed to Angela and Ray's place.

What Jonas needed more than hanging out with us was some rest. I'd noticed the bags under his eyes deepening over the past few days, so I decided to leave him be. Tomorrow I began my piano lessons with him, and he began teaching my students. So, we'd be spending an excessive amount of time together anyway.

21

Jonas

JONAS

I woke up late in the evening, and immediately had an itch to play. It'd been five whole days since I'd touched a piano, and I was beginning to have practice withdrawal. That was a reminder I needed to find a piano sooner rather than later. Even a cheap one was better than not having one at all. It just needed to be able to hold its tune.

I got up and realized just how much I didn't have here. I still needed a coffee maker, and coffee. Orli had taken me to buy some groceries, so at least I wouldn't go hungry. I found a mug, heated water in the microwave left behind by Orli's dad, and dropped in an English Breakfast Tea bag. That should be enough to stave off a caffeine headache.

The apartment was nice. Even the smell of the gasoline and oil had been replaced by one of fresh paint. I'd gotten lucky, very lucky.

I texted Tatiana to see if she was available to talk. We were six hours apart, and she worked with students late in the afternoons, but the woman had never learned to turn her phone off. I'd figured out long ago it was best to text first, and let her contact me if she was free.

When she didn't reply, I figured she was busy, so I flipped open my laptop and began searching for a piano.

There were several that looked promising, not great, mind you, but promising. When I began to get discouraged, I switched to looking for things for the apartment. Sure, I could've shipped my stuff here from New York, but my real life needed to stay safely stored away. I still had no idea if this would work out, or if it would blow up in my face. At the moment, in my face seemed more likely.

So, I'd invest in a few things. A Keurig coffee maker would be fine. No, it wouldn't be my normal cappuccino, but at least when I got back to my life, I'd appreciate those even more. I added the machine to my cart.

I then searched for bedding, specifically sheets with a thread count higher than ten. *I'm a thread count snob.* Although the sheets I slept on last night were okay, if I wanted to rub my face against something that scratchy, I'd date a man with a beard. Even if I couldn't actually afford much, I couldn't afford to not sleep well.

Keeping a tight rein on my spending also meant I'd be doing my own cleaning for the first time ever. Angela had left me a broom and mop, but that was the extent of it, so I added cleaning supplies to my cart too.

After clicking the purchase button, I was prompted to put in an address for delivery. Address? Damn, I had no idea. When the Uber driver brought me here my first day, and even when I'd made furniture delivery arrangements, I hadn't been asked for the street address. It seemed everyone already knew where to find Hancock's Garage.

I quickly flipped over to Google, keyed in the business name plus the town, and came up with the address right away. I finished my purchase, then closed the site, and was just about to close the search engine when some of the results caught my attention. One headline in particular, *Local Mechanic's Son Makes Town Proud*, proved too intriguing not to click.

I quickly read the article that'd been published in the local newspaper, and smiled as it chronicled Orli winning local jazz competitions. He hadn't mentioned that, but from the look of him in the old black and white picture, I could tell at the time he'd been proud.

I scrolled through other articles, including one announcing he was taking over the shop. I also read a much older article noting the owner, Orli's dad, had lost his wife in childbirth.

I couldn't imagine living someplace where your life's history was chronicled for all to read. Despite being somewhat well-known in certain circles, as Stephan Ludwig's piano-playing son if nothing else, I'd never been that noteworthy. Besides Tatiana, I had no one who cared—no friends, no relatives, no lover.

Orli's family were gone as well, for all intents and purposes, but he had friends around, friends who'd all come to help me put this apartment together. Already, I felt closer to these people than anyone I'd known in New York.

Tatiana's phone call took my mind off my gloomy thoughts. "Hey," I answered.

"Hey? Has living in a tiny town already caused you to speak so casual?"

"Tatiana—" I said, ignoring the jab, "—are you teaching?"

"I was, my last student just left. I'm about to go home."

"I don't want anything. I just woke up early and didn't have my piano to practice on, so I was looking for someone to entertain me."

Tatiana laughed. "Well, if you'd come to Germany like I asked you to, I'd be entertaining you by having you help with my students. I could still get you a job, just say the word."

I smiled at the offer. "If this fails, I will probably take you up on your offer, but for now, I'd like to see where this goes."

I took pictures of the apartment and texted them to her, and of course, she was impressed. I'd done the same before work started, and she'd been concerned, but I'd seen her accommodations while attending Juilliard, and this place, even in the state it'd been in before, was better.

"Oh, I have to go, Jonas. The new violin instructor just walked by. I must go and flirt."

I laughed, just able to squeeze in a goodbye before she hung up.

I lay out on the sofa and stared at the ceiling. Maybe Germany was a good option for me. Tatiana worked in an excellent music program there. I was going to be teaching here anyway, so why not teach students with real talent? Someone who would help to bolster my career? As I drifted back to sleep, I had revised my game plan. Once I'd fulfilled the orchestra's contract, and seen Orli through the competition in Salzburg, I'd move to Germany to begin a new life. Tatiana had been right, no future awaited me back in New York.

22

Orlando

J ONAS WALKED DOWNSTAIRS AND waved at me through the door that separated the office from the garage. At first, I didn't know why he was there, but then I looked at the clock, and realized I'd lost track of time. "Ray, I'm going to have to head over to the school. Can you finish Mrs. Bethel's carburetor? She's planning to come pick it up at six."

"Sure thing, boss," he said, and I purposefully ignored the sly smile he was flashing between me and Jonas. The man was constantly trying to fix me up, and damn if he hadn't already figured out Jonas was my type. The harassment would never end now.

I rushed over to clean up as best as I could, and threw on the clean clothes I kept in the back, so I didn't stink of the garage too much. When I came out, Jonas smiled at me. "So, the lessons begin," I said.

He nodded in acknowledgment. When we climbed into my truck and started toward the school, he said he'd like to hold our first lesson after we finished with the kids. "I don't have a piano in the apartment yet, so we'll need to use the one at the school."

"Yeah, that's what I guessed. Is that what you want me to play?" I asked, and nodded toward the sheets of music he held in his lap.

"Yeah, and music I brought along to see where the kids are with sight-reading. I'm assuming you've not done much work on the classics?"

"Well, the books Ms. Phillips gave them include classical pieces, but they usually skip those and go to the fun stuff." He sighed, and I couldn't help but chuckle. "Don't worry, they're pretty easygoing, at least for the most part. Just don't think you can force them to do a piece they hate, 'cause that will shut the entire thing down."

"I'm just not sure I'm cut out for this. The students I work with don't tell me what they want to play, it's the other way around."

"We'll see, but for now, just roll with the punches. It's fun once you get into a groove with them."

He didn't seem convinced, and to be honest, I wasn't either, but if this was going to work out, he'd have to take on the responsibility.

We signed in at the office, and walked down to Ms. Phillips's classroom, where she had the first student warming up with scales. "You two are late," she said sternly. When Mrs. Stewart walked by behind us, Ms. Phillips hmphed, and added, "But, I guess that can't be helped. I've got Kevin started. If you need anything, I'll be in Mrs. Stewart's classroom for a staff meeting."

"We'll be fine, but try not to get arrested," I said under my breath, causing Ms. Phillips to wink at me.

"Kevin—" I said as the kid stopped playing, "—this is Mr. Ludwig. He's going to be giving you lessons for the next few months while I'm taking lessons myself."

Kevin just nodded. The kid was shy, much more than the others. Ms. Phillips had encouraged him to learn piano to help build his self-esteem. "So, can you tell Mr. Ludwig what type of music you prefer to play?" I asked, and Kevin shrugged. "Well, I know you enjoyed playing *The Entertainer* last year, so is that something you'd like to do again?"

He just shrugged again. Jonas smiled, pulled out a sheet of music, and propped it on the music shelf in front of Kevin. "Well, I'd like to find out how much you know. Would you mind playing this for me?" he asked.

The kid looked at the music for several moments, and began playing it almost flawlessly. "Wow," I said. "Kevin, that was awesome."

He smiled at the compliment. "Okay, how about this?" Jonas asked, and switched out the sheet music. Once again, Kevin impressed me with his skill level.

Jonas did that time and time again, until Kevin got to a piece he could only barely play. "Well, sir—" Jonas said, smiling, "—you are quite good. Let's start with this piece, and I'll make comments about what you can do to improve."

I sat and watched Jonas effortlessly guide the kid through ways to improve his playing. Much like he'd done with me, he worked on posture, how to hold his hands, and ways to lean into the music to hit the harder notes.

I guess I hadn't really noticed the level of Kevin's talent, which probably said more about my teaching than anything. Regardless, I was so proud of him when Carla walked in ready for her lesson.

Carla shocked me just like Kevin had, then Randy and Sammy did the same. All four were at different skill levels, but able to sight-read Jonas's music a hell of a lot better than I'd have given them credit for.

What pleased me the most, though, was how well Jonas did with them. He clapped and praised when they overcame something difficult, and the smiles on the kids' faces caused my heart to swell.

Truth be told, that was why I taught the kids. Those smiles and moments of joy when my students managed to succeed at something they'd struggled with made the time I spent teaching them more than worth it.

Before we'd finished with the last kid, Ms. Phillips was back at her desk. She sat silently observing Jonas's final lesson, and I could tell she approved. When Sammy left, Ms. Phillips stood up, shook Jonas's hand, and said how much she appreciated having him. "You are much better with pre-teens than you think you are. I was wrong to underestimate you."

Jonas smiled, though I couldn't tell if he was happy, or just relieved. "I'm more than a little impressed with how well your students play," he said.

"That's all down to this guy," she said, and pointed toward me. "Orlando has the ability to motivate the kids to practice. It's truly a remarkable thing to watch."

"I can see that," Jonas said, and cast an approving look my way. I couldn't deny hungrily soaking up his praise. "Now, I need to get some work out of the wonder boy," he said. That earned him a rare smile from Ms. Phillips.

"Before I go, I think I've found a piano for you. The local Christian Church is moving to a larger facility in Clide, and has already replaced its old piano. When I told the church leaders about the competition, they said they would happily loan it to you for as long as you're here."

I cocked an eyebrow at Ms. Phillips, knowing that church had not been very gay-friendly in the past. "Do they realize it's me who'll be using it?" I asked.

Ms. Phillips chuckled, then nodded. "Orli, son, you know things are changing. They're willing to loan it, *because* it's you who needs it. They've been trying to change their way of thinking since old Pastor Phelps passed away."

I couldn't help but be astonished at the change of attitude. My great-great-grandparents had been dedicated to that church when it'd been part of the Baptist Convention. My great-grandmother even played there a few times after it left the convention and became the Community Christian Church, but attitudes among church leaders had been really sour while I was growing up, and they even protested gay-rights legislation at the state level.

To hear they'd willingly let me, an openly gay man, use their old piano, which everyone in town would know about the moment it was moved to the apartment, was huge progress.

"Well, I'd be very appreciative," Jonas said. "I can't function here long without a piano, and there aren't many viable used options in the area."

"That's what I discovered when I looked too," Ms. Phillips confirmed. "That's why I asked the church. We all know that old one would've ended up forgotten in some basement classroom, which really would be a shame, considering it's still a pretty sound instrument."

I agreed to contact the new pastor, someone from out of town, and who I hadn't met yet, to make delivery arrangements. It was a baby grand, so it'd have to go up through the inside stairwell. The fire escape was too rickety and narrow to be a viable option.

As Ms. Phillips collected her things to leave, I walked out with her, leaving Jonas alone in the classroom. "Hey, that was really decent of you," I said when we were out of earshot.

"No, not really. I realized after my argument with Mrs. Stewart that I was wrong in how I was treating him and you. I was already considering purchasing the church's piano for the school. That they volunteered it for the contest just makes it a better situation. I know they've not always been the most accepting congregation."

I smirked at the ever-crafty woman as we continued down the hallway. "I figured you'd had something to do with their change of mind."

"Oh, no, not me. I think it's their new pastor, who has a son who is out of the closet. You might consider meeting with them now that they've made such a bold move. Unfortunately, not all in that congregation are thrilled with the changes."

I chuckled. "I'm sure that's true."

Ms. Phillips patted my arm as she dashed out the front door toward her car.

23

Jonas

I LET MY FINGERS dance across the keys of the institutional piano. There was a time, not so long ago, I'd never have considered playing such an instrument, but my days of playing the snob were clearly over.

The sound was okay. It was far from the rich sound I was used to hearing when I played, but after so long, it felt good to play anything.

When Orli stepped back in the classroom, I finished playing and turned toward him. "Are you ready to start?" A resigned look crossed his face, and I couldn't help but smile. "It's not going to be that bad. Come over and let me see if you've improved since our first session."

As soon as he sat next to me on the piano bench, I noticed improvements in his posture, as well as the way he held his hands. He still struggled, though, because changing the way one played wasn't easy, even with daily practice. Still, I appreciated the obvious effort he was putting into breaking his bad habits.

"Nice. It gives me hope to see you've been working on what we talked about. And don't worry—" I said, when I saw his frustrated expression, "—your skill will return as you get used to playing correctly. Not only that, but you'll see the slight changes will improve your ability too."

As I'd done with the kids earlier, I placed sheet music of different levels in front of Orli, and had him sight-read to assess how well he played. Because his students were clearly skilled, I already knew he'd play better than I expected.

Sure enough, his skill level was quite high. Nowhere near where it needed to be a year from now to legitimately contend in Salzburg, but at least he already had a good grasp of style and musical theory.

"Good, Orli, very good. So, this piece is where I'd like you to start. Just as with *Für Elise*, I'm not looking for honky-tonk. This needs to flow, so over the next few days, I'm going to work with you on style. You already have staccato down to a science..." I chuckled, and he smiled. "But, your slow classical pieces need to have as much heart as your jazzy ones."

He nodded in understanding, and began playing the piece again without my prompting. Although I was firmly in teacher mode, the few times his shoulder brushed mine sent electric zaps down my arm. Our lesson ended abruptly when the janitor came in and shooed us out, saying he was about to close the school.

"So, when do you think I can have the piano delivered?" I asked. "This really isn't going to work. If we're going to get to where you need to be, we need more than half an hour to practice."

"I'll call the pastor tomorrow," he said, and we both walked out of the building with the janitor on our heels, and locking up behind us.

As we drove back to the apartment, I was in my head, thinking through all we'd need to do to move the students along.

"Hey, are you hungry?" Orli asked.

"Um, I could eat, why?"

"Well, I have food I'd planned to grill over the weekend, but things happened. Wanna come over? I've already asked Angela and Ray."

"Sure, I guess. Why now?"

Orli smiled and drove toward his home. That night, I enjoyed getting to know Angela and Ray better, and got to meet the infamous Ella, who in a roundabout fashion was responsible for me being here in the first place.

Of course, after spending just a few minutes around the girl, I realized how she likely never would have been the star we'd hoped. The girl was all energy, and happy energy at that. She spent the entire time exploring the land around Orli's place, only coming back to tell the adults about whatever she'd found. Young Ella was a free spirit, and tying the poor thing down to a piano for hours on end would've destroyed that spirit.

When I looked at Orli and caught him looking back, a strange thrill passed through me, and I realized just how lucky I was. Not only did I end up with the right student to prepare for the competition, but the student was also a nice guy who'd welcomed me into his world. That he was also delicious eye candy wasn't lost on me either. For the first time since arriving in this town, I was pleased with how things had turned out.

24

Orlando

PASTOR JAMES AND HIS son, Davey, delivered the church's old piano the day after I called to make arrangements. The Kirby baby grand wasn't the best brand on the market, but according to Jonas, it was still a fine instrument. The four of us we were able haul it up the stairs and into the apartment with little trouble, even though the thing weighed a freaking ton.

If the building wasn't literally made out of concrete, I'd have been concerned that it might not hold the weight.

We were about to head back downstairs, when Davey asked Jonas if he could ask him some questions about playing, as he'd lost his piano teacher upon moving to Monongahela. "Sure," Jonas said, with a look of surprise.

They hung back to chat while I helped Pastor James take the straps we'd used back to his truck.

"So, this is a pretty big change for the church," I said, unable to resist getting to the bottom of their willingness to loan us the piano.

Pastor James chuckled. "Well, when they interviewed me for the job, I made it real clear where I stood on the gay-rights issue, and said if they hired me, I'd be pushing for them to become accepting and affirming."

"That just seems impossible to me. I'm sorry if I sound cynical, but you have to understand just how unfriendly the church has been."

Pastor James looked sad, then sighed. "Son, there have been many changes these past few years. I myself had a long way to go, and had to forsake my own religious affiliation when my son came out, but what you might not know is the people in this congregation adore you. When I was being interviewed, your name came up often as witness to someone who's lived the life of a Christian, despite his sexuality."

I looked at the man like he'd lost his mind. "Me? Why?"

He smiled. "Well, you've fixed a lot of cars, and done so when your community couldn't afford to pay. That hasn't gone unnoticed. When I mentioned you needing the piano while Mr. Ludwig was here, the board voted unanimously to loan it to you, and, son, you must know that board doesn't vote unanimously on anything."

That had me returning his smile. It just seemed so impossible that the members felt so favorably toward me. I had a policy to fix people's cars if I could, whether or not they could pay, but that was just me being neighborly, because my business could afford it. I didn't owe anything on my building, and I got paid well for the work I did when customers could pay, so I tried to pay it forward when needed.

"Well, sir, please let your congregation know how pleased I am you're letting Mr. Ludwig borrow the piano. We'll take good care of it, I promise."

Just then, Davey darted down the stairs, and excitedly told his dad, "Hey, Mr. Ludwig said he'd teach me on the weekends if you don't mind."

"Son, you know we're still getting the budget set up. I'm not sure we can afford it right now."

Jonas came down the stairs behind Davey, and said, "Well, my services are being paid for by the orchestra, so my lessons are free."

Pastor James's face broke into a smile, and Davey whooped with joy. "So can I?" he asked.

"If Mr. Ludwig has time, of course, you can."

"Thanks, Dad," he said, and hugged him.

"Saturday mornings, and you'll have to work hard," Jonas said.

"I will. I want to get to the point where I can play at church. Dad said I can lead the youth choir if I can get my piano skills up."

"That's totally doable, from what you showed me today. So, I'll see you Saturday," Jonas said, as both Pastor James and Davey shook his hand before leaving.

"You're getting quite a lot of students. You sure you'll have time for them all?" I asked.

"Please, what else have I got to do? I'll practice myself in early morning, so after that, I'm free as a bird."

"Don't say that out loud, or the entire community will show up wanting lessons."

Jonas chuckled. "Well, we probably should set some limits, but if I have time, I certainly don't mind doing it. In fact, I think I'll be much happier if I'm working, than if I'm sitting around staring at the walls."

"I completely understand. I prefer to be busy myself."

Jonas went back upstairs, and for the next hour and a half, some of the most beautiful music flowed through the shop while Ray and I worked. Usually, we'd listen to the radio, but as soon as Jonas started playing, Ray turned it off so we could enjoy the free concert.

"Damn," Ray said, after silence filled the shop. "The guy is amazing."

"Yeah, he really is," I said, unable to avoid sounding awestruck.

Ray winked, but thankfully, didn't harass me before sliding back underneath Mr. Corvallis's ancient Chrysler LeBaron.

25

Jonas

OKAY, SO I KNEW what it meant to be busy. In New York, I'd spent most of my waking hours practicing, either by myself or with an orchestra to prepare for a performance. Life in Monongahela, however, was a different kind of busy.

I woke up early every morning, as I always did, and practiced. Continuing to work on my skills, so I didn't get soft, as my dad used to say, was a high priority.

Before lunch I'd catch up on corresponding with the orchestra board, who'd demanded I send a progress report at least twice a week, not that I could really blame them, they were paying me to be here after all.

I'd go to the school in the afternoons, and arrive just after school let out to meet with my first student of the day. Ms. Phillips usually worked in her classroom as we practiced, but she never interfered, and the kids didn't even seem to notice she was there. She really did stroke my ego, though, as she assessed each student's progress, and told me how lucky they were to have me.

I guessed I was a typical performer in that way, always looking for praise.

When I'd get back home, I'd meet with Orli for our evening session. He would usually bring along something for us to eat, which was thoughtful, but strange considering he'd worked all day. As time passed, I learned he was incredibly domestic, and would prep our meals before coming to work. We'd eat before practicing, and I tried not to read too much into his essentially fixing me dinner every night.

His skill level improved so fast it made my head spin. "You really are a natural," I told him three or four weeks after Pastor James dropped the piano off.

"Thanks, I think it's more that I like doing it and less about skill."

I chuckled. "Trust me, I've met a lot of people who love it and have no skill."

"Well, I still suck at the classical pieces," he admitted, and I couldn't disagree.

"You definitely don't play them as well as you do the more contemporary pieces, but you're improving."

It was the honest truth. I'd been concerned the first couple of weeks, because of how much he struggled with relearning posture and proper hand placement, but the more we practiced, the better he got. He was improving on the classical pieces too, just not as much, or as quickly as I had hoped.

One evening as we practiced late into the night, he kept struggling with *Clair de Lune*. The piece seemed to give him so much trouble, he kept pounding the keys like he was trying to be heard over a bar full of people. Clearly, we hadn't yet broken him of reverting to his honky-tonk technique, and it gave me an idea for our next lesson.

I went in search of Orli after returning home from school the next day, only to see his backside hanging out of the front of a car. It wasn't a bad view either.

"Hey, Ray—" I said as I walked into the office. "—please let Orli know I'm back."

"I will, but he said he's going to be late. That old Subaru is giving him some problems."

"No problem, we won't be practicing much tonight anyway. I've got something else planned."

Ray looked at me surprised and wiggled his eyebrows. My cheeks heated before I could help it. "Not that!" I laughed, and dashed upstairs before Ray embarrassed me more.

Ray and Angela were becoming close friends of mine, and at least once every weekend we'd all have dinner together at Orli's place, or theirs. The couple was fun, and definitely had an agenda when it came to Orli and me, but only teased us a little, and never in front of each other. Orli had admitted to me a week or so ago that they'd been giving him grief too. "It's like 'cause they're together, they have to fix up everyone who's single," he'd said.

"Well, they are really happy together, so maybe they just want their friend to be that happy."

"I'm happy, but yeah, I think you're right." He'd flashed me a smile while saying it, and I couldn't help but wonder if I was adding to his happiness.

Spending every weekday evening practicing with Orli had begun to build a bond between us. I'd never had a student who was also a friend, let alone a friend I found so attractive, so it was a new experience for me.

Seeing that Orli hadn't brought food for us, because usually he stored it in my refrigerator, I pulled out a frozen lasagna and stuck it in the oven. Those things took forever to cook, but Ray had said Orli wouldn't be able to break away anytime soon anyway.

I poured myself a glass of wine, and ended up finishing it before Orli showed up.

"I think I might have to postpone practice tonight," he said from the doorway, still covered in oil and grime.

I chuckled. "Well, good for you that I didn't plan to practice tonight, but I do have plans. You can use my shower to clean up. By the time you're done, the lasagna I've made will be ready, and we can sit down to watch a movie you need to see."

Orli looked at me in surprise, and I snickered. "You need to learn how to feel the music, and I think this old movie will help."

He shrugged, and said he'd be back after grabbing clean clothes downstairs. There had been a couple times when he was so covered in grime, I'd refused to let him come in, so as a compromise, I'd let him use the shower to clean up before we did our lessons.

By the time he got out of the shower, I'd dished us both a plate and poured the wine. We sat across from each other at the small kitchen table, usually piled high with sheet music.

"So, what was going on with the old Subaru?"

He moaned. "It's Mr. Harris's car. It's old as dirt and the man refuses to replace it. Says it was the first car he ever bought."

"Did you fix it?" I asked.

He shook his head. "No, and I'm almost sure without rebuilding the motor, I won't."

"Ouch, so you need to tell the man you can't fix it then."

He shrugged. "Well, I've told him that several times before, but I'm thinking yeah, this time it's toast."

"Sorry," I said with sympathy.

"Hey, what's this movie you have picked out?"

I laughed. "Well, it's a black-and-white musical from the forties called *Music for Millions*. My dad loved watching classic movies, and this was one of his favorites, because he said the music was so unique. It's got *Clair de Lune* in it, and I think hearing it from a different perspective might help inspire you."

Orli chuckled, but he seemed intrigued. "Is it so bad that I don't want to play it like a funeral march?"

I thought for a moment, then nodded. "Yeah, actually, that is the problem. Not everything—"

"Can be played like you're in a ragtime band?"

I couldn't help but laugh. "Correct, it can't, and you need to learn."

"Well, I guess there's no time like the present," he said, and stood up from the table. He took our empty plates to the sink, rinsed them off and put them in the dishwasher. I appreciated that he never just left the dishes for me to do, like I used to for our housekeeper.

I started the movie, lowered the lights, and poured us both another glass of wine, before I sat down next to him on the sofa. It had taken some online searching that morning, but I'd finally found the movie through a streaming service.

I'm guessing the three glasses of wine, and memories of being snuggled up against my father watching this same movie, must've gotten the better of me. Sometime between the opening credits and the part I wanted Orli to see, I fell asleep.

I woke up to *Clair de Lune* playing in the background. My legs were tucked up under me and I was leaning against Orli. He felt so warm, so solid, and memories of my father floated into my consciousness.

As the song, so beautifully played by the harmonica player, echoed through the apartment, I felt warm tears slide down my face before dripping onto Orli's shirt.

Orli must've noticed, because his rough hand came up to comfort me, rubbing the tears from my cheeks. I sat up and was going to excuse myself to go wash my face in the bathroom, when Orli held me in place.

"Are these for your dad?" he asked. The gentleness in his voice shocked me as much as his question.

I nodded, and admitted, "It was one of his favorite scenes. I-I'm sorry."

"Shh," Orli comforted, and pulled me into his arms. I should've resisted. We had agreed to just be friends. Never mind that I'd fantasized about being in this sort of situation with him, on this very sofa, which would lead to so much more than cuddling. I shouldn't be melting into the warmth of his embrace.

As his hands ran soothingly up and down my back, it was all I could do to pull away. "I-I really shouldn't," I said.

Orli let me go without a word. I returned from the bathroom to find him sitting on the sofa, staring at a blank screen. It appeared our movie night was over.

"You okay?" I asked. "I didn't mean..."

He held up his hand to stop me. "I *felt* you, Jonas. Your sadness. I've had those same feelings, and no one to share them with. I don't mean like a friend... I mean like someone who gets me."

Orli stood up, walked toward the front window, and looked out. "I know we agreed to be friends, and I'm happy to oblige, but I'm also not willing to lie by saying I'm not developing feelings for you," he said, turning around to face me. "I'd like to be more than friends. Would you consider it at least?"

Emotions still swirled around inside me, and many had nothing to do with memories of my dad. I did want more with Orli. I wanted to do so much more than practice piano with him. I wanted more times like tonight where those big strong arms held me, comforted me, and made me feel like for the first time since losing my dad, I'd be okay.

I may have felt like rushing into his arms and kissing him like some cinematic damsel in distress, but I hesitated. "It's a huge risk," I said.

"Life is a risk, Jonas, and whatever this is between us feels like a risk worth taking."

That's all it took. I took the three steps between us, and ended up wrapped in his arms again, his mouth on mine.

Weeks of pent-up emotion and desire burst free as we embraced—need, want, hunger—mine and his.

Orli tenderly stroked my hair when we pulled apart. "Come with me," he said as he took my hand, and led me willingly to my bedroom.

He guided me toward my bed, slipped my shirt over my head, and took his time kissing my neck and shoulders, then he undid my pants, letting them slide to the floor along with my underwear.

"Get on the bed," he commanded, which sent a thrill through me. I did as Orli instructed, while watching him strip off his own clothes.

"I've wanted you so bad, wanted to feel you, touch you." He climbed over me and then lowered himself, pressing me skin-to-skin into the mattress.

"Mmm," was all I could manage to say as I felt the full length of his body touching mine. I was so lost with need.

Orli ground his naked cock into mine, which just caused me to moan louder.

He chuckled knowingly, and began kissing down my torso, not stopping until he reached my cock.

Before taking me in his mouth, he looked up. When we made eye contact, he sucked me into his mouth, and savored me.

"Aaah!" I exclaimed, finally finding my voice. "Oh, God, Orli."

Pleasure flowed through my veins as he assaulted my cock, moving deliciously up and down my length until I thought I might come.

I ran my hands through his hair and gently tugged in an effort to pull him off. "Too soon!" I whined, and got another chuckle, this time with my cock still in his mouth.

"God," I said, unable to resist bucking into his mouth again.

To save me from ending this sooner than I wanted, I managed to pull free and roll him over onto his back, then I slowly moved my body down his, letting my sac glide down him until his cock slid between my balls and ass.

"You are so hot," I said as I moved my hands over his muscular body. He fucked against my taint, sending pleasure through me as I leaned over and savored the flavor of him.

His aroma, a mix between cologne and the soap I had in the shower, heightened my senses, arousing me like some sort of pheromone.

He grabbed my ass and spread my cheeks, slipping his cock up against my hole to tease me. "God, I want you, so much," I said, and would've pressed down, taking him in dry, had he not stopped me.

"Got protection?" he asked. I nodded, suddenly feeling shy. I slipped off his incredible body and dashed to the bathroom, where I stored the condoms. The pack was unopened, of course. I never thought I'd be using them here, but had brought them with me from New York anyway.

I smiled at him as I walked over to the nightstand for the bottle of lube before climbing back onto the bed. "We'll need this," I said, and slipped the condom over his cock.

I lubed my own ass, then crawled back on top of him, slowly slipping his throbbing cock inside me.

"God, oh God," I moaned as I felt his head enter me. It'd been a while since I'd been fucked. Hell, it'd been months, and I didn't do it with just anyone, but Orli wasn't just anyone. I wanted it, wanted him, more than words could say.

Then he thrust gently, and my brain scrambled. "Oh, fuck, yeah, yeah!"

My words encouraged him, and he worked his cock the rest of the way in. "Oh, God!" I yelled, when his balls hit my ass. "More!"

Orli took charge then, pushing inside me again and again, setting all my nerve endings on fire.

"Yeah," Orli moaned as his speed slowly increased. I looked into his eyes and saw the same need I'd felt reflected in his. It felt incredible to be truly seen by this man. *Magic, this is fucking magic*, I thought, as my heart fluttered.

Just then, Orli shifted, and his cock hit my prostate, sending an electrical charge through me. "Fuck!" I yelled. "Oh, fuck! Harder, Orli. Fuck me harder!" I leaned back and closed my eyes, enjoying the sensation of being fucked by a handsome man's perfectly sized cock.

Orli continued thrusting inside me, harder and harder, until I rolled off of him and onto my back. "I need more of you than that," I said, making him smile.

He lay between my legs, lifted them, and thrust back inside. Skin slapped against skin as a thin layer of sweat coated me, my nerve endings once again on fire.

"I'm close," he whispered, while grinning down at me, but not losing pace. I nodded, a bit disappointed because I wasn't, but I should've known Orli wouldn't take and not give. Instead, he shifted, somehow knowing where my G-spot was, and fucked into it.

I all but screamed when pleasure radiated through me, and I shot white ropes of cum all over my stomach and chest.

Orli came shortly after, thrusting hard through the last of my orgasm, and let out a satisfied moan as he emptied inside the condom.

"Fuck," he said as he pulled out, falling beside me. "God damn, that was... it's been a while," he said, out of breath.

"For me too," I said, and desperately wished I'd thought of getting a towel from the bathroom earlier. All I wanted to do now was fall blissfully into sleep.

Instead, I got up, went to the bathroom for the towel, and wiped myself off before coming back. Orli had disposed of the condom, so I handed him the towel, and crawled back in bed next to him.

I was used to men who screwed and left, so I was surprised when Orli cuddled into me. The sensation was almost enough to bring back the tears from earlier. I didn't think I'd ever felt so... so vulnerable and cared for by a lover. I knew that made me sound desperate and needy, but I no longer cared.

As this beautiful man held me, I fell asleep, just enjoying having him near.

I woke up a little while later to find Orli watching me. "Hey, sorry. Fell asleep."

He kissed my neck. "Not a problem for me. You're really cute when you sleep."

I laughed. "I'm sure that's not true, but thanks."

We lay like that for a while, sharing soft kisses and touches, before Orli said, "Tell me about your dad."

"Really?" I asked, thinking it an odd topic after what we'd just shared.

"Well, you seemed so sad earlier, but if you don't want to, I understand."

"No, it's okay. I, well, I'm not used to talking about it."

Orli leaned over and kissed my forehead. "I lost my granny when I was just out of high school, and my grandpa a few years ago. Not one day goes by when I don't miss them."

"Yeah, I was really close to my father. I think 'cause he was so old when I was born, he never felt like a father, more like your grandparents probably felt to you. He used to laugh and say he'd have been ridiculously strict if I'd come along even twenty years earlier, but for the most part, he wanted to show me the world, his world, and the things he loved."

I lay silently then, letting the memories come to the forefront of my mind. Orli absently ran his hand up and down my arm, waiting until I was ready to share more.

"Since he's been gone, I've been a little lost," I admitted.

Orli nodded. "I understand, way more than you know. My dad isn't very paternal. In fact, he's the opposite. He always said we were friends, but damn, he sucked at that too." He chuckled, but I could hear the edge to it. "Had it not been for my mom's family, well, I'd have been lost long ago. Dad wanted to work on old cars, then go play. He didn't want to deal with a young kid. I think if my mom had lived, maybe that would have been different, but..."

I hugged Orli as he trailed off, ruminating in his own thoughts, and we both fell silent. I ended up falling asleep again, and when I woke up, he was gone. I was nervous about what his sudden absence meant. In my experience, an empty bed after having sex meant my partner was gone and would never be seen again.

I was relieved when I heard noises coming from outside the bedroom, and slipped on some pajamas to go investigate. "Hey, what's going on?" I asked as I walked into the kitchen.

"Couldn't sleep. So, I thought I'd make us breakfast."

The man's thoughtfulness had me grinning, as did his timing. "Well, it's only an hour before you have to be at work, so..."

"Yep, and a good breakfast will make the day easier to deal with."

"You feeling okay about last night?" Orli asked, when I sat down in front of the scrambled eggs and toast he'd fixed me.

"Yeah, and amazingly, not too concerned, although, that could change, depending on how you're feeling."

Orli chuckled. "I'm not the one who put the skids on. Well, okay, I did, but I don't have as much to lose as you."

I sighed and took a bite of the eggs, which tasted better than any I'd eaten before. "What's in these eggs? They are delicious."

The smile that lit up Orli's face sent shivers up my spine.

"Just butter, something my great-granny taught me."

"Fat, why does it make things taste so good, but can also make you fat?"

"I think it's a conspiracy."

"Agreed. So, I do have a lot to lose, but we've both already lost people important to us. I mean, I lost my dad, and you've lost your grandparents. I thought about it, and I figure if there's a chance this could be something...

something more…" I hesitated, knowing I was entering territory that would cause most men to run for the hills.

"That if there's a chance this could be something more, it's worth pursuing?" Orli finished for me.

"Does that make you feel anxious? I mean, I'm not one to push relationships on people."

Orli held his hand up and laughed. "I'm a settling down kind of guy. I live in the middle of nowhere, and my friends and neighbors are my family. So, no, thinking about us being in a relationship doesn't scare me. In fact, if you were a player, that would scare me more."

I blushed, knowing what I was about to say was going too far, but I couldn't quite help myself. "Like the twink from the other day?"

"Oh, my god, did you really go there?" Orli asked as he came over, and began tickling me.

"Stop!" I shouted, between uncontrollable giggles. He did, but stayed close, kissing me on the forehead, and wrapping his arms around me.

"Yeah, he was a really bad decision, but in my defense, he was very available when I met him, or at least, that's what he led me to believe."

I leaned back into his embrace, and looked up at him. "I really can't judge you for that, trust me."

"I do," Orli said, and kissed the top of my head before he went back to his side of the table.

There was more in that *I do* than anything we'd said up to that point. He trusted me, and the truth was, for some reason I couldn't even begin to understand, I trusted him too.

After we cleaned up breakfast, Orli said he was going to slip downstairs to start work early. "If I get done early, I get to come be with you earlier, for lessons, that is."

"Only lessons?" I teased.

"Well, we have to maintain some professionalism, but when our lesson is done, who knows?"

"I could find another old movie, if that helps."

Orli smiled. "I like old movies, but I think I've got other things in mind."

I blushed, and he laughed before darting down the stairs.

I really did like the guy, and for the first time in my life, where a guy was concerned, I wasn't nervous. Maybe this was what being truly happy felt like.

26

Orlando

"I'M SORRY, MR. HARRIS. Unfortunately, I can't fix it this time. The motor is toast. Of course, I could rebuild it, but that would cost more than the old car is worth."

"Can we replace the motor?"

"Sure, but then you'll end up replacing the transmission, which probably has six months to a year left on it. The radiator is also close to death, not to mention..."

"Okay, okay," Mr. Harris said, and I had to look away from the disappointment on his face.

"I'm really sorry, sir. I know it meant a lot to you."

He smiled sadly. "My dad helped me buy that old car. It was brand new off the lot. I just couldn't believe the penny-pinching old codger coughed up the cash I'd needed for it. He argued constantly about how new cars were a waste of money."

"You feel like you're letting him down?"

He nodded, and I could tell he was barely keeping it together.

"Well, let me ask you this. If he were with us right now, what would he say about you spending three times its value to keep it running?"

Mr. Harris's eyes grew large, and he shook his head. "He'd have a fit. Everyone in town would be able to hear him."

I chuckled. "Well, maybe it's time you listened to that."

He smiled, a genuine one this time, and nodded. "You're right." He rubbed his hand across the old car and sighed. "I guess it's time to let her go."

Yeah, long, long past that time, I thought.

"I'll tell you what, if you're really ready, the Ellington family is getting ready to sell their mom's car now the estate is settled. They just had it serviced to get it ready for the estate sale. If you want, I can contact them and see if they'll let you come take a look."

"What's the make and model?" he asked.

"Same as yours, a Subaru Outback, but only five years old. Mrs. Ellington only used it to drive to church and the grocery store and barely drove it the year before she passed. The car is like new."

Mr. Harris's smile brightened his face. "My dad would definitely approve."

"No doubt. Hold on, let me call."

Of course, I knew it was a perfect match. The kids felt strange about selling their mom's things, but they were spread out all over the country. The oldest son was the only one left around these parts, and he lived thirty miles away.

"Sure, I can and yes, I still have the keys," I told Mr. Ellington.

I handed the keys to Mr. Harris, knowing the car was completely safe in his hands and that by the end of the day it'd be his anyway.

"You know where Mrs. Ellington lived, right?" He nodded. "The Subaru is sitting under her carport. If anyone asks what you're doing, just call Mrs. Ellington's son," I said, and gave him the number.

"Okay, if you think it's alright."

"It's okay, trust me."

There was that word again. *Trust.*

As Mr. Harris left, I thought about what that word meant to me. Trusting Jonas, a virtual stranger, with something so precious as my heart. Him trusting me with his.

I knew trusting others was something people didn't worry about, but it wasn't so easy for me. When I'd trusted someone before, like Tommy, it almost always seemed to bite me in the ass.

Why then did it all seem different with Jonas? Our shared losses? Need for companionship? Infatuation? Because, damn, he was fine to look at, which had my mind going all sorts of places it shouldn't at work. I chuckled to myself.

"Hey, why are you so happy?" Ray asked as he walked into the office.

"Things are going well. I sent Mr. Harris to look at the late Mrs. Ellington's Subaru."

"Oh, damn, I should've thought of that. That's perfect."

"Hope so. Anyway, I'm going to put his old bucket of rust back together and see if Hank wants to come pick it up as a junker."

"You think he can let it go?"

"Nope, but if his wife has to look at that thing sitting in their driveway, especially if it isn't working, she's going to leave him. I'd like to stop that from happening if I can."

Ray chuckled. "For someone who doesn't fancy women, you sure understand them."

"Ah, that's the gay man's gift to our straight brothers. We know how to keep you out of trouble."

Ray just laughed and got to work organizing the tools we'd left lying around last night. It'd been late when we'd closed up, and I'd sent Ray off telling him we could clean up in the morning.

By the time I finished putting the car back together and contacting Hank, Mr. Harris showed up smiling from ear to ear. "So, is it a match?" I asked and he nodded. "That's great news. I looked the car over recently, and it's in perfect condition. I changed the oil and did a basic tune-up replacing the fan belt too, so it shouldn't need anything for a while at least."

"How much do I owe you on...?" He looked into the garage where his old Subaru still sat.

"You know, I've made so much money off you and that old car." I chuckled at the truth of it. "This one's on the house, but I've called Hank over at the junkyard. He said he'd give you five hundred for it."

At first Mr. Harris looked stunned, then alarmed, but before he could respond, Ray came in and said, "You should take him up on the offer. As a married man my-self, I know even a car you love isn't worth the grief you'll get if you have it towed back to your house."

Ray's face stayed somber, which surprised me. Usu-ally, when two straight men discussed their wives, they laughed good-naturedly, but I could tell Ray was talking seriously with Mr. Harris.

"You're right, of course. What would I do without you boys? Yeah, hold on," he said as he went to the passenger side of the Subaru and pulled out what I assumed was the title. *Who keeps the title of a car in the glove box?* I thought.

That's when I realized Mr. Harris had seen this com-ing, and I shook my head as he filled it out. "You take the five hundred and keep it. It's what I owe you, especially with the amazing deal you got for me with the Ellington car. You know I had to negotiate up on that vehicle? The family's so ready to be done with it, he was going to practically give it to me. As it is, even with my forcing him to take more, I still saved at least a cool grand."

I smiled. "Everyone wins. That's always a good thing."

I had Ray help me push the old car out of the shop and over to the side of the building and called Hank to pick it up. "Glad you made a little off it," Ray said and looked at me askance. He'd been fussing at me for years about selling myself short and giving too many discounts or free work.

"I made more than I would've if I'd have charged him."

Ray nodded. "But is it really a viable business plan?" he asked.

"Not on paper." I stared at Ray for a moment, knowing it was only a matter of time before I asked him to become my business partner. Finally, I decided to come clean about the books.

"So, Ray, when my dad ran the shop, he brought in less than a hundred grand gross. Much less. Since I took over, we've doubled and might even triple that before the year is out. It's only been a year, and we're already making that much more."

"And you think it's because you're giving away your services?"

"I know it is, but I don't see it as giving anything away. We don't live in a huge town, and the people around here, they want to take care of one another, not screw each other over. Like Mr. Harris just said, he negotiated the price of the old estate car up, not down, 'cause he knew what it was worth, and he didn't want to take advantage of someone from here."

"You can't think everyone is like that, though."

I shook my head. "No, of course not, and I more or less already know who I can and can't trust. That's also part of living in a town where you know everyone. Look, my dad never got that. He charged everyone for everything he did. He was miserly and never, at least in my memory, ever just offered to help out. He had weeks where he barely had any work... weeks, Ray. When's the last time we didn't work from sunup to sundown?"

Ray chuckled. "The last day your dad ran the place."

"Exactly. That's the last time we haven't had to turn work away. It goes to show that a little goodwill goes a long way."

"Okay, point taken, I get it. It's a strange business plan and goes against my instincts, but I get it."

"Good, 'cause as my partner, I'd need to know you do."

Ray looked at me funny. "You mean as your employee."

"Dude, you know I was eventually going to ask you to be my partner in all this. We work too well together, and as we're continuing to build the business, it only makes sense you would take on some of the ownership."

"Really? I mean, I was hoping, but..."

"Really!"

Ray rushed me, and the next thing I knew, I was being swirled around in the air. I was laughing when I saw Jonas standing in the office smiling at us. "What's this?"

he asked, when Ray put me down. "You already got you another man?"

"*Another* man?" Ray asked and I didn't miss the twinkle in his eye. "Did you two *finally* hook up?" Jonas smirked and I just laughed. "Well, damn, I'm going to owe Angela a foot massage. I said it'd take at least another month."

"God, man, you're tactless. No, Jonas, my best friend has agreed to be my business partner. He was just celebrating by breaking my ribs."

Jonas laughed when Ray grabbed me again and kissed my forehead. "Just so you can add that to the story you're going to tell for the rest of my life. I'm gonna go call Angela, then we need to go to the diner to celebrate. It's not Saturday, but I'll be damned if I'm not gonna have a cinnamon roll!"

Jonas came over and kissed me as Ray dashed out. "So, that's big, right?"

"Yeah, I meant to ask him before you arrived in town, but things got really busy. I've been approached to purchase a larger and more modern garage, on the other side of town. I haven't mentioned that to Ray yet, but I think we should buy it and hire a couple more guys, or maybe just absorb the guys already working there. I've heard they're all pretty good mechanics, and they'll become even better if they spend some time with Ray. He's a genius when it comes to fixing cars."

Jonas looked concerned, but didn't say anything about it. "I'm happy for you."

"Wait, why the worried look?"

"Well, we just started this," he said, and waved his hand between us. "Now you're going to go into a partnership with your best friend and buying a new business? And we still have to prepare you for competing in Salzburg. Won't that be too much?"

His concern about my taking on more than I could handle was sweet. When was the last time anyone had put me first like that? "Life is always too much. Before you, it was buying the building, figuring out how to run this business, then there were the piano lessons, and the number of kids wanting lessons grows daily it seems, and then..."

"Okay, I get it. Life comes at you fast," Jonas said, cracking a smile.

"Yeah, and me and you dating isn't going to complicate matters. If anything, I'm sure you'll prove a welcome distraction," I said with a wink that made his face flush. "Besides, Ray is much smarter at business than me. He was going to get a freaking degree in business before he left college and went to trade school. He knows more about how to work on modern cars than my dad did, and he's really the main reason we're doing so well."

"Glad you know that," Ray said as he strolled back into the office. The man looked as proud as a damn peacock.

"Been telling him I'm the best thing to happen to him since the day we met."

"Truth," I said, and laughed at my friend's arrogance.

"Is Angela coming?" I asked.

"Yep, she and Ella. Angela was just about to drop her off at school, but she said this news was too good not to celebrate with the whole family. We'll drop her off after we're done."

"We don't have a car scheduled until after nine. I figured I'd be under Mr. Harris's car all morning, so we're free."

"Jonas, join us?" I asked.

He smiled, but shook his head. "No, I need to practice, then I'm going to head over to the school early to talk to Ms. Phillips about arranging a recital. The kids need practice in front of a live audience."

I walked over, tilted his chin up, and kissed him, not caring when Ray let out a low whistle. "I wish you'd come, but I understand. A recital, you say?"

"Yeah, just something low-key, parents only, I think. I don't want to overwhelm them their first time."

I nodded. "Am I going to perform in said recital also?"

Jonas gave me a devilish smile. "You're a quick one, Mr. Hancock, really quick."

He pecked my lips before heading back upstairs. "Hey, wait," I said protesting, but he didn't stop.

Instead, he just laughed, and gave me a little wave before disappearing into the apartment. Damn, I didn't mind performing in Salzburg where no one knew me, and I'd certainly played a lot of the pieces my great-granny used to teach me, but performing classical music in front of half the town? Just thinking about it scared the crap out of me.

27

Jonas

"EXACTLY," I SAID IN response to Ms. Phillips's comment about the recital. "If the parents get used to seeing their kids perform, maybe they'll help encourage them to practice, but also, it's good for them to perform in public, so you think six weeks is enough time to prepare them to perform?"

"More than enough time, and the fact that it'll be right before school lets out for the summer should make it feel even more special," she said.

"Then, I'll let you set up the particulars, and I'll prep the kids for whatever day you decide," I said, and could feel myself grinning. I never would've thought I'd be so excited for a school recital, but the kids were doing so well, making intense progress, and I really did want them to show it off, even if just to their parents.

My students began filing in then, and as they practiced, I got even more excited. Of course, until it was scheduled, both Ms. Phillips and I agreed not to mention the recital. When the date was set, I'd alert the kids and their parents to the performance.

That evening, as I walked down the street back to the apartment, I could hear *Clair de Lune*. At first, I thought maybe it was Orli playing, but the music was beautiful, melodic and flowing. Be it the song itself or the memories it stirred up, hearing the notes tugged at my emotions.

As I neared the building, it became clear the music was coming from my apartment. Could it really be Orli? No, he didn't play the song like that, he still banged it out. Surely someone else was in my apartment.

My heart pounded as I rushed up the stairs, not knowing who I'd find inside. I stopped dead in my tracks when I saw Orli sitting at the piano. Eyes closed, perfect posture, proper hand placement, and fingers dancing across the keys. The man looked as though he had been practicing classical piano for years.

I remained motionless in the open doorway, transfixed, as he continued playing. When he finished, I cleared my throat to let him know I was there.

His eyes opened and he turned toward me, smiling. "How long have you been standing there?" he asked.

"Long enough to be utterly shocked at your progress."

"I had a little motivation," he said, and my smile became even bigger.

"The movie really does help you feel the song."

He shook his head and came over to where I stood. "That's not where I got the motivation for this," he said, and leaned down to kiss me thoroughly.

When he pulled back, my brain was mush. Never in my life had someone kissed me with such passion. I literally felt that kiss deep in my heart.

"So, what're you going to teach me today?" he asked.

"Mmm, something romantic if that's what I can expect once you play it."

"How about something more upbeat?" he said, and pulled me over to the piano. "It's my turn. Since you got me to play your way, let me show you mine. It's time you learned how to play soul music."

I was ready to refuse, since he needed to practice, and if I were being honest, I also didn't want to humiliate myself in front of him by playing badly. I'd already tried and failed, but when I looked into that handsome face, I realized I wouldn't be able to tell him no. "Okay, what do you have in mind?"

He must've expected me to decline, because his eyes lit up even more. "Here, sit down, and I'll show you."

Laughing, I did as he instructed, and he sat beside me on the bench. "Okay, so let's do this in the key of G, just to make it easier to learn."

I couldn't help but bristle a little. "You know I'm a Juilliard graduate and have been playing my entire life."

"And, yet, I still think I can teach you something new."

"I'll have you know—" I said, turning toward him, "—plenty of Juilliard graduates play this type of music."

"Shh, I don't care about them, I only care about what you can do. Now, I'm going to show you a few chords, then I want you to try."

"Don't you just have some sheet music?" I asked.

"No, this is more from the heart, trust me."

Orli played the chords, and I repeated them. "Good, okay, now, let's have you put them together and give it a little oomph."

He demonstrated what he meant, but when I tried, he cringed. "Okay, so this will take some practice. Try it again, and this time don't be afraid to bang the keys. Think staccato."

I played it again, imagining I was playing Stravinsky's *Firebird*.

"Better, but you're trying to play it like a classical piece. This is all feeling, nothing restrained."

I tried several more times before Orli pulled me up and kissed me. "You really do suck at this."

"Wait, what?" I laughed, knowing he was right. "Thanks for the encouragement, teach."

"Okay, listen to me," he said as he took up more room on the piano bench, and began to play. "Imagine there are a hundred people in here all talking, drinking, and creating chaos. You have to play above all that noise, because they want to be entertained."

He played the music, and to be honest, as far as I was concerned, all I could hear was banging.

"Got it?" he asked.

I shook my head. "No, sorry, Orli. All I hear is you pounding the keys, and for no good reason."

"So, have you ever been to a bar?" he asked.

That earned him a raised eyebrow. "Well, of course, I have. Why?"

"'Cause, you don't quite grasp the point of the music. Okay, I have an idea. Come on." He grabbed my hand to pull me up, then led me toward the front door.

"What? Where?" I asked, confused.

"You'll see, come on."

"Wait, we really should be practicing."

"And we will, but if you could try something different for our lesson last night, I can do the same tonight for this one."

I shook my head. "Okay, but let me change into something more appropriate. I'm assuming you're taking me to some bar."

Orli laughed. "You're perfect as you are, and yes, a bar, but not just any bar."

I let him pull me out of the apartment and into his truck. I was clueless as to what was happening, but secretly enjoying the suspense. Everything in me was usually so measured and controlled that I found Orli's spontaneity a major turn-on.

It took over an hour for us to reach our destination. It was a small town, even smaller than Monongahela, if that was even possible. Old buildings lined both sides of the street, and while we parked, I noticed most appeared to be vacant.

"Come this way," Orli said as we crossed the street. I could hear the noise before I saw the building tucked behind the town's main street. When the door opened, I thought my ears would explode, but Orli just smiled and pulled me inside.

"Orli!" I heard several people yell in his direction, and a couple of guys even came up and bro-hugged him, in the stiff way straight men hug other men.

"Why are you here?" one of the guys asked him, and I was surprised I could hear over all the noise.

"Gonna show my new guy what true honky-tonk is all about." That he essentially introduced me as "his guy" to these strangers, all friends I supposed, also didn't escape my notice.

"Perfect, the band called off tonight, so we'll put you on!"

Orli smiled. "I'm gonna put a greasy burger in him first."

"Sounds good. Can you go on in an hour?"

"Depends," Orli yelled back at the guy. "Can you get your cook to get us both a burger and fries before closing time?"

Although I couldn't hear the man chuckling, his big belly wobbled with the action. "I'll see what I can do."

When he left, Orli ushered me toward an empty table, and said, "This place has the best burgers in West Virginia, but they're slow as molasses."

I almost asked him what that meant, but even sitting as close as we were, the noise made it impossible to communicate, so I sat back and watched the crowd. It was mostly what I'd call biker gangs. Rough-looking, middle-aged people, lots of leather, several beards, and tattoos covering almost every inch of skin.

Had I not been with Orli, I'd have felt my life was in danger just being here, but the only ones who even acknowledged us smiled, and nodded their heads at Orli. He must be well-liked here.

The food arrived a lot faster than I thought it would, considering Orli's warning about it usually taking so long. It was greasy, but also delicious. With our burgers and fries came two pints of beer, which were plunked down on the table by a very harassed-looking woman with hair streaked gray and pink, and clothes that looked like they'd been melted onto her body.

"Orli, why are we here?" I asked, tentatively sipping the beer. *Not terrible*, I thought, as I took a long pull.

"You are being educated, but don't worry, these are great people. They just look scary." He winked at me then, which helped me relax some, but there was no denying this wasn't my scene at all.

I shrugged, but knew my expression must've conveyed I didn't really believe him. *What could I possibly learn about music in a loud bar full of tattooed bikers?*

We'd just finished eating when the harassed woman returned to replace our pints with fresh ones. I'd only had a couple swigs of mine before it disappeared. "Damn, what's going on?" I asked, and grabbed my new glass when she came back again to take our empty plates, afraid she'd snatch it away too.

Orli just laughed, like he found the entire situation hilarious.

"Ladies and gentlemen," the same heavy-set man who'd greeted Orli when we walked in said from the stage. "Tonight, we have a special treat. Orli Hancock has returned. Give him a round of applause."

Orli winked at me as the crowd yelled and whistled. "Be right back," he mouthed, but the noise was too loud to actually hear him.

He hopped onto the stage and sat down at the piano. In a way that was clearly making fun of classical pianists, he sat up straight, then stretched his fingers and placed them on the keyboard, just as I'd taught him.

For a moment, I thought he was going to start playing *Clair de Lune*, which I doubted this crowd would appreciate. After hesitating a moment longer, he launched into some raucous music, much to everyone's amusement.

They danced, laughing and carrying on, clearly enjoying the racket he was making. At first, it all made me uncomfortable. I mean, these were pretty scary-looking people, and they all seemed drunk and dangerous at the same time.

But then, I caught a glimpse of Orli's face, and saw just how much he was enjoying himself. That was when my perspective changed. These people were wild compared to anyone and everyone I'd ever encountered at a performance, but Orli was entertaining them. The people were enjoying it, and enjoying him.

The longer he played, the more I enjoyed myself. Hearing him playing to an appreciative crowd, and seeing him lose himself in the music, was something special.

Out of nowhere, I heard my father's voice in my head saying, "Melody of the Heart..." The words he'd told me when I was just a kid hit me square in the chest. I wondered if he'd have been proud of me for venturing so far outside my comfort zone, being in a rowdy bar listening to honky-tonk songs. I could almost hear him chuckling about it.

When some woman old enough to be my mom put her arm around me and asked me to dance, I didn't even hesitate. My father's words had resonated with me. I got up and let her and a few others spin me around the dance floor. Before long, I was laughing along with them.

When the music slowed, so did the dancing, and I turned toward Orli, who still sat at the piano. The entire bar stilled as he launched into *Blue Skies*, his sweet voice echoing around the darkened room.

When he broke into the scatting part of the song, bodies began to move again, almost unconsciously.

At one point, he stood, sending the stool skittering across the stage as he continued scatting and playing at the same time.

At some point, I began swaying to the music as well, but I couldn't take my eyes off Orli. He was truly in his element up on that stage.

As he crooned out the last few words and finished playing, the crowd whooped and hollered. It was a wonder my hands didn't hurt with how hard I was clapping for him. "Thanks, folks. Now, if you don't mind, I'm gonna go hang with my guy."

Orli hit the keys once more and then slipped off the stage, and pulled me into his arms.

All eyes were on us when he kissed me, and the entire crowd cheered. I was so caught up in the moment, not to mention the softness of his lips, to bother feeling self-conscious.

Orli released me and reached for his wallet, pulled out two twenties, and was about to put them on our table when the man who'd greeted us before caught his wrist. "Nope, on the house," he said, and clapped Orli on the back. Orli smiled and nodded his thanks before threading his fingers through mine, and leading me from the building.

"Wow—" I said, after we climbed into his truck, "—that was so much fun."

Orli laughed. "Guessing that's the first time you've had that kind of experience, huh?"

"Um, it's probably unusual for that to exist in the twenty-first century. No offense, but your music is a little out of date."

That had Orli laughing again. "Well, that's what happens when your great-grandmother is your piano teacher. You said you had fun, though?"

"Yeah, and everyone else there did too. A lot of fun, it was really cool. How did you get involved with that place?"

"Oh, that'd be said great-grandmother." He smiled fondly, like a treasured memory was coming to mind. "She used to perform there a lot when she first moved in with my grandparents. Mostly, I think they let her play, because she was sort of a legend around here. Even when younger folks started replacing the older ones in the crowd, they still loved it, loved her."

I reached over and took his hand. "That feeling seems to have rubbed off on you too."

"Yeah, I'm lucky, have been most of my life. Other gay guys I've known really struggled growing up in West Virginia, but my grandparents and great-granny never cared in the least. My dad did for a while, but even he got over it. I guess having honky-tonk kinfolk makes a person more open-minded."

I chuckled and scooted closer to him. "I guess so. Anyway, thanks for tonight. I had a great time."

"And it will continue, 'cause now you understand the reason why I play piano like I do. You can't play that kind of music like you're in a concert hall, you got to put all you've got into it. Think you can do that?"

I shrugged. "Melody of the heart," I said. Orli looked over at me and I smiled. "It means... well, to my dad it meant that no matter what music someone likes, the love of it, the feelings around it, come from the heart." He looked at me with such warmth in his eyes, and before he could respond, I added, "Regardless, right now, I just want to *go hang with my guy*," I said, parroting what he'd said on stage.

"That sounds like the perfect plan," Orli said, and let me snuggle into his side as we drove back home.

28

Orlando

I WOKE UP TO Jonas cuddled into me, and couldn't help but smile. Since the night at the bar, we'd gotten closer and closer. I tended to spend every night with him, even the weekends. Maybe that was too much, but damn, neither one of us seemed to want it any other way.

I untangled myself from him, and slipped out from under the covers. It was only three a.m. but I knew I wouldn't be able to fall back asleep for a while.

The piano technician who was repairing Jonas's Steinway had contacted him a few days ago to say he'd found a place to store it. Jonas had been fixing coffee when the guy called, so he put his phone on speaker, which allowed me to listen in on their conversation. "I'm not going to say it's an ideal facility. You know a piano like yours needs to be babied, and although it's a climate-controlled environment, it's still storage," the guy said.

Jonas asked if the repair shop could store it for the time being, and the guy immediately said no. "You don't want us to keep it. We're a repair shop, not storage. Besides, we don't have room for a piano the size of yours."

"Okay, let me contact the facility and see what I can do to make arrangements."

Jonas seemed stressed as he began looking into the storage facility online and wasn't altogether impressed with its customer satisfaction ratings, but ended up calling the company anyway. I knew how precious his father's piano was to him, and keeping it in a safe and secure place would give him greater peace of mind.

That got me thinking. All of the work on the first floor of my home was basically done. I still needed to install the kitchen and paint the wallboard, but it was otherwise ready to go. The open concept I'd gone with would allow him to store his piano there.

My mind made up, later that morning I informed Ray I needed some time off to work on the cottage. He said he could handle the garage, since we were all caught up at the moment, even though my absence would put us behind again.

"I'm going to be gone for a few days," I told Jonas that afternoon.

"Is everything okay?" he asked, looking worried.

"Perfect, just some classes and stuff for work. Nothing I can't get done fast, and I'll be back soon. I promise to practice as long as you do too."

Jonas's frown morphed into a smile, and he laughed. After going to the bar with me, he'd improved his playing. His honky-tonk technique was still far from good, but his approach wasn't quite as reserved as it had been. "Aye, captain," he said, and I kissed him hard, knowing I was going to miss the crap out of him.

I felt a little bad about not being totally honest, but it was only a little white lie and it'd totally be worth it in the end.

The next day I drove up to Morgantown to get the supplies I needed. Although I hated to pay for help to fix something I'd abandoned several times, I called my buddies Jeff and Lance, who were both private contractors, to help me out.

I knew they'd give me shit about rehabbing the same room again, but at least they didn't know I was doing it for a guy this time, otherwise I'd never hear the end of it.

I mean, I *was* doing it for Jonas. I liked the guy and wanted to make his life a little easier, that was the honest truth, even if redoing my home for someone I'd only just started seeing was just a little over the top.

Thinking about a future with Jonas led to thoughts about the one I'd envisioned with Tommy. He'd proposed just a few months after I'd met him. Deep down,

I knew he and I weren't right for each other, which I guess was why I'd told him I needed to think about it. My gut feeling had been right about him, and I knew it was right about Jonas too. If Jonas asked me to marry him, I wouldn't hesitate to say yes, not that I would be confessing it any time soon, though, since we were still too new for that.

For now, I needed to focus on the project at hand. I had a week to finish renovations on this part of the cottage before I had to go back to work. I'd also heard Jonas tell the storage company he'd be in touch by the end of the week, so the clock was ticking.

Luckily, there wasn't much to do. Jonas had picked a warm white for the apartment walls, so I decided that would work for the first floor of the cottage too. The reality was, I loved color and it would complement my overall color scheme. My bedroom was painted in a soft sage green, the bathroom and hallway were light blue, and the extra bedroom I currently used as a living room was a very light orange that, according to the paint can, was called tangerine.

I'm sure Jonas would notice I'd picked the same color he had, and I hoped it'd please him. It was a small thing, but anything that might make him feel more connected to this place, be it my cottage or my hometown, was a bonus, not that I would ever try to persuade someone to stay in Monongahela for me. Small towns didn't appeal to just anyone. They were for someone who didn't mind people being in their business, and who would lend a helping hand to those same people without question.

If this town wasn't right for Jonas, I wouldn't hold him here. The question was, would I go with him if he ever asked? I already knew I would. I'd miss my hometown, and I'd miss my friends who'd become more like family, but after seeing the amazing relationship shared between my grandparents, and now Ray and Angela, yeah, I'd do what I could to make that happen for me.

If Jonas was the one, then I'd willingly follow him anywhere.

"Orli, are you here?" I heard Angela's voice and smiled.

"Yeah, I'm back here. What's up?"

She came into the kitchen, her coveralls on and hair tied up, and I knew she'd come to help. "So, where's your paint? Ray told me you hired Lance and Jeff." She looked around and seeing they weren't there, spoke quietly. "Those two can build a house from scratch, but they paint like barbarians."

"You've come to save my eyes from the horror of a bad paint job?"

She looked toward the staircase at all the painting supplies. "I'll get started on the walls. Everything the same color?"

"Yep, white."

She stopped, looked at me, and the expression on her face conveyed she knew exactly why I'd picked that color. Without saying anything, she began prepping the living room.

She really was a good friend. She hadn't asked if I needed help, she'd just arrived and got right to work, not unlike she'd done for Jonas. I'd been blessed with my friends.

I went back to prepping the kitchen for the units Jake and Lance would be installing tomorrow. I'd gone back and forth about designing the kitchen, from installing cabinets to choosing appliances, for so long. I wasn't at all sure why that part of the house was giving me such problems.

Nothing I did made the space feel right. I'd hated the choppy original floor plan, but I'd loved how homey it'd felt all those years with my grandparents. I guess I was striving for that same feeling, but I couldn't bring myself to abandon my open concept floor plan by putting the old walls back up. There had to be a happy medium. I just didn't know where to find it.

Oh well, I said to myself as I secured the final piece of wood flooring in the kitchen. *Maybe seeing Jonas's piano here will inspire me.*

I grabbed a roller and helped Angela paint the walls, careful to avoid the natural woodwork I'd salvaged and incorporated into the space. I usually hated white up against traditional woodwork, but the warm white Jonas had used in the apartment caused the deep oak to pop against the walls.

"Wow, that's a lot nicer than I'd have thought. You did good," Angela said as she stood back, looking at the wall she'd just finished under the staircase.

"I think so too, and I think it'll accentuate Jonas's Steinway as well." Angela just smirked, and I knew she wanted to say something. "You might as well spit it out," I said, and resumed painting.

"You're getting really attached, and fast."

I chuckled. "And you're concerned or what?"

"Or what," she replied, and picked her own roller up before turning toward me. "It's just nice to see you happy and after such a long, dry spell."

"Hey, it wasn't that dry."

I could feel her gaze on me, waiting until I made eye contact, to respond, "The guys you dated were not exactly a flow of fresh water either."

I shrugged. "True, and I'm guessing you approve of Mr. Piano Man?"

She winked at me, and as she returned to painting, she began singing, "Play us a song, Mr. Piano Man..."

We chatted as we painted, which made the time fly. There was only one wall left to paint when she left to pick up Ella from school. I continued painting, so that tomorrow, after the kitchen was in, all I'd need to do was install the backsplash. I'd decided to do a simple subway pattern in a herringbone style.

The cabinets were black on the bottom and light gray on the top, so the white backsplash just made sense.

Now that a black piano was going to be sitting in pride of place, I figured the black cabinets would complement it beautifully.

That night, after I finished painting, I almost called Jonas to see if he could come over, but that'd spoil the surprise. As much as I wanted to see him, I wanted to see his reaction when I showed him the fully renovated space, where he could store his dad's precious piano more.

So, instead of calling, I sent him a text wishing him sweet dreams, then showered and crashed early, intent on completing this project sooner rather than later, so I could get back into Jonas's arms.

29

Jonas

"WHAT DO YOU MEAN we can't have a recital?" I asked incredulously.

I'd announced the planned recital to the orchestra board during our regularly scheduled call, which was clearly not going well. "You represent the orchestra, so you can't schedule a recital without our approval," I was told.

"No, in fact, I do not represent the orchestra. You pushed your way into *my* contest, and I signed a contract saying you may be involved in the contest as long as I didn't have to deal with Rodrigo."

"You are not in charge here, young man," I heard Mrs. Covington say. "Our money is funding this escapade, and you will follow our rules, or face the consequences."

"I'm not going to tell the children at Monongahela Elementary that they can't have a recital just because you decided you have the power to stop them."

"We shall see about that," she said, and as I was getting used to, she ended the conference call. I'd swear I was beginning to really dislike that woman.

I was just about to blow it off when my phone pinged with a text.

Rodrigo: *Fucking up again so soon?*

God, I hated that man. His text left no doubt he was still involved and causing more crap to hit the fan. As if the board's phone call hadn't been infuriating enough. I should've blocked his number long ago.

I quickly called my dad's attorney, the one I'd sent the contract to after signing it at the TV station. He'd said it was cut and dried and nothing to worry about, so I hadn't. Even when the board had pushed me around before, I didn't let it bother me, but needlessly taking away what could be a proud accomplishment for my students was where I drew the line.

When I reached the attorney, I explained the situation. "Son, Mrs. Covington is addicted to suing people. The woman is known in the New York legal community for suing anyone she thinks is standing in her way. The reality is she has the money to hire the attorneys to make your life miserable. So, no, the contract doesn't give the board the power to forbid holding a recital, but it does prevent you from doing so, at least to some degree."

"So, what does that mean?" I asked, confused.

"It means you'd be better off not having one."

"Really? They have that much control just because I'm under contract?"

"Yes and no. Like I said, it's more because they have someone who wouldn't hesitate to drag you into court and could smear your name while she's at it."

"Okay, I'll figure it out then."

When I hung up, I felt discouraged, but not defeated. I decided I'd better go to the school to tell Ms. Phillips instead of calling, even though I wasn't scheduled to teach until late that afternoon. She would be fit to be tied over this.

When I signed in, I noticed a flier on the front desk promoting the school's May Day Piano Recital. I groaned, knowing I was too late. The cat was already out of the bag.

Luckily, as I read over the flier, I noticed my name wasn't listed. Maybe if I didn't attend, it would keep the wolves at bay.

I ended up going home instead of speaking with Ms. Phillips and emailed a picture of the flier to my attorney, saying it was too late to cancel the recital. Shortly after, he emailed back noting that at this point, we'd just have to wait and see what happened.

What happened was I got a cease-and-desist letter from the orchestra board. Of course, I sent it to my attorney, who said they were claiming I'd breached the contract by even giving lessons without their consent.

"It's all bull, but you know how it goes, she who has the biggest purse wins," my attorney told me.

"I know, but it shouldn't be that way. So, what do we do?" I asked.

"Well, you will either have to cancel the recital or face the fact that you will be pulled into court."

"And what about my piano?" I asked.

"It's probable they'll ask for it to be held since they paid for its repair."

"God, that's... I can't believe these people."

"I know, son. I'm sorry we have so few options here," he said before hanging up.

So, I'd have to cancel or face the music. Neither were acceptable options, but I refused to be pushed around for the rest of my life by people like Rodrigo and Mrs. Covington. I wouldn't allow people like them to destroy something these kids had worked so hard to achieve. My students deserved their time in the spotlight, even if it was in an elementary school music room rather than a prestigious concert hall.

Would I lose my piano? Because it was still at the repair shop in New York, I probably would. That was the hardest pill to swallow, but I couldn't let them keep pushing me around without a fight. My life was worth more than that, and eventually, I would win this stupid lawsuit. Maybe I could even countersue. I'd have to ask my attorney about that.

Despite feeling determined to finally stand up for myself, the whole situation left me so depressed. I missed Orli, I hated him being gone, and now I was facing nothing but a bunch of shit.

Just then, I heard someone coming up the stairs. "Hello?" Orli called out.

He barely made it into the apartment before I jumped into his arms and began kissing him. "Oh my god, I missed you so much. I can't even..."

As the surprise wore off, Orli pulled me tighter into his embrace and kissed me back, matching my intensity. Our hands were all over each other, heat building up between us.

Before I knew it, he was lifting me into the air as my legs instinctively wrapped around him, and carrying me toward the bedroom.

I wanted fast and furious, and Orli seemed willing to comply. I stripped my shirt off as we went, and the minute we reached the bedroom, we lost the rest of our clothes before I pushed him onto the bed, and took his cock in my mouth.

God, he tasted so good. I decided then and there I wanted to taste all of him, so I deepened my blowjob, making him moan and wriggle under me.

After having lost so much power in the rest of my life, it felt so good to be in control, and I could give my man pleasure while I was at it. It was a win-win I desperately needed.

I slipped my finger under his balls, and began to play with his ass and taint and got exactly what I was looking for. He orgasmed hard, arching his back and letting out a guttural moan, while shooting cum down my throat. "Fuck!" he said. "Fuck, that was too fast!"

I licked the last of the cum off his cock and sat up with a smile. "No, it's what I wanted."

"Come here," he demanded, and when I crawled up next to him, he slid down and took me into his mouth. "Now—" he said after popping off, "—jack off, and let me return the favor."

I smiled down at the hot man, who I could still taste, and complied, stroking myself as he sucked on my head.

"Fuck, that feels good," I said, and stopped jacking off to thrust into his mouth.

He surprised me when he held me firm, then swallowed around my cock, sending a rush of pleasure through me.

He moved my body, so I was straddling his chest, grabbed my ass, and I fucked his mouth with my cock. I might've been in control before, but I clearly wasn't now. Orli was using me, giving me pleasure and doing it from a passive position. "God, fuck!" I yelled as I felt my own climax building.

"I'm gonna come," I said, and Orli shoved my cock deep into his throat and swallowed again.

That was too much. I came, emptying myself into the warmth of his mouth. "Mmm," I said as I spasmed out the last of my cum.

Seeing Orli's smug expression as I pulled out, I couldn't help but lean down to kiss him. I wasn't much on cum swapping, but with him, thinking we might be able to taste ourselves as we kissed sent chills through my body.

We kissed, slow and deep, for a few minutes, until I rested my head on his chest as I lay down beside him. "God, I missed you," I said, still out of breath.

Orli laughed, and tilting up my chin, kissed me again. "I could tell. Now, get dressed. I have something to show you."

"Really?" I asked. "What?"

"You'll see," he said with a flirty wink, and pulled me out of bed.

I laughed, forgetting all my troubles now that Orli had returned. He had only been gone for a few days, and already I missed him like we'd been married for years. Now he was back, and I'd follow him anywhere.

After getting our clothes back on, we headed down to his truck and off we went toward my surprise. "Why are we at your house?" I asked when he pulled up, and put the truck in park.

"You'll see," he replied, and came to my side of the truck to open my door. *Such the gentleman*, I thought.

After I crawled out, I followed him up the beautiful little path that led around the front.

When we reached the porch, he threw the door open and gestured for me to go inside.

"Wow, wow," I kept saying as I walked around admiring the finished space. "This is, um, you did this while you were gone? I thought you had work stuff."

He chuckled. "Well, I lied, but for a good reason. Come over here," he said, grabbing by hand to lead me through the living room.

I followed silently, digesting the fact that he had admitted he'd lied to me. That wasn't something I was okay with, especially considering all my asshole ex had done was lie to me, not that Orli was anything like Rodrigo, but honesty was important.

He pointed to an open space under the big window that looked into the front yard and had a nice decorative fireplace on the adjoining wall.

I looked at the space and tried not to shrug. I mean, it was pretty, but I wasn't sure why it was so special.

"It's um, it's great, it's all great."

"And a grand piano would look really great right here, wouldn't you agree?"

My mouth must've fallen open, because Orli put his finger under my chin, and lifted it up before kissing me.

"Do you like it?" he asked.

The tears that sprung to my eyes as realization hit were unbidden and uncontrollable. "I do," I said through the tears. "You did all this for me?"

"Well, of course, I did. You need the space, and it was stupid for me to have all this unfinished space you could otherwise use."

I was unable to do anything other than melt into his embrace. I wasn't sure if I was crying over his thoughtfulness, getting my piano back, or both, but he just held me while I let it all out. Finally, I pulled back, wiped at the tears, and thanked him. "Thank you so much. I mean, I don't know what to say."

"Well, according to your piano repair guys, you need to call them tomorrow morning. If you decide you agree to it, they'll bring the piano here and set it up. Does that work for you?"

"I, um, how did you get them to agree so fast?"

"Well, as someone who repairs things in a modest space, as I assume those guys do, they really want to get rid of it. They've already been paid by the orchestra, and now they want it gone. They didn't really want it locked away in storage either. People who do this kind of thing for a living have a tendency to get attached to beauties like your piano."

I leaned back and laughed. "So, you talked them into driving all the way from Queens, New York, to Monongahela, West Virginia, to deliver my piano?"

Orli gave a wry grin and shrugged. "Well, sort of. They asked for a delivery address, I gave them mine, and they didn't say no, so when you call, they might have more questions."

"Not a problem. I'll pay to have it moved here if they'll do it."

"Well, apparently, that was included in the repair fees, but you'll find out more tomorrow, I'm sure."

I ended up clinging to my boyfriend again, even though I wasn't sure I could actually call him that yet. As far as I was concerned, though, anyone who'd go to all this effort for me qualified for that title. He pulled me up the stairs and into his bedroom, where I spent the afternoon showing him just exactly how appreciative I was.

30

Orlando

T HE PIANO ARRIVED IN the late afternoon a few days after Jonas had called to confirm delivery, and I had to take more time off work to be home when it arrived. When Ms. Phillips heard what was going on, she took over lessons with the kids, so Jonas could be there as well.

I guess I hadn't really thought about the sheer size of a Steinway concert grand piano. Luckily, I'd measured the room and knew the monster would fit, but its legs had to be removed just to get it through the front door, not to mention, the thing literally weighed half a ton.

Regardless, it really did look amazing in the space. It was almost like it was meant to be there. The black cabinets in the kitchen, the soft oak woodwork, the wooden mantel above the old fireplace, everything drew the eye back to that gorgeous piano.

As soon as the piano was set up, the men stood back and asked Jonas to play it, given the soundboard had been repaired.

The sound that poured out of the instrument sent chills through me. I now understood exactly why this piano was so highly valued.

I caught sight of the tears that fell from Jonas's eyes as he finished playing. "You made it sound like... like it did before my dad died," he said, and the delivery men's faces broke into smiles. "Thank you so much, I-I don't have words for how amazing this is."

"You're lucky," the older man, who I guessed was in charge, said. "That soundboard was salvageable. Not all of them are, but she has her original sound back because of it."

Jonas nodded and turned back around to play. I didn't recognize the tune, but it was full of longing and sadness. I knew he was thinking of his dad.

I glanced over at the men, and more than one was getting emotional as well.

When Jonas stopped playing, he stood up and shook each man's hand before they left.

Once we were alone, I put my arms around Jonas and pulled him into a hug, and held him there. "It truly is amazing to hear," I whispered into his ear. "I've never heard an instrument like that before, certainly not in my home, and you play it so beautifully."

Jonas nodded into my shoulder, but didn't speak. We stood like that for several moments before he pulled back to look up at me. "Okay, I need some time on this, do you mind?" he asked.

I couldn't help smiling so wide my cheeks hurt. "Well, since I did all this so you could do just that, no, I don't mind."

He pecked me on the lips as I released him, and sat down on the piano bench, and within seconds he was lost in the music. I wandered upstairs to give him some space, alone with the piano. I knew his Steinway being here meant Jonas would be spending a lot more time here as well, which was an added benefit to knowing it was somewhere safe and secure.

As I tidied my living space upstairs that I'd been too busy lately to clean, the music flowed up through the floor below. Although muted, it was still beautiful. I could hear Jonas's soul pouring out of that instrument, and it honestly moved me.

I'd heard him play piano several times since he'd arrived, but never with so much passion. I wasn't sure I'd ever heard someone play any form of music with such passion. I knew he was coming to terms with his grief, and celebrating the piano coming back into his life, and I was thankful to have helped give him that.

I ended up collapsing on the upstairs sofa, listening as he played. My thoughts wandered while images flashed through in my mind, as if they were magically tied to the music.

Finally, a long while later, the playing stopped, and I heard footsteps coming up the stairs. Jonas sat next to me on the sofa, and cuddled into my side. "Thank you," he said.

I kissed the top of his head and snuggled into him as well. "You're welcome, and thanks for the concert."

We spent the rest of the day like that, snuggling together on the sofa. I could tell Jonas just needed support as he dealt with emotions he'd kept bottled inside since upending his life by moving here, and I was happy to give him all the loving support he needed.

31

Jonas

THE OVERWHELMING EMOTIONS I'D felt at having my father's piano back in my care, let alone sounding better than it had in years, had left me feeling drained. The fact that Orli seemed to understand exactly what I'd needed, and gave me the space to work through it all stirred up even more unspoken feelings.

The next morning, I got up and played until Orli said he had to go to work. I rode with him to the garage, then practiced upstairs in the apartment after we got there, but my fingers itched for the Steinway. I was nothing if not disciplined, though, so I ignored it, and forced myself to finish my entire session.

Around noon, I got a text from Orli asking if I could come down. I'd just finished lunch, so I headed downstairs.

I stepped into the office to find Orli and a man I didn't know waiting for me. "Hey, Jonas. This is Theo Langford.

He's got a small sedan he's going to sell, and I thought you might be interested."

I stared dumbly at Orli for a moment, trying to make sense of what he'd said. "Interested... in a car?" I asked.

Orli chuckled. "Well, yeah, you're not in the city any longer, and our public transportation is basically nonexistent. Having a reliable car would help you get around, don't you think?"

Unlike many of the people I'd grown up with in New York, I'd actually learned to drive, and had a driver's license, but I hadn't done much actual driving. Owning a car had never crossed my mind, but I nodded and followed the man out to see the little blue Ford. "It's a hybrid, so you get really great gas mileage," he said.

I had no idea what he meant, or if it was important, but the little car looked nice enough. "How much?" I asked.

His price shocked me. I knew nothing about cars, but I would've thought he'd want a lot more than what he was asking. Like, thousands more.

"Um, let me talk to Orli about it, and I'll let you know," I said, and the guy nodded and left.

I walked into the office, where Orli sat waiting for me. "So, what do you think?" he asked.

"What's a hybrid?"

Orli laughed. "It means the car runs partly on electric and partly on gas. The man just bought a Tesla and wants to unload this one."

"Is that a good price?" I asked.

Orli nodded. "It's more than a good price. It's amazing."

"So, is there something wrong with it?" I asked, concerned.

"Nope, I've worked on it myself, or Ray has at least. It's in good shape, the dealership just lowballed him an offer, and he said if he was going to give it away, he'd rather give the discount to someone who needed it."

"Wow, okay. I hadn't thought about it, to be honest. I mean, should I buy a car?"

Orli shrugged. "I admit, when he brought it in, you were the first person I thought about, but that was as much because I'd like you to be able to stay at the cottage with me. I liked having you there last night. And if you had your own set of wheels, you could come and go without having to wait on me."

I just stared at him while mulling over his words. He wanted me with him, at his home, where he'd created a place for my beloved piano. I really wanted to practice more on the Steinway, and now he was giving me a way to do that as well. "Yeah!" I said excitedly. "I want all of that too. Can you set it up with the guy? What was his name?"

"Theo," Orli replied.

"Yeah, Theo. Could you help me do what I need to so I can buy it? Then I might need to have you or someone ride with me a few times. I've not driven in like three or four years."

"Not a problem," Orli said, and before I could stop myself, I was once again in his arms.

"You're the best boyfriend ever," I said, and caught myself. "Well, I mean, um..."

"You said it right, boyfriend. I want that too."

"Really?" I asked, embarrassed when my voice squeaked a little.

"Really. In fact, I've wanted that for a while now."

I kissed him, and didn't stop until I heard Ray wolf-whistling at us from the garage.

I pulled back, flipping him off before kissing Orli again, this time less passionately, and rushed up the stairs to my apartment.

Things were happening so fast, but here, in this small town with Orli, they were good things. Even if the orchestra was trying to make my life miserable, I was happy.

Buying a car turned out to be much easier than I'd thought. Within hours, I was the owner of a little blue Ford sedan, and that evening, Orli and I skipped practice to go for a joyride along the backroads of West Virginia. "This area is so beautiful," I said and caught Orli's smile.

"It is, and have you seen the waterfalls yet?"

I shook my head. "Not since I was a kid, and that was in a different part of West Virginia. Are there waterfalls around here?" I asked.

"Yeah, turn right up here," he said, pointing toward a wide spot along the shoulder of the road. "Mind hiking a bit?"

I shrugged as I pulled over and parked. "I mean, I didn't exactly wear hiking boots."

"No problem, it's an easy hike, come on."

I locked the car and followed Orli up the forested path, and within moments I could hear the distinct sound of rushing water. "Wow, are those the falls?"

"Yep, and you're in for a treat, they're one of the nicest falls in the state."

After a few minutes continuing along the path, we came to a river and followed it up before the waterfall came into view. "Damn!" I said.

Orli slipped his arms around me and kissed my neck as I stared dumbfounded at the beauty before me.

"Pretty, huh?"

"No words to express it."

We stood like that for some time, just enjoying the view and each other. Finally, we walked hand in hand back to the car.

"You know," I admitted as I buckled my seatbelt, "I'm getting rather attached to you."

Orli turned toward me with a grin on his handsome face. "Are you trying to tell me you're falling in love?" he asked.

I smiled. "That's what I'm beginning to feel." He didn't answer for a beat, so I raised my eyebrows in question, hoping I hadn't just said too much.

Orli's grin grew wider, and he nodded. "Yeah, me too. I've never met someone I want to spend my time with like I do with you. I wake up thinking about you. The nights when you aren't in my bed, I miss you terribly. I look forward to our lessons after work. Yeah, I think I'm pretty smitten."

I took Orli's big, callused hand in my own and kissed it. "Good to know we're on the same page."

Orli winked at me as I put the car in gear, and we headed back to town.

Both of us were silent as I drove my new car down the road, still holding Orli's hand. This felt so good, so right. How had this wonderful thing happened to me at the worst possible moment in my life?

I mean, I seldom thought about losing the New York apartment I'd called home for most of my life. I rarely thought about the strife with the orchestra board, or my asshole ex. Mostly, I was just enjoying being with my boyfriend, and teaching my students.

Even Ms. Phillips and I had grown close over the past few months. In between student lessons, she and I would spend time chatting about our lives, music, and the things we'd done. I learned she'd been married long ago to a man who'd cheated on her and they divorced. After that heartbreak, she decided she'd never marry again.

I told her about losing my dad and then our house-keeper, who'd been like a mom to me. I didn't talk about them very often, because I'd get so choked up, but commiserating with Ms. Phillips was somehow easy and comforting.

I felt like was becoming part of this community, and I liked it. I liked it so much more than my life in New York. My father was an amazing man, but I'd had a lonely childhood. He'd homeschooled me most of my life, and I'd spent time with the kids he taught, but it'd mostly just been him and me.

For the first time, aside from Tatiana, I'd made some real friends outside the music world. Angela and Ray were fun people, and had even taken to inviting me over when Orli wasn't around. So, while Orli was spending the weekend in the office catching up on paperwork from his time off, I went to hang out with Angela.

I only found out once I got there that she had ulterior motives in inviting me. Angela announced she was sick of my hair sticking out everywhere, and before I knew it, I was in a chair on her back patio getting a trim.

"It wasn't that bad, was it?" I asked, knowing full well my wild mop needed to be tamed.

"Well, I mean, if you're trying to look like one of those wild-haired composers, all you needed to do was dye it white, and you'd have it down. But since everyone in town knows you're my friend and knows I own the only hair salon and spa for miles around, my reputation is on the line."

I chuckled, then smiled at her as she snipped away the three months of growth. "You know, when I lived in the city, I got my hair trimmed every month, never missed an appointment."

"And you came to West Virginia and became a wild man?"

"Something like that. To be honest, though, I just didn't think about it." I also kind of loved how Orli would absently run his fingers through my hair when we cuddled, but I wasn't about to tell her that.

"Well, we'll be thinking about it from now on, won't we?"

I laughed. "I guess."

"While I've got you here," Angela said, and I cringed, causing her to whack my shoulder with her comb. "Hey, don't act like that, you don't know what I'm going to say."

"Go on," I said, chastised.

"Ella wants to perform in the recital. I know we declined earlier, but her friend Joslin can't stop talking about it, so now, she's convinced she needs to participate."

"No problem, she's ready actually. Just let Ms. Phillips know, she's the one organizing it."

"Yeah, we will. I'm surprised you aren't more upset about us changing our minds."

I was about to ask why when I looked up and saw her expression.

"Angela, seriously, are you still feeling bad about Ella pulling out of the contest?" I asked.

"Well, of course. It's why you got stuck here."

"And I've never been happier being stuck somewhere in my life. Seriously, you can let that go and chalk it up to fate using you to get her way."

Angela smiled. "Good, 'cause you and Orli are great together."

I blushed, but smiled. "I think so too."

She finished cutting my hair and handed me a broom. "Home haircuts mean you gotta clean up after yourself," she said, and turned to go back inside. "Want a beer?"

"Um, I guess."

She came back out just as I swept the last of the hair into a dustpan and dumped it into a garbage can near the door. "What do I owe you?"

"Oh, home haircuts are free, and you're giving Ella lessons for free at school, so it's a wash."

I winked at her and sat down on the porch swing as Ray came out and sat next to his wife.

Here we go, I thought, and laughed as Orli's friends, and well, mine too now, asked a million questions about our new relationship.

Time seemed to be flying. I was spending most nights at Orli's place now, and getting home earlier than him, since his work at the garage had increased. I missed the delicious meals he used to fix us for dinner, but with him working later, I took up that mantle by learning how to cook. My cooking skills still sucked, so I usually ended up serving stuff I could heat up quickly, but Orli always seemed to appreciate my efforts.

My students were practicing hard to prepare for the upcoming recital. Ms. Phillips had complained about the lessons regularly going past four thirty, but I knew they'd feel more confident with the extra time. None of them really needed it, though, since all had improved their skills considerably.

The orchestra board had gone quiet on the recital, and even when I phoned for my weekly check-in, they never asked about it, so frankly, neither did I.

So, it came as a huge surprise when I got a call from the school early Monday afternoon informing me a Mr.

Rodrigo Everett had shown up, demanding to see the students who would be performing in the recital.

"Shit," I said on the phone and then quickly apologized. "I'll be right over."

I hadn't even showered yet. I was glad Angela had cut my hair, so it wasn't flying everywhere. I pulled my clothes on quickly, brushed my teeth, and headed to the school.

When I entered the front office, I saw Rodrigo sitting in the waiting area, looking extremely impatient.

"Rodrigo, why are you here?" I asked, unable to mask my frustration.

"To clean up your mess," he said loudly, causing everyone in the office to look at us.

Within moments, Ms. Phillips and Mrs. Stewart had shown up, along with Principal Jenkins.

"Gentlemen, ladies, if you could all please come into my office," Principal Jenkins said.

Rodrigo stood with a huff, and the pompous ass deigned to saunter into the office. Ms. Phillips gave me a look, and I just shrugged to say I had no idea why he was here.

Once the door shut behind us, we all took a seat, and Principal Jenkins addressed Rodrigo. "I'm sorry, sir, we weren't expecting you. You mentioned that you are here to take charge of the recital?"

Rodrigo glanced at me with a smirk, and said, "Yes, the organization sponsoring Mr. Ludwig's contest is concerned about being cast in a negative light, given the caliber of his students remains unknown. Since the board didn't sanction this... this event—" he said, his hateful smile spreading wider, "—they would like me to supervise and ensure none of the students performing might embarrass them."

I could feel the heat coming off Ms. Phillips, and for a moment, I almost felt sorry for my idiot ex. He had no idea who he'd just royally pissed off.

"So—" Ms. Phillips said, "—you're saying *your* organization has the right to come to *our* school, a public school with its own music program, paid for by the taxpayers of this state and county, and tell us what we can and can't do with *our* students?"

Rodrigo's smile dropped and he shifted uncomfortably. "Well, we are paying Mr. Ludwig's salary."

Ms. Phillips turned to me, and even I cringed under her stare. "Do you represent the organization this gentleman is referring to?"

I shook my head. "No, it sponsored a contest, and agreed to fix my piano and pay my salary while I trained the contest winner. That's the extent of our agreement."

"So—" Principal Jenkins added, "—you didn't tell Mr. Everett to take over the recital?"

I chuckled bitterly. "No, in fact, he's in breach of contract even being here."

At that, she turned to Rodrigo, and said, "Mr. Everett, we don't allow strangers to walk into our school and take over our school-sponsored programs. We also don't take kindly to strangers coming into our school and making demands. Mr. Ludwig is a volunteer in our school. We never agreed to work with your organization, and I assure you that organization will not be mentioned in any of our programs, so I must decline your request for access to any of our students. Now, if that's all, I respectfully ask that you remove yourself from school premises, so that we can all get back to work."

Principal Jenkins left no room for argument, and I'd never seen Rodrigo look so peeved. "We'll see about this." Rodrigo stood and stomped out of the office, slamming the door behind him.

"What the hell was that?" Ms. Phillips asked.

I sighed. "He's my ex. He's an asshole, and he takes pleasure in trying to humiliate me. Sorry, Principal Jenkins."

"Son don't apologize to me, he *is* an asshole. I've never seen someone so arrogant as to think they can come into a school and demand to take over a music recital. Does he really think he has that much power?"

I barked a laugh at her unexpected frankness. "Classic narcissist, yeah. He really does."

"So—" Mrs. Stewart, ever the level-headed one, began, "—what does this mean for you?"

I sighed again. "I'm guessing it means I will get to spend a few days in court."

"Really? They'd sue you over this?" Mrs. Stewart sounded aghast, and all three women were scowling. It was actually quite sweet, because it meant they cared.

"Yeah, the board told me to cancel the recital when I first mentioned it to them."

"And you ignored them?" Ms. Phillips said, smiling.

"Of course, I did. They don't have control over what the school does with its own students. Neither do I. If you want your kids to have a recital, you can do it, and you don't need that windbag's permission."

"Well, if he shows back up, we will probably call the police," Principal Jenkins said. "He left pretty angry, and we won't put our students in the path of someone like him."

"He won't be back here, so you don't have to worry. This was all about trying to destroy me." I stood up to go, and apologized again, "I'm so sorry you all got caught up in this, but I'll make sure it's handled from this point on."

The three women nodded as I exited the office.

As I expected, Rodrigo was waiting for me outside the school's main entrance. "You can't expect us to pay for you to have unofficial performances. This isn't..."

I put my hand up to stop him from speaking. "You've breached the contract more than once. The fact that you're even here talking to me about this is a breach of contract. Please, let the board know my attorney will be drawing up the paperwork to dissolve our involvement."

I opened my car door to step inside, when he said, "You won't get out that easy."

I ignored him. I'd learned long ago it was best not to respond to narcissistic assholes who thought they had the power to force people to do what they wanted when they wanted. Rodrigo thought the world revolved around him and only him. Nothing I said would change that.

As soon as I was at the apartment, I phoned my attorney, and asked him to do what he could to sever the contract. "It won't be so simple. They've already paid for the piano to be repaired, and they will likely try to take it."

"No, it's been delivered to Monongahela. It's in my possession."

"That's good, but that won't necessarily protect you."

"Please, do what you can," I said, and hung up. I had two hours before I had to go back to the school for lessons, so I crawled into my bed and cried it out. Usually, I was one to suppress my emotions until I was nothing but a shell, but I didn't have the energy to bottle this up. Hopefully, a good cry would help me feel better, and clear my head ready for teaching this afternoon. I only wished Orli was here to wrap me in his solid, supportive embrace while tears stained my pillow.

32

Orlando

Ms. Phillips phoned me shortly after two o'clock, and asked if I could come to the school. "Um, sure. What's going on?"

"Well, your guy's in trouble, and I thought I should fill you in on how much."

That set off alarm bells in my head and my pulse spiked. "What kind of trouble? Is he okay? He should be there right now." I was up out of my chair, and about to bolt out of my office before she talked me down.

"Oh, I didn't mean to panic you, he's here and he's safe. This is a different sort of trouble, and he might not mention it. Anyway, come down while he's doing lessons with the kids. I'll meet you in the main office."

I sagged with relief back into my chair, and agreed to meet her at the school shortly. I quickly finished replacing the muffler on the old Jeep I'd been working on, and told Ray he'd have to check it out to the client when they came to pick it up.

"Dude, you are gonna have to hire someone to man that desk."

"*We*, Ray. *We* are gonna have to hire someone," I reminded him. "Let's talk about it when I get back."

He nodded, but looked perturbed as he dove back into working on a car.

He was right, though. Things were getting more and more chaotic as the summer months drew closer. We were so busy we barely had time to breathe, and having to deal directly with customers was a drag on our time spent actually repairing cars, which only put us further behind.

I arrived in the school office just as Mrs. Stewart and Ms. Phillips did. "Hey, come in," Principal Jenkins said from her office doorway, ushering us all inside. "Did Mr. Ludwig tell you about his run-in today?"

I shook my head. "No, I saw him heading up to his apartment just after noon, but then he disappeared. I haven't seen him since."

The three women looked at one another, and as a group, they silently seemed to appoint Ms. Phillips as the bearer of the news.

"So, did you know he was under contract with some organization in New York?"

I nodded. "Yeah, they've been giving him some grief. Is that what this—" I said, waving around the room, "—is all about?"

The women nodded and proceeded to tell me what'd happened. I couldn't believe his ex-boyfriend had shown up here in town, let alone come into the school making demands like some big shot. Jonas was right, the man was an asshole of epic proportions.

"He thinks they'll pull his funding. I'm guessing since he's living above your garage, he can't really afford to lose his income."

"No, he's living off what they pay him. Dang. Okay, so what do you propose we do?"

"Well, if we want him to stay, we'll have to figure out how to replace that income," Ms. Phillips said.

"And how do you propose we do that? I mean, we're doing well at the garage, but not quite that well."

"Oh, hon," Mrs. Stewart said. "We don't expect you to pick up the slack, but we as a community can. I mean, he's teaching all our kids for free, and he's teaching you too."

"Wait, if the contest is off, he won't have to teach me. That'll give him some more time. Maybe we could find him some work." They all nodded again. "Okay, well, keep your eyes open. I will too, and thanks for letting me know."

I walked out and was about to exit the building, when Ms. Phillips stopped me. "Orlando—" she shouted from the office doorway. "—hold up a moment."

I waited for her to catch up to me at the school's entrance. "Listen, I know you and Jonas are getting close, so this is as much for you as for him. We won't let him down. I'll make you a promise about that, okay?"

I smiled at my friend and mentor. "Yeah, okay. I do appreciate it."

"I know you do, sweetheart, now get back to work. I'll let you know what I... well, what *we* figure out," she said as she looked back toward the office.

I knew something big had happened here today. Not only were the three women working to help Jonas and me, but they'd somehow become a team. I didn't know the principal that well, but I did know Mrs. Stewart and Ms. Phillips. The two women had always been oil and water, but now it seemed they were working together. That in and of itself was a miracle.

When I got back to the shop, I immediately told Ray what I'd learned, and asked him to help me think about what we could do to help Jonas, if he was indeed going to lose his income.

That night, Jonas didn't hold back in telling me everything. He said the orchestra board was strong-arming him, and it was mostly his ex's doing. Apparently, the man had accosted Jonas in the parking lot too. I'd love to have gotten my hands on that guy when he was here, but that would've just made things worse. I could still fantasize about it, though.

"I-I think I'm going to have to take a job in Germany," he told me the next day. "I've spoken to my friend Tatiana, and she thinks she can get me hired at the university she's working for."

He'd been in an understandably somber mood since last night, and now he seemed on the verge of tears. He needed to know he wasn't alone in this, and that I wasn't prepared to let him go either.

"You don't need to go committing to anything right now. Can you give us a week before you decide?" I asked. "We're working on some things to keep you here."

He looked a little surprised and confused. "We who? What things?"

"Well, we as in me and some other folks who want to keep you around here, and things like a job. I mean, if you want to stay, that is."

Jonas sighed and walked into my outstretched arms, burying his face in my chest. "I don't want to go to Germany. I want to stay with you and my students," he said, pulling back slightly to meet my eyes. "But, I have expenses, and my attorney thinks the orchestra board will make me pay them back for the piano repair. If I have to do that and survive on my savings this year, I'll be completely broke."

"One week," I pleaded. "Just give us one week."

Jonas cupped my face and pulled me down for a tender kiss, before sighing again. "You can have longer than a week, but I'm going to have to ask Tatiana to start inquiring about the job in Germany."

That night we lay in bed holding each other, but not speaking. It wasn't like I didn't understand why he'd ask his friend to put out job feelers overseas, of course, I did, but at the same time, I couldn't imagine losing this amazing man just when I'd found him.

33

Jonas

THE ORCHESTRA BOARD REACTED by suing me for breach of contract, not that I was surprised. My attorney assured me I had the high ground, but then again, they had Mrs. Covington's attorneys and money. Yet, there was still only so much they could do. Could they force me to pay the money back for the piano repair?

My attorney told me he'd let me know when the court date was scheduled. He said he'd also petition the courts to put the case into arbitration, since I didn't really want to countersue them for the contract breach, although I was the real injured party here, not them.

I wasn't a big fan of litigation, though, and forcing the orchestra to pay me felt wrong. But then again, forcing me to pay them back when they were the ones with absurd expectations and trying to force Rodrigo on me and the school was wrong too.

"

I tried to put it all in the back of my mind as I continued preparing the kids for the recital. I woke up early to an empty bed. It was only five thirty, so I went downstairs in search of Orli, concerned about him. "Hey, are you okay?" I asked, when I saw him in the office, poring over his books.

"Yeah, it's just we're getting really busy. I don't have time to get all the paperwork done between customers."

"Can I help?" I asked, and he looked up at me, clearly shocked I'd ask.

"Um, well, have you ever done accounting?"

I laughed. "No, but if it's just counting receipts, I'm sure I can do that for you."

"And you wouldn't mind?"

"Honey—" I said as I went over to him, "—of course, I don't mind. You let me live here for free, remember?"

"No, you're giving me lessons, it's what we agreed."

I shook my head. "That's what Angela and Ray agreed. You got tricked into this, remember?"

Before he could argue, I kissed him and scooted an old chair over. "Show me what you want me to do."

It wasn't hard. Basically, he needed someone to total up the credit-card receipts, put the information in a spreadsheet on his computer, and then file the paper receipts.

By the time he got done showing me, Ray was walking into the shop. "Hey, what're you guys doing?"

"Orli just taught me how to do the daily accounting, so he can spend more time with me."

"Really? So, are you gonna help with the front desk too?" he asked.

"Um, what are you needing?"

"No, you won't have time," Orli protested. "You have to practice in the mornings."

"Tell me what you need, Ray?"

Ray turned from me to Orli, giving him a sympathetic look. "Sorry, brother, we need the help and if he's willing."

Orli sighed. "I hate to ask, but he's right. We need someone to check in customers and answer the phone, especially in the mornings. We're getting further and further behind, and having to stop the repair work for that is just making it worse."

"Why haven't you asked me already? I'm finished practicing by the time you open, and I usually spend the rest of the morning just preparing my lessons for the kids. I can do that while I'm sitting down here."

"Really?" he asked.

"Of course. Now, show me how to check folks in."

It really was a simple process of filling out some paperwork, getting the car keys, and directing where to park the vehicle. I felt bad I hadn't offered to do this before. Now that I wasn't performing, I was spending less and less time practicing, so I really did have the time to help out.

After checking in a few people under Orli's supervision, he left me in charge of the desk. During a brief lull, I rushed upstairs, grabbed my sheet music and notes, and was then able to plan my day in between customers and phone calls.

At noon, I set the office phone to go straight to voicemail, as Orli had instructed, and went upstairs to have lunch and get ready to head over to the school.

To be honest, I loved being in the office. I got to meet some of the folks I'd heard Orli or Ray talk about and didn't feel quite as isolated as I sometimes felt up in the apartment alone.

I ended up getting to the school early, which was a good thing, since Ms. Phillips needed to go over some things about the recital. "Word's gotten around about your jerk of an ex, and now the entire town wants to show its support by showing up. So, we'll need to hold the recital in the gym instead of here in the music room."

"Are you sure that's a good idea? I mean, will having such a big audience freak the kids out?"

"Nah, they'll be fine. We do a school play every year, so most of them are used to performing in front of a large crowd."

"Okay, well, I'll trust your judgment. What do you need me to do?"

She showed me the space, and I cringed at the acoustics. "It's not going to sound good with all these echoes," I said, and she chuckled.

"You've not done many school events, huh?"

"Um, no," I admitted, and she laughed again. "It'll be fine when the chairs are full. That deadens some of the echo. Trust me, it's a really good thing we're expecting high attendance."

I wasn't sure why we needed a big turnout for a kids' recital, but I just nodded. She knew a lot more about this kind of thing than I did, after all.

34

Orlando

Anxiety, that's what the kids were feeling. I tried to help ease their nerves with silly jokes and playful teasing, but even that didn't work.

Jonas, however, seemed to know exactly what to say. "Listen everyone, let me have your attention."

All the students turned to him, and I watched with amazement as my boyfriend expertly calmed them down. "This is a lot bigger than we expected, and it's completely normal for you to all be feeling nervous. But, remember, nerves are the best thing for helping you perform well. Use them, don't let them use you."

The kids nodded, and I smiled. They really were putty in his hands, as was I.

"Remind me, what happens if we mess up or miss a note?" he asked.

"We keep going," the kids said in unison.

"And what happens if we puke all over the stage?"

The kids all giggled, and some made fake, barfing sounds. "We step over it and keep playing," Jonas answered for them. "And, we do that, because…"

"The show must go on," they all recited with him.

"Right!" He smiled and gave the group a thumbs-up. "Okay, break a leg. Kevin, you're first. You ready?"

The boy nodded, and Jonas put his arm around him as he escorted him out of the room while the other kids formed a line to follow behind.

We all followed Jonas out of the music room and down the hall leading into the gym, which we entered to a round of applause and standing ovation. You'd think the kids were about to play basketball or something.

Kevin walked onto the makeshift stage, sat down at the piano, and blew my socks off. The music wasn't the soft classical piece I assumed we'd hear, since Jonas was the teacher. Instead, it was a fast, intense song, and Kevin was playing it beautifully.

By the time he finished his second song, one that was much quieter and sweeter, the audience roared with approval.

Each kid received the same reaction. With their performances, each student was showing us… me, how much he or she had improved in the months spent working with Jonas.

For his part, Jonas sat smiling from ear to ear, the pride in his students clearly shown on his face.

If I hadn't already fallen in love with him, I would've fallen hard for him now. Here he was, a world-renowned concert pianist, completely wrapped up in the success of a few kids from Monongahela, West Virginia.

Ella was the last to play. Of course, that child wouldn't play any classical, she had way too much Ray in her for that. Her first song was *The Entertainer* by Scott Joplin. When she'd finished with *Black and White Rag* by George Botsford, I was smiling like a proud parent. *That's my girl,* I thought.

Jonas got up, and I figured he was going to thank the audience and conclude the recital, when Ms. Phillips joined him on stage. She whispered in his ear, and he chuckled. "You sure?" he asked.

She nodded and looked at me.

Oh, shit, I thought, as Jonas began addressing the crowd.

"Apparently, there's been some disappointment expressed that our star pupil, Orlando Hancock, isn't performing tonight. But before I ask him to perform, we'll all have to agree to be fine if he says no. So, if he says no, will all of you agree not to harass him?" Jonas asked, and was answered with a combination of claps, whoops, and head nods. One person, who I could only assume was Ray, even let out a long whistle.

Geez, my boyfriend had them eating out of his hand. "So, Mr. Hancock, what do you say? Are you willing to complete our evening with a song?"

I laughed out loud. Like I could refuse. "Yeah, but just one," I said, taking the stage. "You all owe me big time!"

35

Jonas

I FELT BAD FOR Orli. I hadn't expected him to be put on the spot, and honestly, I should've just ignored Ms. Phillips, but this was his town and his people. I figured he knew how to say no if he wanted to.

I applauded with the crowd as he came up on stage, sat down at the piano, and paused in thought for a moment. I figured he'd play one of the honky-tonk songs he was famous for, or maybe *Black and White Rag*, like Ella had just played. But he glanced my way with a little smile that seemed only meant for me, before launching into *Clair de Lune*. The piece that brought us together... our song.

I was shocked at how beautifully he'd captured the melody. Orli played with such emotion, pouring his whole heart into the performance, that I began choking up. I felt so overwhelmed by it, by him.

When he finished, the gym remained silent for several moments, before applause broke out along with whoops and cheers. I laughed at the difference between this recital and most concerts I'd performed in or attended. This was about community. About family.

I wiped away the tears that'd fallen at the realization that Orli's performance was as much an expression of love as saying those three words. When we made eye contact, I knew that'd been exactly what he was telling me.

Ms. Phillips reappeared on stage, and I stood to join her when she took the microphone, and said, "As you all know by now, our maestro, Jonas Ludwig, came to our town as a result of a contest snafu. But, as you can see, his arrival has brought many great blessings."

She patted Orli on the back then, causing him to chuckle.

"But, many of you may not know, the organization that was sponsoring him has pulled out of the contract. So, we are starting a fundraising campaign." As if on cue, the kids jumped up and grabbed fliers from Mrs. Stewart, who was now standing in front of the stage, and began distributing them to the audience. "The money raised will go toward supporting private lessons for our students, and if we raise enough money, we'll send our beloved Orlando Hancock to the competition in Austria, as the original contest had planned."

My mouth flew open. No one had told me. I looked at Orli and saw he was equally shocked. My emotions came pouring out then. Damn, there was something about this town and my inability to control the tears.

I wiped them away and waved at the crowd, many of whom were now looking at the fliers.

"If you wish to donate, you can do so through the website listed on the flier. If you don't have the funds right now, as you can see, we'll be having a series of fundraisers starting later this month. Please, do what you can, and thank you for attending tonight. Let's have one more round of applause for our amazingly talented students, and for Mr. Hancock and Mr. Ludwig!"

With that, Ms. Phillips turned off the microphone, and winked at me before disappearing into the cheering crowd.

Orli slipped off the stage and came to sit by me. "Wow," he said. "You okay?"

"Um, shocked, but, yeah, okay."

He took my hand and kissed my knuckles. "They love you, you know that, right?'

I shrugged. "I think I love them too."

"Yeah, they have that effect on people. Come and meet your fans. The show must go on, right?'

I chuckled, stood up, and followed him into the fray. People shook my hand, parents thanked me, and everyone wanted to talk to me about the fundraising campaign, which I had to admit to only just learning about.

"Oh, that's Ms. Phillips for you," one parent said.

"That woman can get a mouse to hand over its cheese," another said in agreement.

I couldn't help but laugh at that statement. "I know that's true," I confirmed, and smiled Ms. Phillips's way upon seeing her standing in the middle of a crowd.

She winked at me, and went back to talking.

Damn, how had I landed in such an amazing town?

36

Orlando

J ONAS WAS SERVED THE next day. I honestly couldn't understand it. Why would the orchestra board be after him so badly? I mean, he'd all but agreed to pay them back as long as they left him alone.

He ended up crying it out on my shoulder, before he pulled himself together for his lesson with Pastor James's son Davey. Ray and I were still so booked that we barely had time to breathe, so I went down early to start working on paperwork.

Thankfully, since Jonas had started helping in the office, the paperwork I needed to do was a heck of a lot less than before. I was scheduled to sit down with Ray tomorrow, since it was our day off, and discuss the ins and outs of our new partnership.

We needed to talk about actually hiring someone to manage the front desk. Of course, that person might as well be Jonas, since he was already doing the work, only now we'd be paying him. So, even though our wages would never cover all of his expenses, it would at least help.

I'd literally just opened the hood of a Chevy that needed the timing chain replaced, when I saw Pastor James wander in on his way to Jonas's apartment. I waved at him, and he stopped, as if he were considering something, then came into the garage. "Hey, do you have a moment to chat?"

I nodded and walked over him. "What's going on, Pastor?"

He smiled. "Well, I have a favor to ask."

"What's that?"

He sighed and shook his head. "If I understand correctly, your family used to be part of my congregation."

I nodded. "Yeah, until my grandmother died."

"Would you consider coming back, at least occasionally?"

I stared at him in bewilderment, and he chuckled before putting his hands in the air. "I have a reason for asking. I was at the recital yesterday, and heard Ms. Phillips announce that Jonas didn't have a job with his organization any longer."

I nodded. "Yes, but I'm not following how that relates to the church."

"Well, here's the thing, I'm bound by bylaws much older than me that state I can't hire anyone who isn't a member of the church. So, I checked the membership rolls, and was surprised to see your name there, listed under your grandparents' names, that is."

I remained silent as I listened, curious to know where he was going with this.

"Since Jonas is your boyfriend..." he began, hesitating until I nodded my confirmation, "...his association with you would make it okay if I offered him a job as our pianist for the church."

Of all the things he could've said, that wasn't what I'd expected. Never mind my never having felt welcome in that congregation, but now they wanted me back, so they could hire my *boyfriend*? "Well, that's a weird way of going about it. Why don't you just change the bylaws?"

He let out a bitter laugh. "You don't know much about politics, do you? Son, I'm stirring that congregation up. Davey is already a vocal member of my family, and he's forced folks to look at how they teach our teens, and how we communicate with one another. Some are supportive of the changes, and others are struggling."

He paused for a few moments, and it struck me how I wouldn't mind hearing one of his sermons. He seemed as thoughtful as he was impassioned. "I don't mean to diminish member concerns, or their long-held beliefs, but I believe we must change our outlook on equality, or Christianity is in danger of being lost to history. Our church needs to be a welcoming, understanding, and a safe place for all who wish to worship there. Regardless, my board is still full of those more traditional folks, so trying to change bylaws is near impossible. However, getting an exception for a member's significant other should be easy enough."

"But, Pastor, I haven't been there in years."

"That really won't matter, not in the whole scheme of things. The congregation considers you one of their own. If you show up, like maybe tomorrow when I present my request to hire Jonas, I doubt anyone will object."

"I don't get it, but I'm happy to show up from time to time. I'm not a religious man, mind you. I prefer to seek my spirituality out in nature, or playing the piano. Still, my grandmother did love your church, and I care about many folks who still attend, so I don't mind. I guess my question is, though, is it worth it? I mean, how much does it pay?"

When he told me, my mouth flew open. "Really? Why so much?"

"That's the going rate, especially out here in the middle of nowhere. Our old pianist was placed in the nursing home last month, and we've had college kids from Morgantown temporarily filling in since then. They cost even more than what we're able to offer long-term, so hiring Jonas would actually cost less."

"Well, in that case, I'll see you tomorrow. Wait, have you run this by Jonas yet?"

Pastor James chuckled. "I'll ask Jonas if he's interested as soon as he finishes his lesson with Davey today. You can take it from there."

I reached out and shook the man's hand. "Whatever Jonas decides, I'll see you tomorrow. I really do appreciate what you're doing out there. It's something that needed to happen a long time ago."

The man smiled and nodded, then headed upstairs to Jonas's apartment. I still thought it strange a church that'd been so hostile just a few years ago had hired someone as open-minded as Pastor James, but what a welcome change.

If Jonas took him up on his offer, plus what he'd earn working at the garage, he'd be making about two-thirds the monthly salary he'd received from the orchestra. Would that be enough to keep him here?

"We can always hope," I muttered to myself as I began replacing the old timing chain on the Chevy.

Jonas

"YES SIR, I... OF course, I'd be interested, but you need to know, I've never gone to church. My dad was a Lutheran, but he stopped attending long before I was born. I won't even know how to act in a church."

Pastor James chuckled. "It's pretty routine. Why don't you come with Orli tomorrow and see what you think? We've got a replacement pianist coming, so you can get a feel for it, no pressure."

I nodded, confused and a bit excited. The money he was offering was significantly more than I thought I'd be able to make out here in the middle of nowhere, West Virginia. It hadn't even crossed my mind that a church might hire me.

When I glanced at Davey, he was smiling from ear to ear. "Maybe if you take the job, you'll let me play for the congregation from time to time?" he asked.

I laughed. "If you keep practicing like you are, you'll be asked to do it. You're making great progress."

The boy blushed, and I couldn't help but smile. I thanked the pastor and walked them to the stairs. "I'll see you tomorrow at church. I'm anxious to see how it all works."

They both smiled at me, and disappeared down the stairs and out the front door.

I had just gone into the bedroom to make the bed, when I heard the door open. "Billy, did you forget something?" I called out.

"No, it's me," Orli said, appearing in the doorway.

"Hey, do you mind if I bring clothes over to your place tonight? I've got to do laundry."

Orli walked in and slipped his arms around me, then kissed my neck. "Hey, don't get me oily!" I complained, but couldn't help laughing. I loved nothing more than having Orli nuzzle my neck.

"I'm not oily yet," he said, and gave me another kiss before letting me go. "So, did Pastor James mention the job with the church to you?"

"He did," I nodded as I pulled the covers over the bed.

"I'll need to start attending to get around some archaic rule the church has about only hiring members."

"But, I'm not a member," I said, suddenly confused, and Orli chuckled.

"No, but because I'm still considered a member and you're my boyfriend, Pastor James thinks that'll get around the issue."

I shrugged. "Sounds like a bunch of hoops to me, but hey, I could use the money and the gig." I laughed at the thought of a church job as a gig.

"You ever been to church?" Orli asked.

I shook my head. "Nope, so this will all be new for me."

"Well, you'll probably want to attend a few times before you agree. It's not the most exciting thing you could be doing."

I shrugged. "Trust me, I've worked at some of the most boring venues in New York. I can't imagine it would be that bad."

Orli smiled and kissed me. "Well, I'll tell you this much, if it keeps you here, I'd go every Sunday."

"It certainly comes close financially to keeping me here, but I'll need to make a bit more to cover my expenses. Don't worry, though, I've decided to look for a job myself. Who knows, another something like the church job might be lurking just around the corner."

"Possibly," Orli said, and turned to leave. "Oh, why don't you take your stuff on over to the house? I'm going over to Ray's tonight to discuss the business merger. Angela will want you to come too, so when you finish your laundry, come on over."

I laughed. "Have you actually asked Angela?"

He nodded. "Ray told her I was coming over. I think they just expect you to be with me at this point."

"I'll text her, geez, you really are a typical guy. Don't be pushing yourself on someone just 'cause she's a woman."

"Hey, that's not fair," he said.

"Just calling it like I see it. I'll text her."

Orli kissed me one last time before he headed back downstairs to work. I quickly texted Angela to see what her plans were for tonight.

> **Me:** *Orli says he and Ray have business tonight. Do you and Ella want to join me here at my apartment? I'll cook.*

My phone pinged with a reply almost immediately.

> **Angela:** *No offense, honey, but your cooking sucks. Come on over here and we'll leave them in the office while we hang out on the back deck drinking wine and gossiping about them.*

I couldn't help but laugh at her honesty. She really was a good friend.

Me: *Totally offended, even if it's true. Yes to the drinking and gossiping. See you around six?*

Angela: *Perfect.*

I gathered my dirty clothes and some sheets of music I hadn't played in quite a while, but wanted to work on with Orli. I'd mentioned Beethoven's *Hammerklavier Sonata* and *Islamey: Oriental Fantasy* by Balakirev to him originally, but then went a different route with our lessons.

It didn't surprise me that he hadn't asked me to teach him the two notoriously difficult pieces. I mean, they sucked to play. The movements were so challenging, it'd taken a decade for me to master them. Even now, I struggled if I hadn't practiced in a while.

I smiled wickedly at the sheet music. *I'll tell him it's sight-reading practice*, I thought, and grabbed my stuff and slipped down the stairs. I'd have to pick just the right time to spring it on him, so maybe not tonight, but it was going to be fun when I did.

38

Orlando

"WE NEED THE HELP," Ray said, confirming that he'd agreed to hiring Jonas.

"Okay, so it's settled. I'll ask if he wants to officially become our employee."

"We could ask him now," Ray said, and we both looked out the back door to where Angela and Jonas were sitting in Adirondack chairs, laughing over something, while Ella played with the family dog in the back yard.

"Nah, let them drink and be merry. We'll discuss business tomorrow, but you and I need to discuss the possible merger. Mr. Chris contacted me and said he needed an answer about buying his garage across town."

"Man, you know I'm in. Angela supports it, and we have enough saved up to invest, so if it's me you've been waiting on, go ahead and tell him yes."

"For real?" I asked, and when Ray nodded, I jumped up and hugged my friend. "Man, I think it's going to work well. Maybe with more help, we won't have to work so hard either."

"Well, we need to keep the numbers up if we're going to pull it off. I mean, you have no debt right now, but we will after purchasing a new building."

"That's why I'll be selling the shop. With what I expect to make from the sale, we can probably pay the new garage mortgage off fast enough, and still earn what we're making now."

Ray nodded, listening intently, so I pressed on, sharing my plan. "We need to consider keeping the other guys on too. I've been putting feelers out on both of them, and word is both are respected as good mechanics."

"Okay. As long as we can keep the volume high enough to afford keeping them on, I'm for it," Ray said. "But, we'll have to be really upfront with them about that."

"Definitely. So, partner, it sounds like we've got a plan," I said, sealing the deal with a handshake, while we both chuckled at the formality.

"Come on—" Ray said, "—let's tell Angela and Ella, *and* Jonas. I want you to be here when I tell them it's official."

I couldn't help but be happy to share the decision with them. When Ray broke the news, both Ella and Angela rushed him, and then hugged me too. "This is so amazing," Angela said. "My man's gonna be a businessman!"

"Does this make you my uncle?" Ella asked, and hugged me again.

I laughed. "Honey, I'm already like your uncle."

"Okay, then I'm gonna call you that. Uncle Orli and Uncle Jonas."

Jonas's eyes grew large, but he smiled. She hugged him and ran off with the dog to resume their playtime in the backyard.

"You're officially part of the family now, Jonas," Angela teased.

"Especially if he takes the part-time job we're going to offer him," Ray announced.

"Wait? Part-time job?" Jonas asked.

I just sighed. "You suck at secrets, dude," I said to Ray, then turned to Jonas. "Yeah, we're going to hire someone part-time to run the garage in the mornings, basically what you're doing now, but officially."

"Okay, and you want me to do it?"

"Yes," both Ray and I said at the same time.

"I accept, as long as I'm here, at least," he said, worried. "But, if I decide to go..."

I pulled him into my arms and kissed him. "No long-term obligation, but you're already doing the work, so you should get paid, and I really like looking at you through the garage window," I said, wagging my eyebrows.

"He's not lying," Ray cut in. "I have to fuss at him all the time to stop staring at the freaking window."

I laughed and playfully hit Ray on the arm. "So, yes?" I asked Jonas.

He nodded. "Yeah, yes! Yes, I can do that."

I kissed him hard, and when I pulled back, Jonas blushed. He was so cute. He needn't feel embarrassed by our kissing in front of Ray and Angela, though, seeing as their grins were as wide as mine.

I let the conversation shift to other things then. Jonas was still deciding whether to stay or not, and pushing family on the man might be too much. I had no doubt in my mind that if we gave it enough time, Jonas really would feel like part of the family, and Angela's teasing aside, I also knew I wasn't the only one who felt that way.

39

Jonas

"NO, YOUR HONOR," I answered.

"I'm a moderator, not a judge," the woman reminded me again. Damn, I was nervous. Hopefully it didn't show.

"So—" she continued, "—you're saying you didn't agree to the requirement that you weren't to conduct business outside the program while under the employment of the orchestra?"

I looked at my attorney, who'd made that argument earlier. "Ma'am, as I said, the orchestra approached me when I was about to go on-air to announce a contest I'd planned and organized myself. I agreed to their contract, and as you can see, there's no stipulation preventing me from working outside the orchestra's program."

"If I may," the orchestra's lead attorney interjected, and continued once the moderator nodded. "You are aware your contract as a pianist for the orchestra included just such a clause, are you not?"

My attorney had prepared me for this, knowing it was likely to come up.

"Yes, I'm aware of the terms of the employment contract I had with the orchestra."

"Yet, you ignored that rule when you created the contest."

"I was no longer under contract with the orchestra at that time."

One of the orchestra's other attorneys whispered something in the man's ear. He whispered back, then nodded.

"Did you or the orchestra sever that agreement?"

"It's my understanding that when the orchestra stopped paying me, and stopped scheduling me to perform, the contract automatically ended."

My attorney had said that was essentially the way the courts would interpret it, and advised to be careful not to get tripped up about it when they asked. Hell, the orchestra cutting me off financially was what had forced me into teaching private lessons back in New York in the first place.

"Did you agree to accept the money you were paid in the previous contract?" the attorney asked.

"Yes."

"However, that salary isn't mentioned in the contract you signed?"

I shook my head. "No, no amount of compensation was stated."

"But, the amount you were receiving monthly from the orchestra as part of the contest agreement was the same as you got in your previous contract?"

I nodded, and the moderator reminded me I had to speak out loud.

"Yes."

The attorney looked smug, and I knew from my own attorney's pained look that I'd stepped in it. *Dammit.*

At that point, the orchestra's attorney called Rodrigo in to testify. Basically, he told them I had verbally agreed to accept the terms of the old contract as we were preparing to go on the air.

As he recounted it, I remembered our tense exchange at the news station that day, and knew I was sunk.

When it was all said and done, the moderator ruled that I had, in fact, breached the contract. I was ready for her to say I was going to lose it all when she looked over at the attorneys for the orchestra, as if to address them directly. "However—" she said, "—it's apparent that the orchestra is in breach as well. It's also apparent that they breached the contract first, not only when they stopped paying Mr. Ludwig, but when they forced him to take on a client who hadn't applied for the contest. Therefore, Mr. Ludwig, I will not order you to give back the Steinway, as they've requested. However, it's my assessment that you should pay back the orchestra for the income you've received as related to the contest. You will also have to reimburse the orchestra for the money used to repair your piano."

She looked at me then, and asked, "How much can you afford to pay per month?"

I shrugged. Even though my attorney had prepared me for this possible outcome, I hadn't wanted to jinx it by actually crunching numbers. It was just too depressing. "I will have to find employment. I won't know how much I'll be able repay each month until I've secured a job."

She nodded. "In that case, I'll give you six months to secure employment, then we'll reconvene to assess how much you'll pay on a monthly basis."

There were objections by the other side, but the moderator reminded them they'd agreed to let her decision stand, and that was that.

Orli was sitting outside the meeting room when I came out. "You okay?" he asked when he saw me.

I shook my head without speaking, and took his hand as my attorney asked me to follow him, so we could speak in private.

"I'm sorry, Jonas," he said, when we found a quiet corner.

I shrugged and put on the same confident façade I wore like a shield while performing, but my insides felt queasy. "I know you did all you could. Ultimately, I think that might've been the best outcome possible. I won't lose my piano, and I'm not being forced to go bankrupt to pay them back."

Orli looked sad. "So, they won then?"

"Yeah, sorta," I responded.

"I'm so sorry," he said, and drew me into a hug. "It just seems so... wrong."

"It's contract law, and it could go either way. I do think this worked out better than it could've," my attorney said, and after shaking my hand, left.

Orli hugged me for several minutes, rubbing circles on my back, before he finally let go. "Let's go home," he whispered in my ear before taking my hand.

I let him draw me out of the building and down the steps. I looked over as we came out, and saw Rodrigo standing next to Mrs. Covington. When he saw me, he gave me a smug look. The bastard knew he had me. He'd known it when all this started. I should've known better than to trust him. Hell, anytime I had anything to do with Rodrigo, it was to my detriment.

Lesson learned, but it still stung. At least from now on, I'd know to stay as far away from him as possible.

After we returned home, things went from bad to embarrassing. The local paper ran a front-page spread about me and the student recital, featuring photos of several of my students, as well as me and Orli. *Famous Pianist Brings Class to Monongahela*, proclaimed the headline.

I cringed as the article went into detail about how I'd been let go from the orchestra, because I'd defiantly gone ahead with the recital, then it chronicled how the community was coming together on a fundraising campaign, organized by Ms. Phillips and Mrs. Stewart. I was mortified.

On the bright side, at least the two teachers were working together instead of being at each other's throats.

As I walked rather than drove from the apartment to the school that afternoon to help clear my head, I expected to see derision, angry looks from locals about some out-of-towner trying to make money off them. Instead, I saw smiling faces, and people waving and calling out hello who'd never spoken to me before.

By the time I got to the school, I was in an amazing mood. I signed in at the front office, and received congratulations on the article from several staff members before I walked down to Ms. Phillips's classroom.

"Oh, excellent," Ms. Phillips said the moment I walked in, then turned to a young woman I'd never seen before. "Gloria, are you okay watching the students while I go out to speak with Mr. Ludwig?"

The poor woman went pale, but nodded, and I couldn't help but smile in sympathy. I knew exactly what she was feeling. Hell, I'd felt just the same a few months earlier.

"Is she going to be okay?" I asked as we walked out of the room.

Ms. Phillips chuckled. "She will be eventually. She's my new intern. Junior year in college and wants to be a music teacher. Might even be sporting to take over my position."

"Um, you aren't retiring, are you?" I asked, concerned.

Ms. Phillips looked over at me sadly. "Yes. I agreed to this and next year, then I'm done. I'm afraid my poor feet aren't getting any younger, and those kids are, but don't worry about me, I have plenty to keep me busy. It's you we're here to talk about."

We stopped outside Mrs. Stewart's classroom, where she waved us in. "Perfect timing," she said, looking at her watch. "We've got fifteen minutes before my next class."

"Okay," I said, confused about what was going on.

"Let's get to it then," Ms. Phillips said, her face breaking into a smile. Mrs. Stewart nodded, indicating for her to keep going.

"We received an anonymous contribution this morning of ten thousand dollars toward your fundraising campaign," Ms. Phillips said. "I know that's not all you need to survive, but we're hoping it's enough to keep you here short-term."

"I-I can't take charity. I-I..." Of course, I knew about the campaign, but the implications of exactly where those donations would go only just hit me.

"You aren't going to take charity. You're going to work for it." Mrs. Stewart patted my shoulder reassuringly. "Ms. Phillips and I both have a list of students we'd like you to start working with. All of these children have shown some musical prowess, but, well, let's just say they've got less than stellar home lives."

"And you want me to give them lessons?" I asked.

"Yes," Mrs. Stewart said matter of factly. "And since their parents aren't likely to, um, respond, we're going to have you give them lessons during their music class, and physical education if need be."

"Wait, parents are against lessons?"

"No, no, nothing like that. These are great kids, but their parents are notoriously adamant that they are our responsibility when they're here at school. None have ever returned a permission slip, or signed anything we've sent home for that matter."

"I still don't get it," I responded, concerned I was going to end up being sued again.

Neither woman spoke for a moment, before Ms. Phillips finally said, "There are five kids we'd like you to give lessons to. One of them is the child of our town drunk, to put it bluntly. His mom passed away a year ago, and the child is struggling."

"Struggling a lot," Mrs. Stewart added. "I think if my husband, who's a deputy sheriff here in our county, goes over, he can get the dad to sign a permission slip, if you agree to it."

"Okay, and the others?" I asked.

"Foster children, all siblings. The foster parents are good people, but they have their hands full. The three youngest children attend our school, and the fourth child is in the high school. They just don't return paperwork. Never have."

"Can your deputy husband go over there too?" I asked.

"No, that would cause too much of an issue, but we could possibly get the social worker involved. That is if you agree."

"Um, yeah. I'm not comfortable giving classes without parental or official permission. I mean, I've already been sued once, and that's plenty, but if you can work out the permissions, I'm game."

"And you can come in earlier? During summer school hours?" Ms. Phillips asked.

I shrugged. "Sure, I don't know why I couldn't. Yeah, let's do it."

Both women smiled. "We'll let you know when we work out those permission slips, then you're hired."

After the shitty morning I'd had, I felt grateful to be wanted and needed. The women explained how the school would eventually turn this into a formal position, but that required approval from the school board, so for now I'd continue being considered a volunteer. The only difference was I'd receive funding through the fundraising campaign donations, which Ms. Phillips would manage since she'd helped organize it. I didn't follow all the details, but that was the gist of it. All that mattered was I had a job, one I surprisingly enjoyed, that enabled me to pay my bills.

Over the next few weeks, not only did we get all the permissions for the kids, but parents of several other children had approached me about giving private lessons as well. For now, I was just glad that with the money I was now making between the garage, the church, and the lessons, I not only covered my expenses, but was able to put money aside to pay back the orchestra. If all went well, I'd actually be able to pull this off, and most importantly, be able to stay in this amazing little town.

40

Orlando

"WHAT THE HELL?" I asked as the music I was sight-reading during my lesson stopped being music, and became a bunch of random dots and drawings spread across the scale.

I glanced over at Jonas, who was clearly struggling not to laugh. "Dude, what is this?" I asked, surprised to hear the word *dude* come out of my mouth. I usually only ever used it when harassing Ray, but Jonas had me flabbergasted.

"*Islamey* by Balakirev... *dude*," he said with a smirk, and like that explained everything.

"That's the most ridiculous piece of music I've ever seen. That's not playable." I could hear the whining in my voice.

"Here, let me sit down," he said as he slid onto the piano bench.

Within seconds of sitting down, Jonas launched into the song. Fingers flying across the keys. When he finished, I stared at him. "No," I said, and got up to leave.

"Wait," he said, unable to hide a shit-eating grin. "I just wanted you to hear it."

"No!" I yelled as I walked into the kitchen to refill my water glass, and heard him laughing in the living room. He began playing again, and this time the music was soft and sweet. "That," I said as I came back, "I could probably learn to play."

"Same piece, different movement," he replied, not missing a note.

"What's the point of the first part?" I asked.

"Showing off, I'd imagine," he said. "It was written after Beethoven's *Sonata No. 29*, and some say he was trying to outdo Beethoven. Others said it's the perfect piece, because it requires the student to be perfect."

"Or insane," I said with a chuckle.

Just then, the music started back up in a fast frenzy, and although different from the first movement, Jonas's fingers were everywhere on the keyboard all at once.

I stopped watching his hands and started watching him. Not only was his skill stunning, but so was he. The man was truly remarkable, and I was in awe.

When he stopped, I couldn't resist leaning over and kissing his lips. "What?" he asked in surprise.

"You're sexy when you play so aggressively."

Jonas leaned back and laughed. "You're nuts," he said, shaking his head.

"Play another. One of the hard pieces you mentioned to me early on."

He began playing, and I immediately recognized it, though I didn't know the name of it. He stopped after a moment and looked at me. "Who wrote this? Can you tell?" he asked.

I shook my head, then remembered he'd said Balakirev had copied Beethoven, so I took a guess. "Beethoven."

"You cheated, but yes, it's Beethoven. It's deceptive, unlike the Balakirev piece, which sounds hard. Many players of the time weren't even able to play this, because the pianos were different. This piece was considered impossible," he said, and launched back into it.

I watched him, appreciating the music as much as his exertion in making it, and when he stopped, I asked, "Is it strange watching you play like this makes me horny?"

"God, you're weird," he said, but I didn't miss the gleam in his eye. I picked up his hand and was going to pull him upstairs when he laughed, and added, "Nope, got one more for you hear, one I think is just your style."

I moaned. "Can't we make out first, then you show me?"

"No!" he said, and laughed when I pouted. "Listen."

All of a sudden, he switched from a classical piece, which I honestly thought was boring as hell, to a song fit for playing in a honky-tonk bar.

I jumped up and began kicking up my heels like a stage dancer in an old Western saloon, which caused him to mess up. "Stop," he protested, but continued to try and play as I continued to act like a fool.

The music got even rowdier, and I began to flip around the room, twirling and spinning with the music.

As the music got more dramatic, I changed tactics and began to strip. When my shirt was off, I flung myself on the sofa as if it were a fainting couch, acting dramatic like I'd passed out.

He was belly laughing by that point, and totally screwing up the music, which gave me perverse joy. I'd never been this silly and stupid with a boyfriend, and it felt good to see him having just as much fun as me. I kicked off my shoes, and tossed my socks at him as he bobbed and weaved to dodge them, then got even more insane with the music.

His fingers flew over the keys, focus so intense he didn't notice I'd gotten off the sofa. When he hit the final chord, he turned around to find me standing there, stark naked. He all but jumped me then, pulling me up the stairs, kicking off his shoes, and trying unsuccessfully to strip off his clothes as he went.

I straddled him when we climbed onto the bed, taking my time kissing and nuzzling his neck in the way I knew he liked. Undoing his shirt buttons one by one, I kissed and nipped my way down his chest as more and more skin became exposed.

By the time I'd peeled his pants and underwear off, I was ready to taste him.

I took his cock into my mouth and sucked, enjoying the rich moans that rolled out of him in waves. Jonas reacted to my touch as no man ever had, which ratcheted up my own desire to a level I'd never experienced. I wanted... *needed* this man, and I was determined to show him just how much tonight and every night, for as long as he shared my bed.

As I popped off him, he tugged me up and rolled us over, so that he was on top. Grabbing supplies out of the nightstand, I watched as he prepared himself before taking me inside him. I couldn't tear my eyes away from his blissed-out face as I slid in and out of him at his pace, and as he brought us both to orgasm, my heart swelled. In that moment, I could feel in every sense just how lucky I was to call this amazing man mine.

"Who wrote the last one?" I asked once he'd rolled off, and our breathing slowed.

"Huh?" Jonas asked as he lay limp next to me, his body spent.

"The last song you played. The one I'm now calling *foreplay*."

He snorted, then leaned up on his elbow, smiling at me. "We are *not* calling *Islamey* by Mily Balakirev *fore-play*."

"Too late. From now on, every time I hear that song, I'm going to think of getting you between the sheets."

"Remind me to play it often then," he said, and leaned over to steal a kiss.

"No problem. You know, it's nothing like the others. Fast, yeah, but it's fun."

"The others aren't fun?"

"No, not at all. Most of the stuff you play isn't fun, no offense."

Jonas fell back onto the bed, and sighed. "I guess it's how you see it. To me, well, it's not fun, but I do think of the music as poetic. Some of it's highly emotional, like some of Mozart's pieces, but then others... I don't know," he said, and stared at the ceiling. "It's not like they're boring or fun or not, they're supposed to be lots of things."

"You love it, don't you?" I asked as I rolled over on top of him.

He nodded. "I do. I love it for a lot of reasons. I love music, I love that I'm able to create it just 'cause I want to. I love that even now, I have so much more to learn, so many ways to improve. Hell, I don't know if I'll ever be as good as my dad, but I love to try."

He kissed me, and let his hands run up and down my back, before tucking his head into my neck. "I think, though, the thing I love about it the most is how different each piece of music is. Even now, piano and keyboards are part of modern music. So, whether it's Beethoven, honky-tonk, or something from Elton John, the piano still tugs on the heart, and makes us feel."

I took his mouth again and then began nuzzling down his delightful body, until I got to his abdomen, where I laid my head, letting my body rest between his legs. "You amaze me," I finally said.

He chuckled, making my head bob up and down. "You're easily amazed then."

"Stop that," I whispered. "You *are* amazing, not just because of your skill, but because of your passion. I think that's why I and your other students continue to improve. Your love of the music, of your instrument, inspires us to be better."

He stroked my hair, but didn't respond. I didn't really need him to. I wanted him to know I truly saw him and loved that part of him.

When he began to grow hard under me, I lifted my head up and smiled at him. "You know, I like this instrument too," I said, taking his cock in my hand. "But, this is one I don't need lessons on how to play."

41

Jonas

"**O**FTEN LIFE COMES AT you hard," I'd often heard my dad say throughout my childhood. "But, other times, it just works. Those are the times you have to let yourself just enjoy the ride."

Taking my father's words to heart helped me appreciate all that was working right now. It would've been way too easy to get bogged down with worry over paying back the orchestra for years on end, and knowing I'd eventually have to leave here, and get a job making considerably more money. I didn't want to miss all the good stuff, at least for the moment, there was plenty of it to enjoy.

One of the most surprising bright spots was realizing that I didn't actually hate teaching. I would've sworn otherwise, but in fact, it could be quite rewarding. My new students were nuts. I mean, like taking feral animals out of the woods and trying to teach them to play piano, but every one of them, even the surly teenager, lit up like a lightbulb when they played through their first piece of music.

The elementary schoolers all played pieces from one of Ms. Phillips's piano books, and even though the pieces were simple, the look of accomplishment on their faces left no doubt these kids would be lifelong players.

The teenager, Zander, was another story. He called me every name in the book on our first day, and said I had no right to go over his foster parents' heads to get approval for his lessons.

"Hey, listen, kid, if you don't want to do this, then don't," I said, and closed the piano, preparing to leave.

"No. I'll get in trouble. At least teach me something simple, so I can say I tried."

It was then I saw the hunger, the hope, he was working so hard to hide.

"Suit, yourself," I said, and opened the piano back up. "Stick out your hand."

Zander did as I asked and I showed him how he needed to keep his fingers in a bow, then gave him a quick primer on proper posture. It only took a few moments of trying to play before I saw I was already losing him.

"No, hit a C."

"What, man? A what?"

"A *C*. Here," I said and banged out the note. "Easiest key to find on the keyboard. It's always on this side of the two black keys. Now, find me another."

I did that for a few minutes, and as long as he was having some success, I could see he'd keep trying.

Ms. Phillips slipped into the classroom and sat at her desk while I had him do the same with each of the other notes.

"It's as simple as A, B, C, D, E, F, G. Not hard at all."

"Really?" he asked, and I had to try hard not to smile as I nodded.

"Okay, so, next we need to make those make music. I had Zander scoot over on the piano bench, slid in beside him, and played a quick, simple tune that I'd played with the younger kids. "See, every time I hit a key, I'm hitting one of those notes I mentioned to you. Doesn't matter where I'm at on the keyboard, it's the same notes."

"What about the black keys?" he asked.

"Aah, those are when the white ones aren't quite right. See, sometimes I want a C," I said and hit the note. "Sometimes I want something between the C and a D. So, I can hit this, and I get C and a half."

"What?" he asked and looked at me like I was nuts. I did laugh this time.

"Hey, for real, but no one calls it that. They call it a C-sharp."

"So, these are all sharps?" he asked.

"Yeah, unless I go the other way, like when I don't want an A but something less than an A, so then when I hit the black key," I said while demonstrating, "that's called an

A-flat. When I want less than a note, it's a flat, simple as that. When I want a little more, it's a sharp."

"Sounds like a bunch of bull..."

"Zander," Ms. Phillips chastised from across the room, and I bit my tongue as the boy stopped mid-word.

"Gonna get us both in trouble," I said quietly. "Anyway, wanna learn something?"

"Y-yeah?"

"Yeah, you can." I spent the rest of the time showing him how to follow music. I knew Ms. Phillips had taught all this before, but she assured me that although he'd deny it until he died, Zander could actually recognize written music.

I had to hand it to Ms. Phillips, she'd done a very good job teaching the basics of reading music. However, I knew most kids didn't have that kind of skill. Even my more affluent students back in New York often came to me with absolutely no ability to discern a note written on a staff.

When we finished our lesson, I patted the teenager on the shoulder, making him wince and pull away. "Sorry, Zander, I..."

"No, man, it's okay. I get freaked out when people touch me, but thank you for giving me a lesson. I liked it."

"Yeah, me too. Gonna come back?"

He shrugged. "I guess I don't have anything better to do."

"See you tomorrow then," I said and watched him all but run out of the room.

"That went well," Ms. Phillips said.

"You think?" I asked.

"More than. Zander is a great kid. I've been partial to him since the first day he walked into my classroom and tried to steal a cymbal Percy Johnson dared him to take. Foolish boy tried to stick it down his trousers." Then she chuckled, and I saw real adoration for him in her eyes. "Took him to the principal and he confessed and cried like a baby, then begged us not to get him sent away from his family." A dark shadow passed over her face as she told me how his old social worker told him if he got in trouble, they'd take him out of the foster home, and he'd never see his siblings again.

"Anyway, the boy's got a true talent for music. He resists it, of course, like most kids who've been through what he has, but it's there nonetheless. Until you got yourself in the papers, I haven't had any way to pull him into lessons. So, this, you, I'm trying to say, are a blessing."

"He's a cool kid, but I'm not sure I'm all you say I am. However, as long as he wants to come for lessons, I'm willing to give them."

She smiled and began to close up the classroom for the day. As I walked her out to our cars, I thought about what would happen if, or rather, when, I left town.

The fundraising campaign had raised enough money to cover a full year of giving lessons to kids like Zander. I was also going to give another recital and maybe help a couple of my students compete. Still, I seriously doubted my donors would be willing to fund another year beyond that. For now, though, I was happy and loving what I was doing.

42

Orlando

"WHAT COMPETITION?" I ASKED as Ms. Phillips and Jonas both ganged up on me.

"It's the Pittsburgh Amateur Piano Competition. Children and adults can compete, so we'd be entering you and some of the schoolkids. Plus, since it's only about an hour-and-a-half away, the school district is going to let us use one of the school buses."

"But, I didn't think I had to do that now, enter a competition."

Ms. Phillips shrugged. "Orli, we want Jonas to stay for as long as he can, right?"

When I nodded, she continued, "Bringing home a win, even if it's a relatively small one, will give the community something to be proud of. Besides, you've got it in the bag. We've all heard you play."

"I do not have anything in the bag," I said, taking a long breath in resignation before letting it out. "If I get to pick something besides boring classical, I'll do it." When I looked at Jonas, I could tell he wanted to argue. "It's my one requirement. Pick something that shows my skills, but doesn't put me to sleep."

Jonas shook his head, but Ms. Phillips chuckled. "You always have been a pill, but I'm sure our boy here can find something for you," she said as she patted Jonas on the back.

The competition ended up giving us something to work toward, and the piece Jonas picked for me was fun, fast, and not at all boring like I knew he'd have preferred me to play.

It wasn't that easy to learn either, but not because I couldn't play it. Up until now, Jonas mostly worked with me on form, but with this piece he said I lacked style. I took it in stride, and when he was on the verge of getting too serious or frustrated with me, I'd tickle him until he was laughing or wiggling away. With as much time and effort as we were putting into this, I needed it to be fun, and he needed to relax and enjoy the process.

He'd been right, though, I needed to learn to put feeling into the piece. Like when to have a fast tempo, which was what I preferred, but also when to slow down and play quietly, or whatever the music told me to do.

I'd honestly never paid much attention to the dynamics in a piece of music. "Play so they can hear over the noise," I could still hear my great-granny saying.

Now, the dominant voice in my head was Jonas, saying, "Play it with emotion, follow the direction of the composer."

By the time the competition came around, I felt moderately ready. I wasn't really afraid of crowds. I'd been playing in front of them most of my life. People either liked what they heard, or they didn't. The difference was, rather than playing to a room full of folks happy just having music to dance to, I'd be center stage with all eyes and ears on me. Everyone would just be sitting there, listening to every note I played, and judging me for it... this was a competition, after all.

That was more than a little nerve-wracking. I wiped the sweat from my palms as I walked on stage and sat down at the piano. I took a deep breath and pulled my great-granny's face into my mind, because no matter where or what I played, I always thought of her, then I brought up an image of Jonas, and as I thought about him, of how it felt every time he touched me, I let my emotions flow through my fingers.

When the music shifted into the melancholic sadness that ended the piece, I thought of Jonas and all I had to lose if he left town. We'd bonded so much that I couldn't quite picture what my life would be like without him, other than lonely. I all but had tears in my eyes as the final chord fell silent.

Then I stood and bowed. It felt strange to finish a piece that pulled so much emotion out of me only to be greeted with silence. Being a competition, there was no applause or any acknowledgment, good or bad, to indicate how people felt about what they'd just heard.

It was unsettling, and I left the stage feeling sick to my stomach. I immediately saw Jonas, and the expression on his face told me just how well I'd done. When he grabbed me into a fierce hug, I smiled. "Okay then?" I whispered into his ear.

"It was wonderful. *You* were wonderful. I'm so proud of you," he said, squeezing me tighter. "Now, come back with me and let's listen to the kids."

I'd already listened to many of the adult competitors, and it was obvious several were better than me. Well, more controlled, at least. We wouldn't know how I officially stacked up against them for a long while, though. Rather than announcing a person's score following their performance, as I'd expected, scores were posted on a board in the back of the auditorium after all competitors in an age group had performed.

My nerves, however, quickly slipped away as one after another of Jonas's students got up to play. There were different levels, of course. Everything from beginners to the kids I used to teach, who played much more complex stuff than when under my tutelage.

"Wow," I said, when his final student finished. "They did amazing."

Tears had filled Jonas's eyes throughout the performances, and now they slipped down his face. "They really did, didn't they?"

I hugged him to me and kissed the side of his head. "Yeah, baby, they really did."

I ended up scoring high, only getting dinged on my posture, but not high enough to win. *Damn posture.* I always seemed to forget myself while playing and slipped back into my old ways, but the music had been good, at least, according to my scores.

After the competition, we all went to a local pizza place. Between Jonas and myself, the kids, several parents, and Ms. Phillips, we took up a good portion of the available seating. After everyone had settled down with their food, Ms. Phillips stood to speak. "You all, I know Jonas wants to speak to you, but before he does, I just wanted to say how proud I am of each of you. You were top-notch tonight, kids, even the big kid back there. Great job."

Everyone cheered, while I chuckled at being called a big kid, though I certainly felt like one at the moment.

Then Jonas stood and immediately got emotional. He laughed as he wiped the tears from his eyes. "Like Ms. Phillips, I'm so proud of you. You each played exceptionally well and showed your skills, not just at playing, but at performing, which I know I've been beating into your heads for the past few weeks."

Some of the kids nodded while others seem to hang on his every word, and all soaking up his praise, as he continued, "You've also done so much for me these past few months. I love helping you grow and learn, and this afternoon, as I listened to each of you show your skills and talent, it struck me just how lucky I've been to be a part of all this, so before I get too mushy, and Zander starts yelling at me..." he said, as the teenager rolled his eyes dramatically, but was smiling. "I'm gonna stop and say, you're the best students I've ever had, and I'm so happy I get to be your teacher."

I glanced at Ms. Phillips just as she looked over at me, and she chuckled as she wiped a tear. I'd never seen the woman cry before, so I was a bit surprised. Then again, she was more than a little attached to Jonas, so it made sense she'd been moved by his words.

I walked over to her as the kids dug into their pizza, and putting my arm around her, I whispered, "You are my hero, Ms. Phillips. We all know without you, none of this would've happened."

When she started to argue, I picked up a piece of pizza and put it on her plate, and said, "Don't argue, eat, and accept the compliment for what it is—the truth."

She smiled, and without saying a word, picked up the pizza and took a huge bite. We sat together, eating and chatting, as Jonas mingled around the room talking to students and parents.

I realized that in all these years, I'd never told Ms. Phillips how much she meant to me. First as her student, then as a volunteer pulled into her world to help teach our kids the joys of music. She embodied compassion and a love for community we should all strive for, and I knew there was still so much I could learn from her.

43

Jonas

SOMETHING CLICKED INSIDE ME as I listened to Orli perform. It wasn't like I wasn't already falling for him, but watching him pour his soul into that piece of music, knowing how far he'd come these past few months, left no doubt about the depth of my feelings.

That night, after we got home to his place, we made love like there was no tomorrow. As we lay bathed in the moonlight, I wondered if he felt the same way. Did he love me the same way too?

Before coming to this town, I'd been so alone. My life had become devoid of people who cared, a purposeful career, and a place to call home. Desperation had almost led me to throw away the most important thing I had left of my dad—his piano—because it felt like the best things in my life were already behind me.

Now, in just a few months, my life had completely turned around. I had friends, people who were beginning to feel like family, and colleagues who respected me, and students who wanted to learn, *and* I had Orli, a man silly enough to do a ridiculous striptease just to make me laugh, and strong enough to spend hours holding me as I cried.

I leaned over and looked at him as he slept. He was so handsome. When I'd first arrived, I'd felt that instant spark of attraction, but ignored it. Really, what could a New York concert pianist have in common with a small-town mechanic? But, after we'd spent some time together, it became more apparent that our differences were all on the surface. We had only appeared to be opposites.

I rolled over on my side, and Orli, almost on autopilot, snuggled up behind me, pulling me close. I almost moaned at how good it felt to be wrapped in his arms. It was too soon for me to confess my love, so I'd wait until the time was right to tell him. The only question that plagued my mind was, how would we handle a long-distance relationship?

Would he come to Germany with me? No, that was out of the question. His life was here. He and Ray were opening a new shop together. There was no way he'd leave his friend in the lurch.

Would he visit me in Germany? That was the real question. I was guessing he would if he could, at least initially, but not for the long-term. I knew that too.

"Why are you thinking so hard?" he asked quietly, his arms tightening around me.

"How do you know I'm thinking?"

"'Cause it's hurting my head," he replied, and nuzzled my neck the way I liked. "Go to sleep. Stop worrying about everything."

I sighed. Even half-asleep, the man was able to figure me out. "Night, Orli," I said, and almost, just almost, told him I loved him.

"Night, sweet Jonas."

As I struggled with my predicament, knowing I was in love with a man whose world I might have to leave, sleeping became more and more difficult. On Sunday night, I told Orli I wanted to stay alone in the apartment to see if I could catch up on sleep. That proved a mistake, because damn, between missing him and worrying about the future, I practically had insomnia.

I dragged myself out of bed Monday morning feeling horrible. I managed not to snap at anyone as I checked in Orli and Ray's customers, then I only got in about half an hour of practice before my head started pounding, and I decided to let practice go for the day.

So, by the time I had to go to the school for lessons, I was more than dreading it. Bone tired and irritable, I still pasted on a smile, though. After the success of the competition, I didn't want to sour their experience by being, well, sour.

I decided to walk there rather than drive. As much as I appreciated Orli helping me get a car, I'd been conditioned to walking everywhere back in New York, and it usually helped clear my head anyway. I'd just come around the corner of town that led down to the school when out of nowhere, Rodrigo stepped in front of me.

"You son of a bitch, what did you tell them?" he snapped.

I stopped in my tracks and stared at him for several moments before it even registered that he was actually here, in the flesh, let alone what he'd asked.

"Tell who? Rodrigo, I'm in no mood to deal with your bullshit today. Leave me alone. In fact, you shouldn't come near me ever again."

Between the two of us shouting at each other, we were beginning to attract attention. I stepped off the sidewalk and onto the street to walk around him when he grabbed my arm and spun me around. He shoved a magazine into my chest and said, "You'll be hearing from my attorney."

The asshole stalked off to his vehicle without another word, so I stepped back onto the sidewalk and glanced at the magazine. I almost laughed out loud seeing his picture splashed across the front of it.

It was a snapshot of Rodrigo dancing in the middle of a crowded bar, wearing some ridiculous outfit and surrounded by several men. He was standing on something, which put the men at eye level with his crotch, and all were looking their fill.

The Grell Chronicle was a small publication that featured the classical music scene in New York. Usually, the magazine was as boring and dry as a stale cracker, and I doubted few people actually read it in general. I'd certainly never seen a cover as scandalous as this one.

I flipped the magazine open, turned to the article, and began to read.

Celebrated New York orchestra conductor Rodrigo Everett has been raising as many eyebrows off-stage as on in recent years, multiple sources say. I read on as it chronicled how he'd been romantically involved with more than one of the orchestra's musicians, and had used his influence to destroy the careers of others.

My face must've glowed as I read in very clear detail a recounting of that horrible night Rodrigo had deliberately brought his new boyfriend to my dressing room minutes before my performance, in order to cause a scene and break up with me.

Reliable sources overheard Mr. Everett state as he walked away, "That should be enough to rattle the loser. He should fuck up enough that we can easily get rid of him."

I felt sick. I sat down on a bench not far from where I stood, and finished reading the article. Supposedly, the guy he'd been with that night, a pianist named Joseph Stanfield, had only lasted with the orchestra a few weeks before he was dumped. When Rodrigo had tried to oust him, though, he'd hired an attorney and sued the orchestra for sexual harassment. I continued reading, unsure if I should be pissed at, or proud of, this man I'd only met that one horrible time.

Repeated requests for comment by Mr. Stanfield, who remains under a gag order, were denied. Mr. Stanfield's attorney also declined to comment on his client's behalf at this time, citing the pending litigation.

I read a bit more about other musicians Rodrigo had allegedly taken advantage of over the past several years. I had no doubt it was all true. "Wow," I said as I stared down the street. "It wasn't just me."

"It seldom is," a woman I'd never seen before said as she sat down next to me. "Olivia Starling. Mr. Ludwig, I presume?"

I nodded, but didn't say anything.

"I'm with the *New York Post*. I wondered if you'd be willing to comment on that magazine article about Rodrigo Everett that you've been reading."

"Um, no," I said, and got up to walk away. Since Rodrigo had just left, I assumed this was another effort on his part to pressure me into helping clear his name.

"You know," the woman said behind me, "I can help." I didn't even look over my shoulder at her as I began jogging toward the school. "If he did this to you, he'll do it to others!" she yelled, just before I was out of earshot.

By the time I got there, I was in no condition to teach. When Principal Jenkins caught sight of me in the main office, she said, "Mr. Ludwig... Jonas, you don't look well. Can I get you something to drink?"

"No, um, can you let Ms. Phillips know I can't make it today? Something's come up and I need to go."

I opened the Uber app on my phone, and it showed no cars available. That meant Sally, still Monongahela's only Uber driver, was either busy or not taking calls today. Not knowing what else to do, and not wanting to run into the reporter or Rodrigo again, I did what I should've done already. I called Orli.

"Hancock's Garage," he answered on the first ring, which made me wonder why he was in his office rather than working on cars.

I swallowed around the lump in my throat. "Um, Orli..." I croaked out.

"Jonas, baby, are you okay?" he asked.

"No," I whispered into the phone and couldn't hold back my tears. Principal Jenkins quickly put an arm around my shoulders, and pulled me into her office. "You can sit in here as long as you need," she said, and gave me some space, but didn't go too far.

"What's wrong? Where are you?" Orli asked, sounding increasingly worried. "Was that Principal Jenkins's voice?"

I wiped the tears and answered yes. "Orli, I need a ride home from the school. I-I didn't drive 'cause I…"

"Shh, I'll be right there, okay?"

"Thanks," I said, and hung up.

A few moments later, Principal Jenkins came back into her office, and sat beside me. "Honey, are you okay?" she asked.

"No, my ex is causing a stink. I'm stuck in it again. Damn, I can't get away from the fucker," I said, and more tears slipped out.

"Oh, don't I know just how you're feeling," she said. "A bad relationship in college turned ugly and I had to get a restraining order, but even that didn't stop him. Only thing that did was a few nights in jail."

I shook my head. "I doubt I can get a restraining order against him, just because he comes here picking fights, he's too smart. Oh," I said and looked around, "God, I'm so sorry, making such a scene in school. I'm going to go outside and wait for Orli."

"You are gonna do no such thing. You're going to wait right here with me, then when Orli picks you up, you'll go have a big glass of wine with him, and drown that miserable jackass ex out of your mind."

I actually chuckled then. "Thank you. God, I feel like such an idiot, though. I'm really sorry."

"No need. You're among friends here, so just relax."

I nodded, feeling moderately better. Orli arrived a few minutes later, and I finally had myself under control enough that I could leave the office without making more of a scene. Orli didn't press me, but when we got back to the garage, I handed him the magazine and thanked him for coming to get me. "I'm going to head up to the apartment and call my attorney. I'll fill you in on the details when I come back down."

I left him sitting in his truck, and felt guilty for not having it in me to explain further just yet.

When I got through to the attorney, he said he'd look into the article and contact the *New York Post* to get to the bottom of why its reporter had shown up right after Rodrigo. Even though I hadn't been one of the unnamed sources in the article, the whole thing left me feeling like I'd been fucked over once again. Hell, I'd been willing to just let it go, instead of suing the orchestra for sexual harassment myself.

However, reading about Rodrigo using his position to screw with men's hearts and careers, that it was a pattern, rather than a one-off with me, sparked something inside me. It was time to fight fire with fire. Yes, it was likely to destroy my chances of ever working in a professional orchestra again, but *c'est la vie*. I was tired of playing Rodrigo's victim.

44

Orlando

I WENT UP TO check on Jonas about an hour after picking him up, and found him passed out on his sofa. Even now, his face registered the frustration of his day. I wish I knew how to help, but the article I read, well, it just seemed to highlight his asshole ex's many faults. I didn't think it cast Jonas in a bad light at all.

I went back downstairs to work and found Ray eyeing me. "Did you find out what happened?" he asked.

I shook my head. "No, he's asleep, but from the way he sounded when he called, it had to be pretty bad."

"Well, you'll be there for him, and we will too if he needs us," Ray said.

I went over and put my hand on his broad shoulder and squeezed. "You really are the best friend a guy could have," I said.

"Truth," Ray said with a smile, and turned back to work on the Chevy Impala.

I knew Jonas hadn't been sleeping well, and he must've made up for it, because I didn't see him the rest of the day. When I went upstairs after closing up that evening, for what normally would've been my lesson, I heard Jonas on the phone. I was just about to leave when he saw me, and motioned for me to come in.

"Yes," he said into the phone, while I sat down next to him on the sofa. "So, you think I should speak with her?"

I couldn't tell who he was talking about, but he didn't seem to mind my eavesdropping either.

"Okay, thanks. I'll think about it and let you know."

When he'd hung up, he leaned into me. "My life is a fucked-up mess."

I lifted his chin so I could make eye contact and asked what was going on.

He recounted in detail how Rodrigo had shown up just to push the magazine on him, threatening him with his attorneys and generally making a scene, then he told me how a big-city reporter appeared immediately after Rodrigo had left, which raised more questions.

"Yeah," I agreed. "The timing is more than a little suspicious."

"Well, my attorney contacted the *Post*, and they said it was just a coincidence. She'd come to ask me about the article, and found Rodrigo stalking the streets waiting to cross paths with me. He must've been keeping an eye on the apartment to time it that well, plus I decided to walk instead of drive today. He was probably too afraid of you to come anywhere near here."

"Afraid of me? Well, I'm not sure why, but I can live with that. That asshole needs to stay away from both of us."

Jonas kissed me, and pulled out of my embrace to sit upright on the sofa. "I'm so tired of Rodrigo. I'm tired of watching my back. I'm tired of him controlling me. I-I think I'm going to do the interview, tell them everything Rodrigo has done, not just relating to our relationship, but the contest contract and the legal case as well."

"Can you do that without getting into more trouble?" I asked.

Jonas nodded. "I'm not under a gag order. Besides, I lost, remember? There was no settlement where I'd be locked down with a non-disclosure agreement."

"Then do it," I said, and kissed him. "The son of a bitch doesn't deserve your protection. Tell the world what he and the jackasses he works for did to you."

Jonas nodded. "Yeah, that's what I'm going to do." He leaned against me and sighed. "I gave up my career over this. I doubt I'll ever get hired to play in any of the large organizations again. More than a few musicians have been blackballed over things like this."

"I'm sure that's true, and it's beyond wrong. Sounds to me like it's about time one of those old toxic organizations is held accountable."

"It helps to hear you say that. Anyway, I'm going to take a trip to New York next week. The reporter said she'd interview me with my attorney present, so he can keep me from saying something that might get me sued in the future."

"Then, I'll come with you," I said, not even having to think about it.

"What about work?"

"It can be put off. What Ray can't handle himself, we can reschedule for the following week. There's no way in hell I'm letting you face that by yourself, Jonas. You need support, and I'm going to be the one who gives it to you. If you want me to, that is."

Jonas kissed me, and when he pulled back, he had a small smile on his face. "I really do want you to, need you to, even."

"Aah, baby, same here," I replied. "Same here."

45

Jonas

"**W**HAT MADE YOU AGREE to the interview?" the reporter asked.

I looked at my attorney, and he nodded, telling me to go ahead. "When I read the article in *The Grell*, it struck me how if we don't stand up to Rodrigo, he'll continue using his position to professionally harm other men... maybe even do worse than he's already done to me. Anyone who abuses their power and influence should be held accountable, and that's why I'm here."

"Are you the one who leaked the information about your pre-concert incident with Rodrigo to *The Grell?*" she asked, and I shook my head.

"No, I've not told many people what happened that night, and to be honest, this is the first time I've spoken to a reporter."

"Can you confirm what *The Grell* reported about the incident?" she asked, and I nodded.

"Yes, it was largely accurate. The source must've witnessed it."

"Do you think that witness was the man Rodrigo kissed in front of you?" she asked, and my attorney gave me a purposeful look. I needed to be careful how I answered.

"I can't say, because all I really remember from that night was Rodrigo and his new, um, boyfriend."

"Joseph Stanfield?" she asked.

"Yes, Joseph was new to the orchestra. He'd been hired to replace the first chair position that'd just retired."

I didn't mention it, because my attorney had advised me to just speak to the facts, or my own feelings about what had happened, and warned against giving my personal opinions about Rodrigo. I'd admit, I was finding that difficult. As I looked back on all the time I'd known him, his pattern of pursuing the most talented musicians became obvious, and so did his trying to destroy their careers when the relationships inevitably ended. I couldn't exactly say that to the reporter, lest my attorney have a coronary, but I knew it was the ugly truth.

"And you didn't notice anyone else in the room?" she asked.

I shook my head. "No, but as I said, I was so taken aback by Rodrigo's actions, I apparently didn't notice, or don't remember if someone else had been there."

The reporter came back around to asking why I thought Rodrigo posed a risk to other men. My attorney gave me a very pointed look, reminding me of the statement we'd practiced to answer any questions concerning Rodrigo's behavior.

"One can't know for sure, but it does concern me that he targeted me as well as Mr. Stanfield as romantic partners, then made a concerted effort to destroy our careers. I'm not saying this is his trend, but it's something the orchestra should investigate, and if warranted, directly address before he damages anyone else's career."

That seemed to satisfy her, and she switched to the court case.

"Can you tell us why the orchestra filed a lawsuit against you?"

I could tell she was hoping to catch me off guard, and I almost returned her vicious smile. My attorney had prepared me too well to be surprised by anything in this interview.

"I can, yes," I responded without missing a beat, shocking her, exactly like my attorney and I had practiced. I simply stated the facts as they would appear in the public record, then I told her the outcome. "Because Rodrigo was in breach of contract by involving himself in my contest when he'd agreed not to, the orchestra didn't get everything it wanted—like my father's piano. However, I will have to repay the cost of piano repairs as well as any income I received over those past months."

She asked for the amount, and when I told her, she asked if that was going to cause me financial difficulties.

"Yes, of course. My father's expenses were significant. After he passed away without an insurance policy, I was forced to sell most of his belongings. I barely had enough money to cover my living expenses, then, of course, I lost my job with the orchestra."

"So, is it fair to say that because of Rodrigo's actions, you are now having financial difficulties?"

She'd said Rodrigo rather than the orchestra, and while he was mostly fair game, I had to be mindful of not saying too much. I'd been advised to avoid any mention of him, but I'd been skirting that line. "Yes, I doubt I would've messed up the night of the concert if he hadn't set me up to do so. In my entire musical career, I had never performed so badly, and it was entirely out of character for me. Had I not messed up, I wouldn't have been put in the situation that I was. So, yes, I can confidently say, I would never have been in this financial situation had it not been for Rodrigo Everett."

The genuine smile on the reporter's face told me that was what she'd wanted to hear, and my attorney remained calm, so I figured my calling out Rodrigo hadn't crossed any boundaries.

She asked a few personal questions, then about my dad, growing up under one of the greats, and my success as a pianist prior to my work in the orchestra.

She ended by asking me why I didn't sue for sexual harassment. I confessed it was because I feared for my career, then acknowledged my career had probably been destroyed anyway. She finished jotting down some notes, then thanked me and my attorney before leaving his office.

"So, was that okay?" I asked my attorney. He nodded and assured me I had done well.

Orli sat waiting in the attorney's lobby, and stood up as soon as he saw me. "Thanks for being here," I said, walking across the lobby, and straight into his arms.

"Of course. Everything go okay?"

"I think so. As well as it could. I want to go home, though. I just need a long weekend at my apartment or your cottage to get myself back together," I admitted.

"No problem," he said, and steered me outside. We rode the subway to the airport, and once we got through security, I snuggled into Orli's side, and thanked him for springing for airline tickets. "I don't think I have a full day's ride on the train in me this time," I said.

Orli had surprised me by purchasing the tickets for us, which I'd chastised him for at the time, saying it was too much money, but now I was so happy he'd done it. I slept for most of the flight to Martinsburg.

It had been a draining several days leading up to this, but it was a relief to finally have my say. While it would likely come with repercussions, I hadn't realized just how beaten down I was by what Rodrigo had done to me, personally and professionally, until I'd finished that interview.

I'd been playing the victim game too damn long, and I was mentally and emotionally exhausted. I'd let the bastard get inside my head, and had messed up a concert as a result, but that didn't mean I had to own all of it. Telling my side of it to the reporter was liberating.

Orli left me at the apartment after I said I needed time alone, and I crawled into bed and just stayed there thinking about my life. The two articles would probably end what little hope I had of ever having a professional career performing. Six months ago, that would've destroyed me, but now I felt like teaching gave me an unexpected path forward, not teaching the entitled brats I'd given private lessons to before, but the kids here in Monongahela. I loved piano and I wanted to teach kids to master that art, kids who actually wanted to learn. That inspired me.

Did that mean I needed a teaching degree? Probably. It was too bad Ms. Phillips wasn't going to stick around a while longer, and it seemed they already had her replacement in mind. I would have to talk to her about that later. I was sure she'd have advice for me.

I rolled over and closed my eyes, and ended up sleeping a full twelve hours before waking up feeling refreshed. The interview and sleep seemed to be exactly what I needed. I stumbled to the kitchen, fixed myself a coffee, and texted Orli asking if we could go back to the waterfall we'd visited before. I felt liberated and free, and right now, I wanted to put my past behind me, and just enjoy the beauty of West Virginia, and this time, I'd bring my swimsuit.

46

Orlando

S UMMER ROLLED GENTLY INTO fall, and my relationship with Jonas continued to grow and blossom. The interview he'd given had changed him, made him more confident.

Even when the *Post* published the article, and people trolled him or the orchestra, he was able to completely shrug it off.

While in bed one night, shortly after the article came out, I asked why he was so calm, and he gave me a smile. "It's like that all exists in the past, like it was a different life than the one I have now."

He kissed me then and climbed on top of me. "I'm happier right now than I've been since, well, since I was a little boy, so it doesn't matter what the trolls say. It doesn't matter what Rodrigo says, or what the orchestra folks say. The only thing that matters is that I've got you." He kissed my forehead. "I've got Monongahela."

He kissed my lips. "And I've got this," he said, grinding himself into me, causing me to laugh and flip him onto his back.

I lay on top of him, and nuzzled into his neck before kissing my way up to his mouth. "You know I'm in love with you, right?" I asked, concerned that I'd picked the wrong time to confess what I'd been feeling for months. I'd been struggling to keep it to myself for so long, though, that seeing him so happy just made it impossible to keep my mouth shut any longer.

Luckily, he smiled, leaned up and kissed me deeply, before saying, "I love you too, so much, it doesn't even feel real."

Happiness swirled through me, and I couldn't hold back a relieved sigh. Had we been standing, I'd have picked him up and spun him around the room. Instead, I ground into him, kissing him long and hard before moving down his body to show him just how happy he made me.

47

Jonas

W E WERE GETTING READY for Christmas break at school. All the kids were going nuts, but in the funniest ways. The teachers were about to pull their hair out trying to get all the pre-holiday stuff done. If I'd thought about being a teacher before, seeing them all like this convinced me even further that it wasn't the career I wanted. I wanted to support them, not be them.

The kids were all talking about how they wanted to do a recital or play next year for the holidays, and for the first time since I'd arrived, I was excited at the possibility of doing more. "I think that's a great idea. We can combine the two, music and drama, perhaps in a musical."

Just a few months ago, I'd have been concerned I wouldn't be here long enough to plan that far ahead, but now, I had already committed to the school. Once the fundraised money was gone, I had no idea how I'd be able to afford to stay, but who cared. I was living in the moment and letting the adage, *where there's a will, there's a way* fill me with hope.

Ray and Orli were planning to take over the new garage, and fully move all of their operations there sometime in the next few months, which concerned me a bit about where I was going to live, but I pushed even those worries aside. Maybe whoever bought the building would let me stay in the apartment at least a few months, while I found more permanent accommodations.

Maybe, if enough time passed, it would be with Orli. I was so in love with him. God, I had never experienced anything like this. It was like everywhere I looked, I saw things that made me think of him, reminding me of things he'd said, or ways he'd touched me. My heart felt so full, all because of him.

Even Angela teased me the last time I'd gone to get my hair cut, after I'd mentioned him to her too many times. "Man, you've got it bad."

I laughed. "Yeah, well, he's worth having it bad over."

The other women in the salon chuckled, and turned the conversation to how they'd felt when they first fell in love. I'd begun meeting her at her salon, instead of getting my hair cut at her house, which meant I'd become acquainted with many of her other regulars. Oh, and I was required to come in frequently, because, as she didn't hesitate to remind me, "It looks bad on me to have a friend looking shaggy."

I'd become so integrated into Monongahela life that hanging out at the salon, talking about my man, and hearing the latest town gossip, had become natural. Truly feeling like a member of the community still bewildered me when I thought about it.

"Oh, are you coming for the Christmas Eve celebration at the church?" I asked Angela. "I'd love to have Ella join the youth choir."

"Yeah, I talked Ray into it. By the way, you should know that's a big thing. Ray hates church, so, you know, if he didn't love you, he wouldn't even consider it."

I chuckled. "Well, I'm not asking for him to get baptized, just make it so Ella can play the bells."

Angela hugged me before she sent me on my way. I couldn't say I'd become a major church person, but I liked my Sunday job. It paid well, but the community also seemed to rally around me there. I'd also started giving lessons after Sunday church services to several kids who didn't live in Monongahela, and was also helping with the youth choir.

Pastor James had finally relented in letting his son Davey assist me, after I'd said he was more than ready to do it. So, Davey was handling the bell choir, but because he was still a kid himself, I tried to step in to help when I could. Mostly, working together brought him, his family, and me closer.

At least once a month or so, Orli and I would get invited over to Pastor James's house, or we'd have them over to Orli's for a meal. They were just one of the many families here in Monongahela who'd welcomed me into their homes and their lives.

The forecast was calling for snow, so I decided to drive to the school instead of walking. Not that I was prepared to drive in snow, but I much preferred walking, because it did give me a little exercise during the day. I parked the car and walked inside to sign in, when I spotted Mrs. Rita Covington speaking with the office secretary.

"Oh, shit," I muttered to myself, just as Ms. Phillips was walking by from getting her mail.

"What's going on?" she asked.

"See that woman?" I asked, knowing she hadn't spotted me yet. "She's one of Rodrigo's main supporters. This can't be good."

"You don't have to see her. I can go tell her so, if you'd like me to."

I chuckled. Ms. Phillips would do just that if I let her. "No, I need to see what she wants, if for no other reason than to get her to leave. My god, you'd think since we are so far from New York, these people would leave me alone."

"Hold on," she said, and pulled me toward Principal Jenkins's office. "Let's do this in here, so as not to make a scene, then she and I can be your witnesses."

"You have class," I said, and she shook her head.

"No, the kindergarteners are spending extra time in the gym with Mrs. Stewart today, so I'm all yours," she said, smiling.

Principal Jenkins immediately agreed, probably to avoid another meltdown that tended to happen when the orchestra people showed up. I waited while she went out and brought Mrs. Covington in.

"I'm sorry to drop in unexpectedly," Mrs. Covington said as she took a seat. She looked warily at Ms. Phillips, whose determined look conveyed she wasn't about to leave. She took a deep breath and let it out slowly, before turning to me.

"Jonas, I'm not someone who is used to apologizing. In fact, my husband would tell you it's my most ardent flaw. However, I don't think I can live with myself without personally apologizing to you." She shook her head, and taking a Kleenex out of her purse, wiped at her nose. "Rodrigo had us all fooled. I know we should've seen the red flags when he kept pushing us to fire you, then again when he did the same with poor Joseph."

I sat stunned by what I was hearing. Not in a million years did I think Mrs. Rita Covington would ever admit to being in the wrong, let alone apologize to me.

"I'm not sure what to say. I guess, in some way, you're a victim here too, but you and the orchestra board enabled Rodrigo to do what he did. There's no sugarcoating that it's destroyed my career, and I'm sure Joseph Stanfield is never going to fully recover either." Mrs.

Covington continued dabbing at her eyes and nose as I sat for a few moments to collect my thoughts, before I found the words I wanted to say. "Mrs. Covington, organizations like the orchestra should be building up the careers of their musicians, not intentionally tearing them down. Unfortunately, there will always be men like Rodrigo who destroy others to feel better about themselves. I guess it's best that you finally figured that out." She nodded and I could see her true feelings in her expression. "Thank you for coming to apologize. It does make a difference. Shocking, but it does help."

She looked over at me and sighed again. "There's no fool like an old fool," she said. "I wanted you to know I've removed myself from the board, and I've withdrawn my financial support as well, at least until they can replace Rodrigo and implement policies that prevent this kind of harassment from happening again. I'd also like to offer an olive branch to you. If you're still interested, I'd like to fund you and Mr. Hancock's trip to compete in Salzburg, as was the original plan." She chuckled a bit before she admitted she would've been the one paying for it anyway.

Principal Jenkins and Ms. Phillips both made noises of approval at that, and I couldn't help but chuckle. "I'll have to speak with him, and we'll let you know. How would you like me to contact you?" I asked."

She handed me her card, and apologized again before she left. "Wow," I said as I sat back in my chair. I looked over at Principal Jenkins, and felt the need to apologize again myself. "I'm so sorry the school keeps getting dragged into my personal drama."

"Oh, honey, don't be. This is the most excitement I've had in years."

That made me bark out a laugh. "Okay, well, I've got a student in five minutes."

"Wait, are you going to go to Austria?" Ms. Phillips asked.

I shrugged. "That depends entirely on whether Orli wants to or not. Me personally? I no longer care one way or the other."

As I walked alone down the hallway, I thought more about the competition that was only about two months away. It'd be fun to go to Austria, but I really would be fine not going. Yes, it would likely help my career to enter a student, particularly if that student might place well, but it no longer seemed the be-all and end-all achievement it used to be.

But it sure as hell could be a lot of fun, I thought as I sat down with Kevin to go over a piece he was planning to play as a Christmas present for his family.

"Dropped the lawsuit? Like, I don't owe them money any longer?" I asked, stunned.

"Exactly like that," my attorney said.

"Okay, so... oh," I said, remembering Mrs. Covington's visit the week before. "Is this to do with Mrs. Covington pulling her funding from the orchestra?"

The attorney chuckled, which I took as a good sign. "Well, not completely, though I'm sure that's part of it. I think it's more because the orchestra wants to merge with the Nissequogue Philharmonic, and that isn't likely to occur with the self-inflicted black eye of the lawsuit hanging over their heads."

"Well, I support that. This is the best Christmas present ever!" I said, and we shared a laugh.

"I'll forward you all the paperwork when they send it to me. I'm expecting that won't happen until after the holidays, but yeah, it's over. You're free."

Emotions caught in my throat at his words. *Free*. Last I heard, Rodrigo was fighting his termination, and his job prospects were dismal. Cleary, bad press and word-of-mouth about his conniving against me, Joseph Stanfield, and likely others had spread throughout New York and beyond, but that wasn't even the best part. The best part was I was finally free of him, the orchestra, and a financial burden that would've hamstrung me for years.

"Thank you," I managed to squeak out.

That night, I ordered take-out from the Monongahela Café, because I still cooked like shit, and I wanted tonight to be special, a celebration. The dropped lawsuit not only wiped away my debt, but it also eliminated the only reason I could foresee that would force me to leave Monongahela.

Orli remained fully committed to our practice sessions, and all the more so upon agreeing to compete in Salzburg, after I'd told him about Mrs. Covington's offer. So, when Orli came upstairs for his lesson right on cue that evening, I was prepared. I'd decorated the table with candles, and set the food out on two china plates I'd found in Elmer Frank's antique store on my walk back from the restaurant.

"What's all this?" Orli asked.

"It's a celebration," I said, and rushed into his arms, ignoring his greasy clothes.

"And what're we celebrating?" he asked as he leaned down to kiss me.

"Mmm, that right there's enough," I said as he pulled back. "But, go get cleaned up, then I'll tell you my great news!"

His eyes lit up, and he gave me a quick peck on the lips before disappearing into the bathroom. I glanced down at the huge black stain on my white t-shirt, and couldn't help but laugh. I would just have to add this to the growing pile of what I now thought of as my *cuddle clothes* for when Orli came home from work. They doubled as my work clothes on the mornings I worked in the office too.

I quickly slipped a clean shirt on, and lit the candles, and when I heard the shower shut off, began warming up the food.

He stepped up behind me, still slightly damp from his shower, and wrapped his arms around me. I couldn't help but moan and lean into him, like I usually did when my man held me. "God, I really am over the top in love with you."

"That goes for both of us then," he said, and looked over my shoulder at what we'd be having for dinner. "Oh, you got the roast beef. I love the café's roast beef."

I chuckled. "So you've said, which is why I got it. Now, sit down, and I'll serve us."

Once I plated our food and sat down at the small table, I took Orli's hand, and said, "The orchestra is forgiving my debt to them. I'm free."

Orli's eyes went wide, and he squeezed my hand. "Really? You don't have to pay them back?"

I shook my head. "Nope, my attorney called this afternoon with the good news. No more debt. You know what that means, right?"

"It means you can finally flip the fuckers off and go on with your life," he said adamantly.

I laughed. "Yeah, it means that, but it also means I'm okay financially. I still need a permanent job, but I can make a living here in Monongahela. It means I won't need to leave."

Orli jumped up and rounded the table, then pulled me up as well. "Oh my god, really? You've decided to stay?"

I chuckled into his neck, and let him kiss me, then hold me as we both celebrated the moment. "I'd already decided I wanted to, just wasn't sure how to make it happen with that debt hanging over my head. Now, it's not, so there's no reason not to stay."

"I'll give you a reason to stay," he said, and gave me just enough time to blow out the candles before he pulled me back to the bedroom.

48

Orlando

"YOU'RE STARING AT THE buildings like a tourist," Tatiana said as we walked through the old medieval parts of Salzburg.

"Um, I am a tourist. Besides, I might just be frozen... it's so freaking cold here!"

Tatiana laughed, like I'd told the funniest joke ever.

Jonas's friend was tall and lean, with a short crop of blondish hair. Her accent was unique, sounding like something between Russian and German, not that I was an expert on accents or anything.

"So, how did Jonas talk you into entering this big competition?" she asked.

I smiled at the fiery woman in front of me, and admitted, "It wasn't really him. If anything, he tried to talk me out of it, but I figured, why not? I get to spend time with my handsome boyfriend in a country I've never been to, and it's all paid for by the evil witch that helped bring us together."

Jonas playfully hit my arm, but laughed. "Behave," he said conspiratorially. "Mrs. Covington could be lurking around any corner."

I acted like I was afraid for a minute, then laughed. "I'm not afraid of the big bad wolf."

"Well, I still am. She's formidable. Anyway, Tatiana, are any of your students competing?" Jonas asked, mostly to change the topic. For real, though, our benefactor could be lurking, and Jonas didn't want to create any new issues where she was concerned.

"I have three students and one former student competing," Tatiana responded. She looked at me then, and asked, "So what are you performing?"

"That..." Jonas began.

I interrupted him. "Is a big ol' not your business," I said, causing her to laugh. I was secretly relieved by how well the two of us were getting along, which put Jonas further at ease as well.

"Oh, sweetheart, don't be afraid of my students. They are just the best in Europe. I'm sure you'll beat them hands down."

"Indeed," Jonas said, and winked at me, not taking her bait.

We spent the entire morning together wandering through the streets of the old town. Tatiana and Jonas took turns pointing out the sights, like the bell tower on the old city hall, and a huge golden ball in a city square called Kapitelplatz.

When Tatiana left us, we toured the Hohensalzburg Fortress, and ended our day at the museum marking Mozart's birthplace.

I'd traveled a bit with my great-granny and grandparents to places all over the US and Canada, but I'd never experienced anything like Salzburg. The buildings were so old, it seemed inconceivable they still stood. History was such an integral part of this city, and Jonas appeared to relish exploring it as much as I did.

We made the most of our day before going back to practice in the room assigned to us. I'd agreed to play a traditional piece by Beethoven, because, as Jonas had put it, "The judges won't tolerate anything written in this century or the last."

I honestly didn't care what I played. I loved practicing with Jonas, and I'd come a long, long way under his tutelage in the past year. I might not love the classical piece he'd chosen for me, but I did feel confident I could play it well, and put the right amount of emotion into it, even if it didn't fully speak to my heart.

As the hours ticked by and the competition drew closer, I could tell Jonas was getting more nervous. To be honest, I really wasn't nervous at all, at least not for myself. If anything, I was nervous for Jonas, and for him, I'd do my very, very best.

The night before my first performance, he kept asking if I was okay. I finally told him my nerves weren't the issue, then flipped him face-first onto the bed, and gave my very-tense boyfriend a massage. "Don't worry," I whispered as I straddled him ,while massaging his neck and shoulders. "You've taught me well. I'll be fine."

"I hope so," he said, his voice muffled in the pillow. I kept working my fingers into his muscles, until I felt his body relax beneath me.

I sat back, so he could roll over, and I asked, "What does this competition mean to you? Are you afraid I'll embarrass you?"

"No, God, no. I think it's just my own nerves getting the best of me. I mean, I competed here too, you know. My father was normally a mountain of soft love and support, but he'd been fully freaked out, which told me he cared how well I did. I placed, even the first time, but I was too nervous to even enjoy it. Being here brought all of that back up, and I guess, in a way, I'm still afraid of disappointing him."

I lay down beside Jonas, and pulled him flush against me, so we were spooning. "I don't want to disappoint you, but you've forced me to play this song like what, a million times? At this point, sometimes I dream I'm playing it. Unless something bizarre happens, I think I'll be okay, and I'm determined to enjoy myself regardless."

He turned in my hold to look at me. "God, Orli, I'm so sorry. I'm supposed to be supporting you, and I'm making you nervous. There's no pressure, trust me. I'm already so proud of you, and it'll be great, no matter what happens."

We snuggled until Jonas fell asleep, but I remained wide awake with my thoughts. He'd said he didn't want to disappoint his dad, which I didn't doubt was true, but I bet trying to impress the people who'd shunned him was also fraying his nerves.

This was Jonas's way back, a means to regain the reputation and career he'd worked his whole life to achieve, and I played a key role in that.

I fell asleep a little while later, despite feeling a new twinge of nervousness. The pressure really was on me. I needed to do well, for Jonas's sake.

The crowd in the small performance room was enough to make anyone nervous. Five judges sat in front of me, while a few rows of people sat behind them, Jonas and Tatiana among them. I wiggled my fingers to prepare for the performance, forcing myself not to think about the judges, Jonas's needs, or anything other than the music. I played with all my heart, letting the boring classical piece flow through me.

Normally, I'd have inserted elements of my own style, just to add some personality and keep the piece from sounding too dry, but not today. Today was for Jonas, so I stuck to the script, playing it exactly how he had instructed me.

When I finished, there was a smattering of applause from the crowd as I got up, and joined Jonas and Tatiana in the audience.

We listened to the rest of the competitors in my age group perform, then Jonas and I went to dinner. "We'll get the results any minute," he said as he kept looking at his phone. He'd praised me, saying I'd done well... not *great*, but well.

Just as we paid for our meal and were about to leave, Jonas got a text, and grabbed my hand. "You made it to the next level. I knew you would, you did well, very well."

It gave me pleasure to see Jonas's face, his expression a mixture of joy and relief. He seemed so pleased I hadn't flunked out on the first round. Well, I guess I was too. I honestly hadn't expected to get through to the next level, because so many entrants in my age group proved to be incredibly skilled performers.

Jonas had explained that the competition consisted of three elimination rounds, the first one having been today. The day's results narrowed the field from more than three hundred entrants to just one hundred competitors.

The second round, taking place tomorrow, would further narrow the field to just ten competitors per age group, who would go on to compete in the final round, in hopes of placing in the top three. I was under no illusion that I would even make it into the top ten. That was an achievement reserved for people like Jonas, dedicated pianists who practiced for hours each day. Not honky-tonk weekend warriors like me, who taught schoolkids in their spare time.

I didn't share my thoughts with Jonas, though. I didn't want to disappoint him, but he had to have known. I would play my best, do my best, but without any expectation I'd place high, let alone win.

After dinner, we joined Tatiana and her students for drinks. The men she taught, all college-age and competing in my age group, mostly spoke in German, but I didn't need to know the language to recognize their belittling glares, when they noticed my oil-stained hands.

I did my best to ignore them, reminding myself I wasn't and never would be a part of this world. I was here for Jonas, so they could see how Jonas had transformed some grease-stained honky-tonker into a polished concert pianist. I didn't really think Jonas thought that, not even a little, but hadn't that been the gist of our original agreement for his contest? These guys were certainly treating me like I was some kind of circus act.

"You can't play the same old way and win," one of the men said in English. "It's like sticking any idiot on the bench, and expecting him to win playing like a teenager."

His broken English was hard to understand, but I'd gotten his drift. I wasn't in the same category as they were. I was the idiot. Of course, my interpreting it that way was the whole reason the jackass said it in English, since most of their conversation had been in German.

Apparently, I wasn't the only one to pick up on their trash-talking. "It seems the idiots are bountiful this year," Jonas said, while staring down the three men. I stifled a chuckle, until I looked up at Tatiana, who burst out laughing as soon as she made eye contact with me.

"You are a great sport, Orlando, unlike Jonas here. I love seeing him wanting to protect you, though. But, Jonas, my dear, I think your sexy Orlando is strong enough that you don't need to protect him."

I put my arm around Jonas, and leaned over to kiss his temple. "I like my brave protector, Tatiana, don't be ruining my fun."

She laughed again, and Jonas elbowed me. "Ass," he said, but his smile eliminated any heat from the word.

Mostly, Tatiana, Jonas and I ignored her students after that and had our own conversation, while they prattled on in German. It made for a much more enjoyable evening.

All insults aside, though, what the jackass who'd been trying to intimidate me had said actually made sense.

Jonas had pushed me to play the piece, using only the dynamics as they were written in the music. "Don't veer off of the basics," he'd told me.

I didn't question him, because, to be honest, he knew much more than I did, and I trusted his advice. However, the musicians who'd stood out the most had demonstrated much more heart than I had. I had no intention of turning Beethoven's *Six Bagatelles* into a honky-tonk song, but after hearing the other performances and then that jerk's sneer tossed at me, I decided I needed to add just a wee bit of myself to the music. Would it prevent me from getting into the top ten? Probably, but it was extremely unlikely I would make it that far anyway. *Just don't embarrass Jonas*, that was my only requirement.

For round two the next day, I was placed in a room with ten other contestants. Only one of us would go on to perform in the final round, having made the top ten in our age group. Listening to the other performers, only solidified my decision to put my own spin on the piece. It was a gamble, but playing entirely by the rules had never been my style. "You gotta be yourself," my great-granny used to say.

I was the next-to-last performer to play. I could tell the crowd was tired, as were the judges, and that just spurred me on even more. I let the piece start slowly, playing it precisely as Jonas had taught me, but as I hit the fast movement, I added my own twist that came from my great-granny's teaching.

I imagined myself performing in front of the old honky-tonk bar crowd, and for the first time ever, had fun playing it. When I finished, I stood and bowed as all the contestants had, then walked off the stage. I glanced into the audience and saw Tatiana's face first. She was smiling, almost like she was biting back laughter, while everyone near her appeared to be talking in hushed whispers.

Fuck, I thought as I made my way to Jonas. Tatiana's smile was very likely an indicator that I'd really fucked up. Jonas looked over at me when I sat down next to him, his face registering shock. I hadn't thought I'd gone that far off track, though, admittedly, I had lost myself in the music. He was about to say something, when the next and final contestant began his piece.

I felt marginally better when Jonas took my hand. At least he didn't hate me for botching the whole thing. *God, I'm an idiot*, I kept thinking over and over.

When the contestant finished, the judges filed out of the room first, like they had the day before, and the rest of us followed. I was ready for the tongue lashing that I expected was coming my way, when Tatiana came over and pulled me into a hug. "You did fabulous. I can't believe my tight-arse friend let you play that way. Mr. Rules isn't one to let loose. Oh, it was fabulous, just fabulous," she said, giving me another squeeze before spotting one of her students. "Oops, gotta go promote my own troops." Then, she pecked my cheek, and headed across the room to where her student sat fuming.

"I'm sorry," I said, when Jonas grabbed me, and pulled me into a hug.

"God, no. Sorry? For being amazing? No, I-I've not got words, you made that piece sing."

"Really, you aren't mad?"

He looked at me like I was crazy, and cupped my face, as he said, "I can't be mad at you for playing like that." Then, he pulled me down and kissed me deeply, right there in front of everyone. "Now, let's go to the hotel and order room service. I want to show you how amazing you were."

I laughed as he all but pulled me out of there, and across the road to the hotel.

For me, that was the perfect ending to the madness, and secretly I promised myself I'd never enter another competition, no matter how much Jonas might want me to, but at least I'd put myself out there, playing music I didn't really relate to, but could still make my own. I'd had fun, and was proud of myself for trying, and that was all that mattered.

49

Jonas

ATIANA WAS RIGHT. I played by the rules and seldom put myself out there, at least not without hours and hours of practice. *Be unique, but in a socially acceptable way*, had always been my philosophy, and it'd served me well as a performer, as well as a competitor.

But, the moment Orli hit the second movement in his performance, I knew I'd been wrong by holding him back. I'd never heard that movement of *Six Bagatelles* played that way, but it fit the piece so well. I think if Beethoven had been alive, he'd have approved of the subtle stylistic shifts.

The moment Orli and I entered the hotel lobby, we were stopped by person after person singing his praises, and telling us how much they enjoyed his performance. So much for the quick roll between the sheets I had planned before the lunchtime break ended and we had to be back for announcements.

We ended up grabbing a quick sandwich, and a glass of wine for me and a beer for him in the hotel's restaurant, before we headed back over.

To add to the fanfare of making the top ten, and since the second round had far fewer competitors, the results were being announced as part of an in-person ceremony, rather than through online postings and text messaging. In my experience, the announcements usually lasted about an hour as they went through each category and age group. Piano often came last, or close to, then we'd go to the party one of my dad's former students always held at his massive home located a short distance from the hotel.

The party was typically a high-brow affair, with a significant number of past competition winners in attendance. My dad had enjoyed a standing invitation, which meant I'd been welcome to attend by default, and Tatiana used to go with us. I hadn't received an invite this year, which was no surprise given the orchestra debacle, but Tatiana had, and invited Orli and me to accompany her.

I rarely saw the party host, since Tatiana and I usually hung out in the giant solarium, and gossiped about all the snotty attendees. I'd have declined even going, had I not wanted to share a part of my old life with Orli. I wanted him to see it, understand it, so he could understand me, not that it was a life I wanted ever again, but at least he'd get a better idea about the type of world I came from.

So, against my better judgment, I'd accepted Tatiana's invitation and hoped the night would be filled with excitement, then Orli and I could slip out early, head back to our hotel room, and make up for everything we didn't have time to do to each other over lunch.

Tatiana had already planned to sit with me for the announcement ceremony, which was our tradition. We found her waiting for me at the entrance, ready to go inside. She hugged Orli and praised him again, before we all meandered down the walkway to our seats.

As always, fellow musicians we'd known for years greeted us. This year, however, several people intentionally ignored me, only saying hi to Tatiana. I was amused when she turned her nose up at more than a few, not even acknowledging them. It struck me how I had become such a pariah to some, but also how lucky I was to have Tatiana as a friend. When I then gazed at my handsome boyfriend, and was met with his loving smile in return, I counted myself double lucky.

The announcements were as boring as I'd expected, like watching paint dry boring. We watched and clapped respectfully as the results were announced for each instrument category, and the top ten competitors in each age group therein were called to the stage. While it was thrilling for those in the top ten, my heart went out to everyone else who didn't make the final cut, and I remained hopeful Orli wouldn't be among them.

"Now for the piano categories. Age group one," the announcer said.

Age group one included the youngest competitors, all elementary age. As they announced the kids' names, I smiled, reliving pleasant memories of the earliest times I'd stood on that stage among the other finalists. They were always so excited at that age, and I knew they were barely containing themselves. They reminded me of my students in Monongahela.

"We should try to get a scholarship to bring some of our students one year," I whispered to Orli, making him smile.

"Good luck with that," he whispered back.

They went through the teens next, before finally getting to Orli's age group. I reached over and grabbed his hand. It floored me how calm he was, which just showed me he took this very differently than I always had. Of course, he didn't have an award-winning, world-renowned father whose reputation he had to live up to, even if my dad had always told me not to compare myself to him.

One by one, the finalists were called to the stage. I recognized all of them, I realized. People who'd been performing almost as long as I had. The ninth person called was a young woman from New Jersey. This was her first year competing in the adult category, and I was so happy for her.

"And our tenth competitor to earn a spot in the final round is..." the announcer said as we all sat on the edge of our seats, "Mr. Orlando Hancock."

Orli's grip tightened in mine, and a look of shock and a bit of terror reflected on his face. "Go," I said, and pushed him to his feet. His face was flushed as he rushed down the aisle and up the stairs to join the other nine competitors on stage. "These are our top ten finalists in the piano soloist category."

Applause rang through the auditorium, and the shock was almost more than I could bear. Tatiana was hitting me on the shoulder, and I barely even noticed. "He did it," I said, and she giggled.

"Yes, he did."

As Orli slipped past the row of people congratulating him to get back to his seat, he stopped in front of one of Tatiana's students, and I heard him whisper loudly, "Thanks for the advice the other night. You were totally right." Then, winking at the jerk, he walked past and pulled me into a hug, before we both sat down as they completed the announcements.

50

Orlando

"**Y**OU'RE IN THE TOP ten," Jonas said, and jumped up and down once we got outside. "You made it into the top ten!"

I laughed. "You sound surprised."

"You have no idea, Orli. I mean, I knew you were good, but you can be the best and *still* not make it into the top ten in Salzburg. It's amazing, you're amazing!"

"Thanks, sweetheart," I said as I kissed him, and hugged him to me.

"How can you be so calm?" he asked, when he pulled back.

"Um, calm on the outside, but definitely not on the inside. I think I'm just dazed. It's not like I expected to make it this far. I sure didn't expect to be competing with the best of the best."

"You got this, seriously, you proved that today. You have that certain *je ne sais quoi*."

I kissed him again, and let him lead me to the hotel. Interestingly enough, no one spoke to us as we walked back. Earlier today, people were coming from every angle to congratulate me. Now that I'd actually made the final round, it was as if no one could believe it.

When I asked Jonas about it, he chuckled. "Let's just say you're less approachable now than you were a few hours ago."

"Huh?" I asked. "It's still the same me."

"Who placed in the top ten in one of the most prestigious piano competitions in the world."

"Okay, now I might be freaking out," I said, feeling a bit queasy all of a sudden as we entered our room.

Jonas closed the door and hugged me, rubbing calming circles on my back. "Honey, you accomplished something magnificent today, but you're right, you're still you. Don't let the fame go to your head."

"Easy for you to say, Mr. Superstar."

Jonas just laughed. "Come on, get ready. The party started half an hour ago. It's fine to be fashionably late, but rude to be too late."

"Remind me why we're going to this?" I asked.

"Many reasons. First, because as a top contender, you should be seen somewhere tonight. It's part of the whole package. Second, because I want to thumb my nose at the host who intentionally didn't invite me this year," he said, chuckling. "But, I promise we don't have to stay long. Everyone knows you'll want to spend most of the evening practicing and resting before tomorrow's competition."

"Do I?" I asked with raised eyebrows.

"Do you what?"

"Do I need to stay here and practice?" I asked nervously.

"No. To be honest, if you don't have it by now, you're not going to have it tomorrow. Most of us would be freaking out at this point in a competition, so it's natural to be nervous. Dinner parties are fine, but no partying hard until after the competition."

"So, why aren't they doing this tomorrow night?"

Jonas laughed again. "'Cause once the winner is announced, no one will come to see the losers."

"God, it's so competitive. I guess I didn't realize that."

"It's beyond competitive, and childish, and snarky, and, well, it's a bunch of creative sorts with huge egos trying to navigate around each other. It is what it is."

I took a deep breath and let it out. "I'd rather just stay in, order Salzburg-style take-out, and watch a movie while cuddled up in our bed. I don't want to meet the rich assholes that thumbed their noses at you."

"A quick in just to be seen, and then we'll leave, I promise."

I slipped on the tuxedo Jonas had insisted I rent in New York before flying here. Of course, he already owned one, which I could only imagine cost more than several months' income for me. I didn't mind that I stood out as the poor mechanic, but I didn't understand at all why we needed to get all dressed up just to go hang out with assholes.

The bright side was I got to see Jonas looking hot as hell in his tux. I mean, I'm not into fancy clothes or anything, but damn, he looked fine.

He whistled at me too when I walked out, and seeing his eyes travel up and down my body made wearing the penguin suit worth it... well, almost.

The party was everything I knew I'd hate. Live soft music played in the background, while people in ridiculously expensive outfits paraded around each other in an equally ridiculously expensive house. Unlike earlier in the day, everyone seemed eager to shake my hand, ignoring the grease stains and welcoming me, as if I'd elevated my social standing by getting into the top ten.

Of course, those same people whispered into each other's ears as I walked away, so I knew they were only being nice on the surface. Hissing snakes was the analogy that came to mind.

I was not enjoying myself, even when Tatiana came over and congratulated me, genuinely meaning it. "I'm so glad you did well, but with Jonas as your teacher, I guess I should've known you would."

Jonas was working to pry himself away from the people talking to him. "Just a few hours ago, these assholes wouldn't give him the time of day," Tatiana said, shaking her head. "Now they are all over him."

"Just because I did well?" I asked, confused.

"Yes, they are fickle little people, and your success is his success. You did very well today."

"How are your students?" I asked, thinking of the three men I'd met last night.

"Angry, frustrated, typical men who have bruised egos," Tatiana replied. "But, it was fitting they didn't make the final, because they are lazy and refuse to practice. This is what they needed to kick their butts. Now maybe I can teach them to meet their potential."

I laughed. "You're a tough one, Tatiana," I said, before I excused myself to go find a bathroom.

The ground floor bathrooms were all being used, so a waiter pointed up the stairs and told me to go down the hall. I heard voices as I passed by one of the upstairs rooms, catching only a snippet of conversation spoken by someone with a thick French accent.

"You will do fine, *ma chéri*. Besides, if you do bad, at least you won't place last. This year they have reserved that position for a grease monkey."

My face bloomed. I knew people were thinking that, but at least no one had the audacity to say it within earshot of me. Suddenly, I was like the teenager dreaming of being in front of his classroom with no pants on.

I managed to get downstairs and out the door into the abandoned winter gardens, and leaned up against a tree to catch my breath. "You're fine, you'll be fine," I said under my breath.

I heard a group of people come out of the house and walk in my direction, thankfully stopping before they reached me. I was sure they couldn't see me, still leaning against the tree below the patio, because when they began to speak, it was about me.

"It's a shame he did so well. That prat Ludwig should be sent home, what with all the chaos he caused in his last job. Now he parades the grease monkey in front of us, as if he can compete with the top amateurs in the world. It's an embarrassment to his father."

I listened as the group threw one insult after another. I wasn't really the one they were insulting, although they certainly didn't have anything nice to say about me either. They were tearing down Jonas, *my* Jonas, and that upset me beyond words.

"And Beethoven's Bagatelle, what a simple piece to play. It will be an embarrassment for everyone for him to play that when his competitors are playing much more advanced music."

"It's like he did a boogie-woogie, and the judges went nuts."

"They must want to get him in the sack. I hear he has a big cock."

The group laughed, and that was when I decided to make my presence known. I walked around the partition and smiled at the assholes, before saying, "That's something none of you will ever know," then left them gawking after me as I walked back into the house.

I found Jonas and told him I was leaving the party, then I set out on foot back toward the hotel, still too upset to stick around to see if he'd follow me or not.

"Wait!" Jonas called out as he jogged up behind me. "What happened?"

"What happened is that party is full of judgmental jackasses. I don't allow people like that in my life, and I'm surprised you'd want them in yours either," I said as I kept walking, despite how the horrible shoes were beginning to hurt my feet.

"Damn, Orli, wait a fucking minute," he said as he ran to catch up to me. "Did someone say something to you?"

"To me directly? No, but I certainly heard enough, and not just about me. Jonas, they were being hateful about you too. *Really* hateful. I don't want to be around those people. Can we just go home?"

"Like to the hotel? Yes."

"No, home. I don't want to compete with these idiots, they aren't worth my time."

Jonas stopped. When I turned around, he was staring at me. "You want to blow off the competition?"

"I don't know what I want," I said, and put my head in my hands. "Not to go back to the party from hell, that's for certain, but why stay here? Why does it all matter? You know your skills, your abilities. I know mine. I knew I played well before you arrived in my life, not like you or these pretentious snobs, but I could hold my own playing my kind of music. I know I'm a better pianist now because of you. I knew that before we came here. I don't need those horrible people to acknowledge me, Jonas. Why would you?"

He shook his head. "They represent the world I grew up in, the world my dad lived in. Most of them even knew my dad, respected him, envied his career. I didn't need you to compete. In fact, you're here, because you said you wanted to come."

"I said that for you," I admitted.

He nodded. "I know that. I've known it all along, and yes, if you want to go home, we'll go, but you'll just be proving them right. I don't know what they said, but I can imagine, and I'm sure it was all just to make themselves feel better, to feel superior, but the judges are impartial. I believe that, and you're proof of that as well."

"You want me to continue?" I asked.

Jonas shook his head. "I want you to do what makes you happy, but it seems such a waste to be here, to have accomplished so much just to leave now, because those windbags offended you."

I turned and we began walking, but slower now, and side by side. "Is it true the piece I'm playing, *Bagatelle*, is a simple piece?" I asked.

"No, it's an adequate piece to perform."

"But, people are playing more complex pieces?"

He shrugged. "I honestly haven't paid attention to who is playing what. My attention has been only on you."

That made me smile. I reached down and took Jonas's hand in mine as we continued walking. "What if I played *La Campanella*?"

"Um, no. Are you crazy?"

"Yes, but you said I've been doing better with it. You even said you wish I could've performed it in front of Rodrigo, so he had to eat crow."

"I didn't mean it about Rodrigo, though he deserves to eat crow. Besides, you can't just go changing your music selection at the last minute."

"Is that a rule? I didn't know," I said.

"No, damn it, Orli, it's not a rule, but you, you'd… ugh. Why would you want to play one of the most difficult pieces ever written at a competition where you've placed in the top ten?"

"'Cause these mofos need to be taken down a notch or two, and because I can. I know I can. If I'm going to place last anyway, like that French fucker thinks will happen, why shouldn't I go out with a bang?"

I stopped and smiled at Jonas, and gave his hand a squeeze. He looked at me for a long time before he shook his head in exasperation. "Do you have it memorized?"

"Close, at least close enough. Come on, let's grab one of those practice rooms, and you can help me memorize the parts I don't remember."

"You know you're nuts, right?"

I shrugged, then pulled him into a kiss. "No risk, no reward. Either way, it's going to be epic."

51

Jonas

I T'S MY OWN FUCKING fault. God, I'm an idiot. I chastised myself as I walked with Orli down the narrow road toward the hotel. I knew not to take him to that stupid party. I *knew* it, but my own ego got the best of me, and I wanted to shove my uninvited self in the face of my dad's former pupil. Some party host he was, practically fawning over me and Orli, like he hadn't snubbed us. I wanted to show him and the other arrogant assholes that I wasn't easily dismissed.

What did I get for my ego trip? A rightfully pissed-off boyfriend teetering between quitting the competition altogether, or playing one of, if not the, most difficult piece of piano music ever written. Yeah, either option sucked.

He could play it, that was something, at least, but it wasn't anywhere near ready to perform. Maybe I could convince him of that before he went in front of the judges tomorrow. For now, I'd take my lumps for having taken him to that stupid party, which meant spending the evening practicing.

For three hours, instead of being cuddled up together in bed, under the lovely satin duvet, I listened to Orli banging out *La Campanella*. "No, you keep overcompensating when you get to the fast parts," I said for the thirteenth time, and squeezed the bridge of my nose.

There had to be some way to get him to see it, to hear it in his head, then it came to me, and I was surprised and little frustrated I hadn't thought of it before.

"*Redneck Rag*."

"Huh?" he said, his eyes showing the fatigue I knew he was feeling.

"Play *Redneck Rag*."

He did with ease and then turned to me. I smiled, because my idea might actually work. "Now do it as fast as you can, like you were trying to beat a competitor."

He smiled back at me then, finally getting it. His hands sped across the keyboard, and as he ended the song, I made him play it twice more. "Consistency, you need consistency. Play it exactly the same as you did last time."

When he finished, the fatigue was gone, replaced by my happy man, the one who loved playing piano his way.

"Now, play *La Campanella* like you did *Redneck Rag*."

He laughed out loud and began playing. "Don't forget the dynamics. Keep playing, but remember how Liszt wrote it. Honor the maker."

He laughed again and played it, not perfectly, but better than he had since we'd started.

"That's it, you're headed down the right road now, but play it again, this time, just enjoy it. Imagine *La Campanella* is the song someone requested down at your honky-tonk bar."

His rendition was so fucking perfect. Even better than I could play it.

I kissed him, then said, "Now play some stuff you want to play. Whatever makes you happy."

He launched into several different ragtime tunes, and I laughed as he stood and shook his booty as he played.

When he stopped, he grabbed me into a hug. "We did it."

"No, *you* did it, but now, let's get out of here. At least you know you know how. There's no point in beating this poor, dead horse any longer."

We walked back to the hotel room hand in hand, and even though we passed several people who'd been at the party, neither of us acknowledged them. Our spirits were too high now to waste time and energy on all those snobs. It felt like the two of us had turned an important corner together in between leaving that party and spending time practicing.

For him, I hoped he now knew I was there for him, no matter what, be it forgoing the competition, staying in it to play his way, and in life in general. For me, I'd learned a lesson that had escaped me from day one. Let go, and let people be who and what they want to be. It didn't have to be perfect, and sometimes that imperfection might reveal a unique perfection all its own.

I fell asleep the moment we lay down, and woke to the delicious smell of freshly made coffee. "Room service has already been by," Orli said as he stood in the doorway. "Get up and let's go walk down by the river. I don't want to come back here, until it's time to get ready for the competition."

I nodded and got up, taking the cup of coffee from Orli's hand as I passed him, and then grabbed a couple of pastries before collapsing on the room's sofa. "You ready?"

He shrugged. "I'm as ready as I'll ever be, thanks to you."

"Thanks to your great-grandmother, you mean. If you hadn't already had a love for her music, you wouldn't have conquered *La Campanella* in time to perform it, so here's to your great-grandmother!" I said, and raised my coffee mug.

Orli had just finished pouring himself a cup, since I'd taken his, and clinked it to mine. "She'd have liked that," he said, smiling.

"She'd have been pissed as hell that I dragged you here, is more like it."

"Nah, my great-granny loved to stick it to the man. That was her first and most passionate mission in life."

"Then maybe you're right, maybe she'd have loved this after all."

52

Orlando

THE SHIFT IN OUR plans made for a much better day. We left the hotel right after breakfast, walked along the river, and had lunch in a sweet little restaurant, before we went back to the room to change for the performance.

"You ready?" Jonas asked as we walked through the front doors of the auditorium.

"I guess," I said with a wink, hoping to relieve some of his tension.

"You'll do great, just remember, have fun."

"Aye, captain," I said, just as we were swept into the paperwork, and registration for the day.

"You'll be number six," the very harassed-looking woman said, giving me a terse smile. "Good luck!" I tried to ignore the expression on her face that silently added, "Because, you're going to need it."

No, I thought. *I don't need luck. I have skill, and a terrific teacher*. That, and feeling Jonas's hand squeeze mine in support was all the reassurance I needed.

The first competitor bumbled the first chord he played and had to start over, his nerves tight enough to snap. Even though the others who performed ahead of me didn't mess up, and tried to hide their nerves by appearing overly confident, even arrogant, their true feelings of stress were obvious if you looked close enough.

I wandered up on stage, waiting to the side as I'd been instructed when the fifth contestant had started. I had enough time to admire the choreography it required to keep a process like this moving. There was no announcement, no fanfare, just one person performing at a time, while the next waited in the wings to take their place.

My competitor finished, stood and took a quick bow, and as he walked off stage, I walked on. I searched the crowd and, despite the bright lights, found my handsome boyfriend in the audience, sitting alongside Tatiana. I smiled at them both, then sat down at the piano.

I closed my eyes, bringing my great-granny's image into my mind. "We got this," I could all but hear her say, then I imagined Jonas, with his sweet smile, nervous eyes, and love that shone out of him when he was around me. This was for him, well, for both of us.

I played the first chords, and like some telenovela, I heard a shocked gasp when the audience realized I wasn't playing the piece they had expected. The competition rules dictated that when there was a music change, the judges must be notified before that round started, which Jonas had done before we left the hotel room.

I'd expected the crowd's surprised reaction, since it was too late for the printed programs to be changed. Jonas told me people would accuse us of grandstanding. That had made me laugh.

The thing I loved about Liszt's *La Campanella*, especially now after last night's practice session, was it sorta felt like ragtime. I'm sure the composer would roll over in his grave at the comparison, but it made sense to me. The piece broke the rules, and continued breaking them from start to finish, a hallmark of ragtime music.

I couldn't help but wonder, besides the intensely difficult notes and fast tempo, if pianists struggled with the piece, because it was so out of the norm for most classical music of its time. It was certainly why I had struggled with it, but not today.

Now, the notes just flew out of my hands. The audience disappeared; I was playing for Jonas. Only him. I didn't give a damn about judges, or pretentious assholes in the audience. I just cared about my sweet, sweet Jonas, and as I banged out the last frantic notes, I think I showed him that.

I got up and heard whispering all around the auditorium, but I just bowed and walked off the stage.

One of my competitors sneered as I walked by them, and said to another something in a language I didn't recognize. I couldn't understand the words, but the intonation certainly conveyed how he felt. I smiled at him, though, and found my way back to my seat in the auditorium.

I noticed Jonas's eyes were wet when I sat down. He immediately reached over and took my hand. I leaned into him, kissed his temple, and whispered, "Thank you," before the next competitor began playing.

Three more competitors came after her, but I didn't hear them. I was too lost in thought about how much I loved the man next to me, and how much I wanted him in my life forever. I would've loved to have pulled him out of that auditorium and onto a plane bound for home, and back to our small-town lives, but that wouldn't have been fair to him.

This *was* Jonas's life, at least until moving to Monongahela. Piano competitions, fancy dinner parties, and concert performances that took him all around the world. I regretted my breakdown last night, knowing I'd rebelled against something he'd striven for his entire life, but I wasn't upset at knowing I'd never fit into that world. I was angry at the assholes at that party who didn't see Jonas for the wonderful human being he was. Maybe my playing *La Campanella* would help open their eyes.

There was a brief intermission, and the competitors were allowed backstage to use the restrooms there, so we didn't have to mill through the crowds. Everyone seemed to be ignoring each other now, and the complete lack of congratulatory comments or sportsmanlike handshakes felt weird and petty.

I did my business, then went back to find Tatiana standing in front of Jonas. "You disappeared last night, then again this morning. I searched everywhere for you," she said. When she noticed me standing there, though, she immediately told me how amazing I'd been, and kissed both my cheeks.

"Come meet him, at least," Tatiana said as she excused herself and headed to the back of the auditorium. The lights blinked, which was my cue to go back on stage with the rest of the competitors to await our fate. "What was that about?" I asked.

Jonas smiled. "I'll tell you after you win," he said, and gave me a wink.

I just laughed. Winning was unlikely, but at least the grease monkey shouldn't be on the bottom like the French man had predicted last night.

"Third place—" the announcer said once we were all standing shoulder to shoulder, "—goes to Lena Muller." At least now there was clapping.

"Second place goes to..." He paused and looked out into the audience, drawing it out to ratchet up the anticipation. "Jordon Moreau."

People clapped more enthusiastically now, and I even heard a whistle or two.

"Finally, in first place, and the winner of this competition in the adult piano soloist category is... Orlando Hancock."

I stood rooted to the spot for maybe a moment too long, because the young woman standing next to me put her hand on my arm, and gave me a gentle shove.

I stumbled up to the front of the stage, took the trophy handed to me, and shook the announcer's hand. Had this really happened? Had I really just won this... entire thing?

The auditorium was awash with applause, and even more ear-piercing whistles as I bowed once, then again before we were all escorted from the stage.

Unlike not twenty minutes earlier, all of my fellow competitors were quick to shake my hand and congratulate me. Only then did it really begin to sink in that I'd actually done it. *I've won the fucking competition*, I kept thinking. *How is that even possible?*

Jonas flew up the stairs. I met him halfway across the stage and he flung himself into my open arms. "I won it. I fucking won it!"

"Yeah, so I heard," Jonas said, and I leaned down and kissed him hard. "We're so gonna display this."

Jonas just laughed, glancing at the trophy. I didn't quite notice the sadness in his demeanor, until after the euphoria began to wear off. "What's wrong? Are you okay?"

"Yeah, I'm good. I'm so proud of you! Come on, we're going to party with Tatiana and a couple of her girlfriends to celebrate. None of the crap from yesterday, we're going out to a club, and celebrating like real people."

We partied the night away. Tatiana and the two women she'd dragged along were more than fun as we danced, drank, sang badly, and had a blast.

I woke up the next morning extremely happy, despite the hangover-included headache that persistently banged against the back of my head. Our fun night didn't leave Jonas faring much better this morning either.

We managed to get ready, despite those hangovers, and met Tatiana for brunch. As soon as coffee was served, she asked, "So, did you think about it? What do you think? It's an amazing job, and of course, with this handsome fellow's win, I know you can ask for more compensation."

"Job? What job?" I asked, looking at Jonas.

"Tatiana's boss offered me a teaching position at her university."

"And you didn't tell me?"

"No, we were out, and I didn't..."

I stood up. "This hangover is something else. I'm feeling queasy, I think I should go lie down," I said, making up the first excuse that came to mind. Really, I wanted to rant and rave that after all this, Jonas was still going to leave me, but I couldn't do that. He deserved more, so instead, I made my excuses.

"I'm going to head back to the hotel, take more pain medication, and maybe another nap. I'm sorry, Tatiana."

I left before she could respond. This couldn't be happening. Why did I insist we come to this wretched place full of snobs for a competition I didn't care about? Why wasn't I happy just letting things be? I mean, had I just said no, then... then he'd be staying, staying with me.

I got back to the hotel room, and lay on the bed face down. My head was still pounding, and I felt so overwhelmed with the impending loss of the only man I'd ever loved, the only man I'd ever wanted like this.

By the time Jonas came into the room, and sat on the edge of the bed, I was asleep. "Hey, you okay?" he asked softly, waking me up.

I rolled over to face him, but didn't respond for several moments, thanking the heavens my headache had settled down, at least.

"No, I'm not okay, Jonas. I don't want to lose you. I don't want you to move to what? Germany? Isn't that where Tatiana is working?"

He nodded. "Yes, it's Germany, but..."

He stood up, walked to the window and stared out. "I don't want to teach in Germany, or New York, or anywhere but Monongahela." He chuckled sadly, before continuing, "Tatiana says I'm an idiot throwing my old life and career away, but..." He turned toward me, then came back over to sit on the bed, where I could see his face. "If I left Monongahela now, I'd be throwing away my new life. I don't really fit in Europe, or even New York now. In fact, I don't think I've ever fit anywhere except Monongahela." He took my hand and pulled me up, so I was sitting next to him. "I've never fit anywhere except with you."

My tears flowed freely, maybe aided by the hangover, but mostly because the man I loved so much was saying he was coming home with me. I wasn't going to lose him, my sweet Jonas.

"So, what? You're settling for good in Monongahela?" I asked, desperately needing the confirmation.

He nodded, then dropped to his knees facing me, still holding my hand. "I'm coming back to Monongahela no matter what, but it would be so much better if I was coming back with you as my fiancé. Orlando Hancock, will you marry me?"

I fell to my knees too, and kissed him hard on the mouth. "My God, you proposed to me? Like with a hangover and everything?"

He chuckled. "Splitting headache or not, I want you in my life as my husband, forever."

I hugged him tightly. "Yes, fuck, yeah, of course! And, oh my god, you're coming home, and you just asked me to be your husband, and..."

He leaned back in my hold, cupping my face and kissing me to shut me up. I moaned happily as I deepened the kiss, before things grew hotter as we began tugging each other's clothes off, and I spent the afternoon making love with my beloved fiancé.

53

Epilogue: Orlando

"**H**ELLO, I'M ELLISON ATCHISON. Do you have a moment to speak?" the man asked, when I answered the front door.

"Um, yes. Come on in," I said, feeling a bit antsy, thinking maybe I'd just invited in one of the religious recruiters who tended to proselytize in the area, although, most avoided my home, knowing I was gay.

"Is Mr. Ludwig available as well?" he asked, and then I did get suspicious.

"May I ask why?" I asked, before I went to get Jonas.

"Yes, of course, I should've introduced myself," the man said and pulled out his card. "I'm with the West Virginia Appalachia Foundation. We're mostly funded by one donor, and he's quite impressed with both you and Mr. Ludwig. I'm here at his bequest to make you an offer."

"Um, okay. Please, excuse me for a minute, Jonas is upstairs."

The man nodded and I rushed up the stairs. I couldn't help but chuckle when I saw Jonas, wearing his grease-stained *cuddle clothes* and sorting through a mountain of cardboard boxes.

Jonas had moved in with me the day we returned from Salzburg, and we were still creating spaces to put his stuff. Between that and the more precious belongings we'd retrieved from his storage unit in New York, our second floor was a glorified mess.

"Um, we have company," I said.

"Really? Like now? Who?"

I handed Jonas the business card, and told him what the man had said about an offer.

"I haven't even brushed my teeth yet. I'm going to do that and get out of these," Jonas said, and waved up and down his body.

"Okay, but make it quick. I'll do my best to distract him in the meantime," I said, and went back downstairs.

"Is this a bad time?" the man asked as I entered the living room.

"No, we only have Sundays off, so usually this is when we catch up on housekeeping. Jonas will be down in a moment."

I showed the man over to the sofa, then went to get us both a glass of water as I stalled for time.

When he came down, Jonas quickly introduced himself before we both sat across from the man. "So, as I told Mr. Hancock, I'm Ellison Atchison and I represent the West Virginia Appalachia Foundation," the man said to Jonas. "The foundation isn't very well known, but it was founded by Samuel Clifton. You may know the name?"

I didn't know who he was talking about, but Jonas apparently did, because his eyes grew large at the name-drop before he nodded.

"Mr. Clifton has been a benefactor for a couple of your previous campaigns, including the fundraiser your friend, Ms. Phillips, organized on your behalf. You seem to be in the right place at the right time because Mr. Clifton very much wishes to invest in a music program that builds on the natural musical talent of the Appalachia area, especially in West Virginia, Virginia, and the Carolinas."

My feeling of shock at the revelation of who had enabled Jonas to remain in Monongahela this past year matched the look I saw on my fiancé's face. When neither of us responded with words, Mr. Atchison continued, "We've been exploring programs in the area, and because so many public schools are defunding and eradicating their music programs, especially in under-served communities, we've had a hard time finding an area to begin our efforts. Of course, that's not the case here. Not only has the music program been supported in Monongahela, but with previous community-based lessons and now Mr. Ludwig's instruction, it's actually expanding."

We both nodded, and Mr. Atchison finally got to the point. "We want to model what you're doing here in Monongahela to create an official school. Sort of like a pilot program to start. We'll use your successes to build other music education programs throughout the Appalachian Mountains. Of course, it can't just be piano, we'll want to hire teachers to come down from Martinsburg to teach other instruments and vocals as well, but we'd like your help to lead the project."

After letting out a long breath he must've been holding, Jonas finally spoke, "Honestly, I'm not sure what to say. This is an amazing opportunity, and it seems exciting, but you must know both of us work. Orli has a full-time job running his own business, and I work several just to make ends meet. I'm not sure we have the extra time to launch and run a music program."

The man chuckled. "Well, we're offering you a job, at least one of you. Mr. Ludwig, with your experience, as well as that of another person I'll be visiting later today, we believe you can help make this a success. You'd be an employee of the foundation, and Mr. Clifton is aware of your prestige, Mr. Ludwig. He's happy to compensate you for what you're worth."

He told Jonas what he was willing to pay, and I almost laughed when Jonas's mouth fell open. He fish mouthed a couple times, opening and closing, but no sound coming out, before he said, "I-I need more information."

"I'm sure you do. That's why Mr. Clifton would like to invite you to spend a few days with him at his home in Charlotte. He'll answer all your questions then. And, Mr. Hancock, if you can get away, we'd like you to come as well. Your win at the competition in Austria as an amateur player has created quite a stir in the musical community. Mr. Clifton believes there's a lot of unrealized talent like yours in these mountains. You are the personification of what he's been saying for years, so we'd very much like to have you involved as well."

"When do you need an answer?" I asked.

The man smiled, appearing pleased that Jonas and I were at least considering the offer.

"We are in the planning stages, but Mr. Clifton is free next Saturday. He'd like to spend some time with you both then. As I said, I've got one other person to visit before I leave town, and if she agrees, she'll be asked to join us as well."

I knew immediately he was talking about Ms. Phillips, and I secretly planned to call her this evening to get her opinion.

We all shook hands as he left, after which Jonas and I stood in the living room just staring at each other. Clearly, the shock of it all hadn't worn off for either of us. "Do you think it's real?" I asked.

Jonas shrugged. "No idea, but I'll tell you this much," he said as he walked back upstairs, "I won't be signing any contracts without a *lot* of attorney oversight."

It turned out that Ms. Phillips was indeed the other person Mr. Atchison had come to Monongahela to visit. We all ventured to Charlotte on Saturday to meet with the benefactor, Mr. Clifton, and were floored by what he had planned. The incredibly detailed process was actually well underway, and included state universities, several school districts, and community music programs, as well as private tutors and teachers.

Ms. Phillips was as impressed as we were by the plan and Mr. Clifton's vision, and things happened fast after that. Jonas was put in charge of the program, and part of the job was to create a place for kids to receive music lessons. Principal Jenkins immediately offered to let us use the school, which worked okay, except the janitors got fussy when they couldn't readily get into the rooms after hours to clean.

Ms. Phillips had already agreed to take over as the head teacher and administrator since she had the education experience. Her retirement from teaching at the elementary school would be official in May anyway, and she made it clear she was happy to take the position as long as she didn't have to chase a bunch of kids around a school day in and day out.

The pilot program launched with such success, bringing kids in for lessons, and helping set up a local band, choir, and orchestra, that Mr. Clifton sought to expand it further. He planned to open a music school here in town, but needed to find a suitable building first.

I'd put the garage up for sale in February, not long after returning from Salzburg, and had only gotten a few nibbles, so when I'd received a full-price offer on the place the week before Clifton's announcement, I had no idea he was the one who'd made it.

"My garage?" I asked, when he told me the news. "That's, well, that's perfect, although you know it needs a lot of work to transform it into anything resembling a school."

The man just laughed. "I assure you all that's well in hand."

In the end, I barely recognized the building I'd spent all my life either living or working in. The first floor was opened up and turned into a small multipurpose space that included a place for small performances. The entire upstairs apartment was converted into classrooms and practice rooms. I couldn't have envisioned a better use of my old garage.

With Jonas fully employed and working in a position he loved, our relationship was ready for its own kick-start.

It seemed apropos to get married at the new school. Its architect had retained the big garage doors on the front of the building, with the idea they could be opened for performances that drew audiences larger than the space normally held.

That ended up being exactly what we needed, because most of the town turned out for the wedding.

Tatiana flew in for the occasion and stood with Jonas, and Ray stood with me. Ella had insisted on being our flower girl, so she completed our little wedding party.

The ceremony actually took place in a large tent we had set up in the parking lot, and the reception in the building.

The plan was for Jonas and me to meet in the building and walk together hand in hand to where Pastor James awaited us in the tent.

When Jonas came down the stairs, wearing the tux he'd worn in Salzburg, I lost it. "You're really gonna be mine?" I asked when he reached me.

"You sweet man, I'm already yours, but let's make it official, shall we?" he asked, lacing his fingers with mine.

We walked hand in hand as Tatiana and Ray followed behind. Pastor James smiled when we reached him, and he launched into the ceremony.

"Would you like to speak your vows?" he asked Jonas first.

Jonas smiled, then nodded before turning to me. "Orli, I've lived so many years alone, lost without friends, without family. Then, like a miracle, I found my way to this remarkable little town, and into your life. From the moment you met me, you've comforted and supported me. Even when I didn't know what was coming next, you were there, and that hasn't changed. You've continued to be my support. I had no clue that day when my life was falling apart around me that I was looking at a man who would lead me into a better future."

Tears slipped out of Jonas's eyes as he hesitated. "You are my savior, in so many ways, but more than that, you're my friend. I know it sounds cliché, but you really are the person I want to fall asleep with every night and wake up next to each morning. You're the light at the end of any day, no matter how hard that day may be. You are everything to me, Orlando Hancock, and I pledge to do everything in my power to be the best husband to you a man can have."

I heard a few sniffles from the guests behind us as Pastor James turned to me and nodded.

Emotions had built up inside me so much while Jonas was speaking, it felt like beavers had built a dam in my throat. I cleared it, hoping I could get past it enough to speak my vows.

"Um, Jonas," I said, and when my eyes locked with his, the nerves melted away. "You came into my life like a hurricane," I said, and heard chuckling behind me. Even Jonas smiled.

"But, it was the very thing I needed." I broke down before I could get the next words out. Jonas reached up to wipe away my free-flowing tears as I struggled to regain my composure. "I know these are our vows, but I don't think I've told you that I'd planned to spend the rest of my life alone. I didn't dare to hope I'd find someone to love me. I'm still so surprised that you, someone who appeared in my life out of the blue, angry, frustrated, and I feared close to being decked by my best friend, would be my perfect match."

More chuckling came from the crowd. "But, here you stand, willing, for some bizarre, crazy reason, to marry me, willing to help me better myself, better the community we call home. Of course, I pledge my life to you, to honor you, to love you, and to sing your praises to anyone who sticks around long enough to listen. You are my teacher, my lover, and my friend, and I'm yours, Jonas Ludwig, for the rest of my life." I took a shaky breath and let it out slowly. "Besides, you show me every day the melody of the heart is more than just the music that makes us happy. It's also how being with you fills me with a happiness I never knew was even possible."

I'd deliberately chosen to use the words his father had instilled in him about music, not only because I meant them wholeheartedly, but as a way to include Jonas's dad in our special day. It wasn't lost on him, because tears slid down my handsome man's face and I could see the intense love I felt for him reflected in his eyes.

We kissed to cheers and whistles from the crowd as Pastor James pronounced us husbands. As the rest of the day spun past at our reception, I felt like I was floating on a cloud. We never left each other's side and danced for hours in the building where it all began.

All I wanted to do was hold this incredible man, look into his beautiful eyes, and tell him over and over just how much I loved him, how appreciative I was to have him in my life. Music had brought us together, had strengthened our connection, and in him I'd found the melody of *my* heart.

Family inheritance or his own passion... Can he have both?

When an inheritance pulls him back to his family's ski resort in the Rockies, he's faced with a difficult decision. With his heart pulling him both directions, will he choose his singing career or a life of love and legacy?

Melody of the Snow
by Blake Allwood
Available at your favorite bookstore.

Join Blake's email list to get advance notice of new books and receive his occasional newsletter:

www.blakeallwood.com

<u>Transitions Series</u>
Aiden Inspired
Suzie Empowered (An MF Romance)
Bobby Transformed

<u>By Chance Series</u>
Love By Chance
Another Chance With Love
Taking A Chance For Love

<u>Big Bend Series</u>
Love's Legacy (1)
Love's Heirloom (2)
Love's Bequest (3)

<u>Romantic Series</u>
Romantic Renovations (1)
Romantic Rescue (2)
Romantic Recon (3)

<u>Melody Series</u>
Melody of the Heart
Melody of the Snow

<u>Road to Rocktoberfest Anthology</u>
Changing His Tune (2022)

<u>Novellas</u>
Tenacious
Moon's Place

bibliopride.com

Books by LGBTQ+ authors